WINDS OF THE NIGHT

JOAN SALES (1912–1983) was born in Barcelona to a Catalan family. In 1932, he earned a law degree from the University of Barcelona and in 1933 married Maria Núria Folch. At the outbreak of the Spanish Civil War in 1936, Sales was working for the Catalan government as an advocate for the expanded use of the Catalan language. A former member of the Communist party, he fought in defence of the Republic on the Madrid and Aragonese fronts. In January 1939, as the Fascist forces advanced, he crossed the French border and was interned in a transit camp, before continuing an exile that took him from Paris to Santo Domingo in 1940 and Mexico City in 1942, where he trained as a typesetter and founded a magazine devoted to writings by the exile community. He returned to Catalonia in 1948 and he cofounded the Club Editor publishing house, where he would edit and publish some of the most important authors of twentieth-century Catalan literature, among them Màrius Torres and Mercè Rodoreda, as well as his own work, including a book of poems, *Viatge d'un moribund* (1952); a collection of letters from his wartime and exile experiences, *Cartes a Màrius Torres* (1976); and a Catalan translation of *The Brothers Karamazov*. He died in Barcelona.

PETER BUSH has translated, among other books, Josep Pla's *The Gray Notebook*, which was awarded the 2014 Ramon Llull Prize for Literary Translation; Ramón del Valle-Inclán's *Tyrant Banderas*; Luis Martín-Santos's *Time of Silence*; and Joan Sales's *Uncertain Glory*, of which *Winds of the Night* is a continuation (all available as NYRB Classics). He lives in Bristol, England.

PAUL PRESTON is the Príncipe de Asturias Professor of Contemporary Spanish Studies and the director of the Cañada Blanch Centre for

Contemporary Spanish Studies at the London School of Economics. His many books on the Spanish Civil War include *The Spanish Holocaust*, short-listed for the Samuel Johnson Prize in 2012, and, most recently, *The Last Days of the Spanish Republic*.

WINDS OF THE NIGHT

JOAN SALES

Translated from the Catalan by
PETER BUSH

Afterword by
PAUL PRESTON

NEW YORK REVIEW BOOKS

New York

In Memoriam
Juan Goytisolo 1931–2017

THIS IS A NEW YORK REVIEW BOOK
PUBLISHED BY THE NEW YORK REVIEW OF BOOKS
207 East 32nd Street, New York, NY 10016
www.nyrb.com

First published in the Catalan language as *El vent de la nit* in 1983 by Club Editor.
First published in Great Britain in 2017 by MacLehose Press, an imprint of Quercus
Publishing Ltd.
First published as a New York Review Books Classic in 2025.

Library of Congress Cataloging-in-Publication Data
Names: Sales, Joan, author. | Bush, Peter R., 1946– translator.
Title: Winds of the night / by Joan Sales ; translated by Peter Bush.
Other titles: Vent de la nit. English
Description: New York : New York Review Books, 2024. | Series: New York Review Books classics
Identifiers: LCCN 2024003199 (print) | LCCN 2024003200 (ebook) | ISBN 9781681378763
(paperback) | ISBN 9781681378770 (ebook)
Subjects: LCGFT: Novels.
Classification: LCC PC3941.S336 V4613 2024 (print) | LCC PC3941.S336 (ebook) | DDC
849/.9354—dc23/eng/20240524
LC record available at https://lccn.loc.gov/2024003199
LC ebook record available at https://lccn.loc.gov/2024003200

ISBN 978-1-68137-876-3
Available as an electronic book; ISBN 978-1-68137-877-0

The authorized representative in the EU for product safety and compliance is
eucomply OÜ, Pärnu mnt 139b-14, 11317 Tallinn, Estonia, hello@eucompliancepartner.com,
+33 757690241.

Printed in the United States of America on acid-free paper.
10 9 8 7 6 5 4 3 2 1

CONTENTS

*Quant à moi, je serais bien content
si un jour on venait à prétendre
qu'Henri Bergson n'a pas existé.*

HENRI BERGSON

I

I found out quite by chance because I was in touch with a small group of Catalan nuns who were surviving in semi-clandestine conditions while waiting to be shipped off to the Caribbean; they were sending our poor nuns really a long way from our country, to South America, Africa, and the Philippines. And one of these nuns happened to be his sister. They had transported him from the frontier to Barcelona heavily manacled, on the 3rd; but she didn't find out until the 8th, nor did anyone else who wasn't in on the secret. She tried several times to get into Montjuïc castle that day and the day after, all to no avail. Finally at 7.00 p.m. on the 10th she did manage to see him, three metres away, and behind bars: "He was very calm; he spoke to me clearly, as he always did." She saw him again two days later; they allowed her to go into his cell. He hugged her, she sobbed, he cheered her up; he could barely stand because of the injuries inflicted on his back and legs when he was interrogated: "I'm fifty-eight," he told her, "could I have ever dreamt of a more beautiful death?" The military trial was held on the 14th; they didn't allow her in, she had to stay outside by the door. The officers began to leave at eleven o'clock; one of them was the defence lawyer, who told her: "He was the calmest person in the whole room; his serenity shames us all." At 9.00 p.m. the defence lawyer appeared on the doorstep of the flat where the nuns had found refuge: "Start the preparations for his burial." She decided to go back up to Montjuïc: she had no authorisation, but got in anyway. He stuck his head through his cell skylight: "Where are you going, my child? What do you think you are doing at this time of night?" Because it was almost midnight. When she said she wanted to give him one last hug, he replied, rather taken aback: "But if they were going to do it now, they'd be getting me ready." A jailer then said: "They'll read out your sentence very soon."

"Oh, will they?" he responded calmly, "I thought they'd have got me ready first."

They let her go into the cell and spend three hours with her brother; then she had to leave. Dawn was breaking over the sea on a new day, October 15; he was executed at 6.30 in the moat of the old castle. He had taken his shoes off so his feet could touch the land for which he was dying. I still have the letter Sister Ramona wrote to me in my yellowing papers among a few items from those distant days; my eyes always mist over when I reread it:

> They gave his corpse over to my care; there was a smile on his face. It was the morning of St Teresa's Day and I told myself I had to be as strong as the women described in the Gospels. By his niche I offered my life if needs be so that all upstanding men who are living far from our country or rotting in prisons could return to their homes; I prayed to St Teresa for our country, so foreigners don't put an end to it and to us all. Then I declared out loud to all those present: "*Senyors*, may God forgive you, for you know not what you do." I said that without clenching my fist or holding out my hand: I said that, crossing my arms over my chest, on that day of St Teresa, on the mountain of Montjuïc, facing the sea.[1]

1 The person referred to here is Lluís Companys (1882–1940), president of the Generalitat of Catalonia during the civil war. Arrested by the Gestapo in France, where he had gone into exile in 1939, he was extradited and executed in 1940.

It is natural for us now to see that war as having been banished to the mists of the past, a war as remote as our own youth – and yet, like our youth, it seems as if it were only yesterday. Or perhaps it is because I am a pendulum that has come to a halt; perhaps every pendulum halts for ever once it has marked the hour of glory, of uncertain glory. I am ashamed to confess that I have never put my youth or my war behind me. I carry them, and always will, like an infection in my blood! I long regretfully for both with a sorrow that is as guilty as it is relentless . . . the scent of youth and war, of burning woods and drenched grass, that life of wandering, those starry nights when we found such strange peace in our sleep; everything seems carefree in that realm of uncertainty, with uncertain glory in our hearts, at war when we are twenty, the war and our hearts so fresh and full of hope! War is a foolish thing, perhaps that's why it is so deeply rooted in men's hearts; boys play at war even though nobody ever taught them. War is a foolish thing, a thirst for glory that can never be satisfied – but what of love? Glory and love in this world? And all youth is but the uncertain glory of an April morning, dark storm clouds criss-crossed by lightning flashes of glory, but what kind of glory? What kind of glory, Lord? You wake up, and how sad it is to wake up after a night of feverish delirium. Perhaps the worst of war is the peace that follows . . . You wake up from your youth and think you have been feverish and delirious, yet you cling to the memory of that delirious madness, of those stormy shadows, as if they were the only worthwhile things this world possessed. I am but a survivor, a ghost; my only life, my memories.

After the delirium I entered a Tunnel. Groping my way in the dark, I could hear muffled shouts as I moved forward; the tunnel was so long, the darkness so black, the shouts so muffled! And that lasted for years.

We floated like flotsam from a shipwreck, cut off from all friends and acquaintances. If you happened to recognise someone else marooned, adrift among the scattered debris, a face you identified among so many cadaverous faces drifting down streets, you were more likely to feel uneasy. You never knew what that individual might have done in his delirious madness, or what he could be doing now; you would try to slip into the hungry grey crowd before he spotted you. We mistrusted one another; conversely, everybody was crushed under the weight of their own selfish worries. The port was deserted, the rail-lines mostly destroyed, there were neither lorries nor petrol; hunger ruled. Whoever bothered to listen to the pompous speeches the radio endlessly spewed out? You only aspired to survive another day, to make it to the next morning. They had had to bring back into service old trams withdrawn as useless years earlier; more than once I saw one such contraption from another era fall apart under the burden of so many passengers, people rushing to clamber into the next tram, fighting those already inside tooth and nail; they simply had to get to work, whatever it cost, to work a sixteen-hour day so they could buy a few mouldy potatoes!

Some people had crossed the Pyrenees. Far away, another war had begun, and for my sins I sometimes felt tempted by that other war, by that fresh hope. But I soon lost heart. I wondered if it is even possible to fight more than one war. Can we love more than one woman? Can we burn again, if we are burnt out already? Can another love, another war, exist beyond that one and only love and war? What does it matter whether you win or lose? I have lost on both counts and can never be anything but a ghost; I can only live on my memories! And if I dreamt of war – and dream of it I did, my God, in those years – it was always the same one, our war, the one we fought, just as I could dream of no woman other than the one I still dream of and will for ever.

A gasogen . . . it is as if I could see one now, an unsightly device made of iron that perched like a tumour on the back of the stray cars still in circulation at the time, allowing them to run on coal dust or hazelnut shells. There was no petrol. The odd car with this hump, and a few peculiar trams that had survived from the past century, were all one ever saw on the streets of Barcelona. It was war, always war, that had now spread over the continent. You wished it had never broken out, that you could open your eyes one fine morning and rediscover the unsullied hopes of a country reborn.

The war now was . . . it was like re-encountering a girl you'd once known full of innocent dreams transformed into heaven knows what, her aged, wrinkled face caked in make-up, cruelly illuminated by the streetlight on a stinking street corner. You wished the orgy of hatred of those first post-war years had been only a nightmare, because it was like a nightmare, the memory of which has stuck. Smoke was already spiralling from the gas chambers in Germany, and those ugly lorries driven from the desolation on the other side of the river to a remote end of the city, to that huge common grave, their progress slow, they were so overloaded; they passed by in the night, covered in tarpaulins that bulged in places, as if hiding sacks of potatoes. Some people followed them, hoping a sack would fall off when they hit a pothole; once, when I was standing by the roadside near the bridge over the river, one did fall off, but it wasn't potatoes, it was an old man.

They didn't bother picking him up; a blow from a rifle butt cleared that excrescence from the middle of the road.

Smoke was already spiralling from the gas chambers in Germany; Himmler[2] was no dream. He paid a visit. There was one name I knew only too well among those who went to welcome him, it appeared on the front pages of the newspapers: Lamoneda. He had become an important person.

I only spent nine months in the concentration camp. They let me out so I could go back and finish my studies in Barcelona, because, in spite of everything, I wanted to complete my studies. I wanted to be a priest.

It was as if I had been stunned by someone; Auntie Llúcia talked and talked and I never could understand what she was saying: "Why do you stare at me like that, with your mouth gaping wide?" she asked testily, but I kept on, my mind far away. I felt severed from everything that was my previous life. I had sunk into a kind of stupor, which meant I spent hours staring into space, my mouth agape. Three years later, I had still not managed to find out anything precise about what had happened to Dr Gallifa, just as I knew nothing about Lluís, Soleràs, or any of my friends and colleagues. Of course, I had roamed the carrer de l'Arc del Teatre and nosed around the houses there looking for the anarchist's widow; finally, some neighbours told me she had left months ago, they did not know where she was. I had written to her brother, who was now a permanent fixture on their farm; he replied that he had had no news of her since the end of November 1936. Everything

2 During his brief Spanish tour, Himmler visited the monastery of Monserrat and was pleasantly surprised that "la Moreneta", the medieval Virgin venerated there, although black, "had Aryan traits".

was like that at the time, lost traces, evanescent lives, people you weren't sure were dead or alive; I did at least dredge something out to a certainty: Dr Gallifa had lived in that attic. Without Dr Gallifa, Lluís, and Soleràs I felt cut off from everything and everybody. I was blown about by the winds. I was a mere wraith. I became so utterly oblivious of everything that was happening – and things were certainly happening – and so close to losing my mind that sometimes I spent hours thinking only about my telescope, the childhood instrument that had accompanied me throughout the war and that I had lost in the last days of the final debacle. I never thought of buying a new one; it wouldn't have been my childhood gift, or the one Lluís and I peered through to find the stars in those days – those days of war – which now seemed as happy and as remote as Paradise Lost.

As far as Soleràs was concerned, all I discovered, three long years after the war, was that his octogenarian aunt now lived in Grenoble. Apparently it was where the Soleràs family was from, something he had never told me, and some distant cousins of theirs were still living in the city; from what I learnt, his aunt went off to live there at the start of the war, a detail Soleràs had concealed from us. After her nephew disappeared, she evidently decided never to return to Barcelona, where everything would have reminded her of him – though that's only my conjecture. I never got a reply to the letters I wrote her asking for news of him – unless it was that cheap coloured religious print of the vulgar and sentimental kind I received from Grenoble inside an envelope showing no sender or any written clues apart from my address (which was, again, my Auntie Llúcia's mansion in Sarrià). It was a picture of St Philomena.

I had to wait until the end of a rainy December before I finally had more precise information concerning Soleràs and Dr Gallifa. The news reached me most unexpectedly, via another ghost who was floating adrift, just like myself.

I had just finished my studies and was waiting to be assigned to a living. In the interim I stayed on at my aunt's and went for strolls around Barcelona, where I had very little else to do. One morning I sat down in a bar on the Ronda de Sant Pau; I hadn't had breakfast so I ordered a croissant and a cup of malt. There was no coffee or milk at the time, or they were in very short supply and extremely expensive; neither was there any bread, but you could eat as many croissants as you wanted, provided you could pay for them. Because of my soutane I had taken a seat in the shadowy depths of that establishment to dunk my croissant in peace. At the time a priest in a café was bound to be frowned upon, and I could hardly tell passers-by that I had just fallen out with my aunt; nor that while looking for a suitable boarding house I had not given up my room in the Sarrià mansion, where I was still sleeping, and otherwise leading a bohemian life dunking croissants in cups of malt.

I was at the back of the bar with a good view of the goldfish bowl at the other end – I mean that glassed-in extension some bars erect on the pavement during the winter months.

My ghostly alter ego was sitting at a marble table and dunking a croissant in his cup of malt, just as I was.

He was looking through the panes of glass at a street still bustling and full of colour in spite of everything, with those peculiar trams that passed to and fro like gigantic dinosaurs, their rickety iron cages almost disappearing under loads of passengers clinging desperately on. A few huge black limousines with monstrous gasogen humps also occasionally drove by. The huddled masses walked endlessly along the pavements, and it all had a rather melancholy air. The overburdened trams reminded me of carcasses being devoured by a whole anthill, and the neon advertisements, extinguished at that time of day, bore the sickly pallor of someone waking up after a night-time orgy: "Rexy Mura, goodbye bald pates", "Rexy Mura, farewell unsightly hair", "Barcelona by night", and so many others, equally sad and ridiculous with their laconic slogans.

Nevertheless the pavements *were* full of people, however badly dressed and hungry-looking, and that was life! My ghost stared at the flow through the glass wall of the goldfish bowl: a man well into his fifties. I could only see him at an angle, against the light and from a distance, so I couldn't make out his face. He looked like the survivor of a shipwreck now marooned on a reef, contemplating the despairing vastness of the ocean. Only that glass stood between him and life, but he sat there as if separated from the outside world for ever; you also felt the soles of his shoes had worn thin and could no longer keep out the mocking damp of that December morning passing through him like an electric current.

He threw bits of his croissant into his cup like someone throwing crumbs to fish, without conviction, that is, well aware that fish are ungrateful creatures. A steamboat hooted, something unusual in Barcelona, now mostly a deserted port. My attention was distracted from the ghost. At the time – this was before I was sent to the Caribbean – I had never been outside Spain, apart from my few weeks in the French concentration camp, and that ship's siren sounded like a fantastic summons from remote, tropical lands, from islands eternally in flower on the other side of the ocean that I had only known in my dreams and that, one day, poor me, I would have to experience first hand. When the last vibrations of the blast had evaporated in the cold air, I gave him another glance. Imagine my surprise: the phantom ghost was walking towards me with his cup and his croissant.

It was Lamoneda.

A strangeness about his gaze made me think of a dead man staring at me from the shores of the beyond; shadowed by several days' stubble, his pallid face communicated only disillusion. You would have said he was an abandoned dog expecting only to be kicked and beaten.

He sat next to me, muttering: "I suppose you don't mind," and not waiting for my response – a response that wasn't forthcoming because shock had silenced me – he added: "We last saw each other in July 1936; the fact is . . . I have just reached fifty, idiot that I am."

This was what he said, word for word, as an opening gambit, and he even repeated: "Yes, idiot that I am." More than ever it felt as if we were simply two ghosts, and I remembered Soleràs (I still thought he was alive, though nobody knew where he might be): he had reminded me of a time when we'd been arguing about ghosts and Picó had said people in the Science Faculty did not believe in them. Soleràs had interrupted: "But is there anything that isn't ghostly?" And here was the ghost of Lamoneda by my side, sticking a finger up his nose while glancing sideways at the goldfish bowl. The stream of humanity seethed without end along the pavements and I did some quick mental arithmetic: if this idiot had just made it to fifty, he must have been forty-three on the eve of the war, when he was still loitering down corridors in the Pharmaceutical Science Faculty, embroiled in eternal studies that did him no good at all – he was once arrested on suspicion of dealing in cocaine. He embarked on a long monologue which I did and didn't listen to; I felt he had set a trap by sitting at the same marble table as me, lowering a croissant identical to mine in a cup of malt that was twin to mine, and Soleràs came to mind again, taking me back to the occasion when he told me about the paintings covering the walls of his aunt's flat. Apparently she had a horror of light and open spaces and was made unhappy by bare walls. One of the pictures was a print with all the kings in the world – before the 1914 war, naturally – depicting them all gathered together – "there were fifty or sixty," said Soleràs – like one big family around their patriarch, Emperor Franz Josef; but the juiciest detail, Soleràs added, was that his aunt had deliberately pinned over the figure of an adolescent Alfonso XIII a picture of a bearded individual who was none other than Don Carlos María of Bourbon and Austria-Este, the Carlist Carlos VII. And now that memory returned because it really did feel as if someone had played the same trick again, replacing Soleràs with this ghost rehearsing his monologue beside me; he rambled and I didn't catch what he was saying because it was all so knotted up! I couldn't grasp what he was talking about – bitter disappointment, disillusion, ingratitude, and time went by, no trace remained of his malt or croissant, and still he kept on and on. I had a vague intuition that my soutane had made him think I'd been on his side – a general misconception at the time – and I was about to disabuse him when I realised that if I stayed warily silent he might tell me lots I was interested in finding out.

First and foremost I wanted to know what *he* knew about the end his uncle had met.

"What do you want to know?" he interrupted, as if the subject made him nervous. "You probably know too much already: that he's assumed dead, and about there being signs that speak of miracles. I'll tell you about it all in due course; first let me tell you the story of my tenant farmer. He's the one who has sunk me into poverty . . . dire poverty!"

Dire poverty . . . But wasn't he an important personage? Or were those front-page articles a dream? The ghost eyed me suspiciously: "You didn't dream them . . . as you see me here, I was one of the leaders of the land; this man here before you . . ."

And he pointed to his shabby coat that gave him a shipwrecked look.

"But you have a big farm," I said, "A big farm on the plain of Vic, if I remember correctly."

"Not as big as all that," he replied, bitterly and scornfully. "Not so big. Behind my back, my father mortgaged some bits, and sold off others. As he set out in his will, he'd been forced to do that to pay for my studies in Barcelona. He lied. He was intent on reducing my inheritance in order to increase that other fellow's. Let me explain myself, it's rather complicated, but it is scandalous too; it transpires that my dear, dear Papa had enjoyed a bit of fun on the side, unbeknown to his family; he was incredibly discreet. We only learnt of the existence of a natural son after his death: he put in an appearance in the will. So it turns out the man sitting opposite you now has a brother. A brother! Isn't an illegitimate son what they vulgarly call the son of a . . . ? Papa made me his heir on condition that I diverted five hundred pessetes a month for life to my . . . brother. And there was more to come: if I were to die without an heir, the farm would go to him; so all I am is what they call a 'rotten heir'."

"Even so, apart from this brother who came as a surprise, you are the only son . . ."

"And orphan, without mother or father!" exclaimed that fifty-year-old orphan, starting to chuckle softly. "They pay me ten thousand pessetes a year rent for the farm, but let me tell you the rest of the story. I have to give five hundred a month to the other fellow. Do your sums, dire poverty! It's a joke when you're fucked because your father had a bit of fun on the side ages ago . . . If I could only tell you how much I have suffered . . . Firstly, I never knew my mother, as you know."

I thought how I had not known my mother either, and how Lluís and Soleràs were in the same boat, but at least Lamoneda had known his father, had watched him live into old age on the ancestral estate.

"My father? Hmm . . . my father . . . best to forget him. You are aware that my mother was the sister of this Dr Gallifa who preoccupies you so, and that she died accidentally soon after I came into this world; well, if you know that much, you know as much as I do. My father never told me any more about her. My father, hmm . . . never mentioned her."

He jumped from one subject to another and for no discernible reason began telling me about the way he had been deceived and bamboozled by envious colleagues the minute he was given an important position in some office or other: "You wear your heart on your sleeve and they gobble it up, horrendous things happen, things that cry out to heaven! I sacrificed myself, I risked my life in so many dangerous situations, I carried out highly important secret missions, the man sitting opposite you was the man who welcomed Himmler . . ." – he would return to that episode time and again as one of the most glorious memories of his existence – ". . . I was one of the leaders of the land . . . but there was so much slander, you know, lots of slander; they tricked me in all kinds of ways! The spirit of those early days quickly faded; never mind that we were the genuine article, before you knew it we'd been sidelined and persecuted by envy and the newcomer upstarts had stuck their claws into us. If you were to believe them, we were all fifth columnists! Every man jack of us! If you added them to those who were republican once and have now joined our own ranks, you'd double the population. I've even come to suspect . . . yes, there are moments when I am haunted by this terrifying suspicion! . . . let me tell you in confidence: I truly suspect that the new chief of police is a liberal."

He extracted from his inside jacket pocket a wallet that was swollen fit to burst, and from what I could see it only contained press cuttings: "I keep things, you know, I keep everything! Look at this communiqué that was issued after they got rid of me, and you tell me if this man isn't a Mason!"

I kept the cutting, because he gave it to me; he carried several copies in his wallet and evidently gave one to every acquaintance he came across in order to persuade them that the new chief of police was a highly dangerous red. The communiqué went as follows – in Spanish, of course:

I have decided hereon not to accept any denunciation that isn't written and duly signed, in any case giving those who decide to inform every assurance of total secrecy concerning their written statements, which will be returned to them once the facts reported have been clarified, because anonymous denunciations, by phone or letter, have caused and continue to bring turmoil to people's minds and anxiety into homes that day after day see their peace and quiet disturbed by incessant, unjustified denunciations. I hope everybody will understand the motives inspiring my words and that from now on, when someone makes a denunciation in the name of our holy cause, they won't sully it by using the techniques of calumny . . .

"I was sacked on the telephone because of that denunciation farrago. Dumped on the street! The fact is I am too good and sincere and idealistic, and that was my downfall. Nobody else could furnish a C.V. like mine and the envious took their revenge by making my life impossible in every way. Here you see me, in dire poverty; I'm poverty-stricken, whereas that chemist . . . Do you remember the chemist I worked for on carrer Sant Pau, where I was an assistant in 1930, the fellow who informed on me because he claimed I was helping myself to his stocks of cocaine? Well, despite that, despite informing on me in 1930, he's now back retailing his potions on carrer Sant Pau as if nothing had happened! The new chief of police didn't think twice about releasing him . . ."

He was obviously worked up on account of such nefarious doings, but then something else caught his eye: one of the *habituées* of the Rondas de Sant Pau and Sant Antoni had just walked in, heralded by her lurid red hair and stiletto heels. This houri skilfully mounted one of the swivel stools by the bar and ordered breakfast, smiling cheekily in our direction.

"That woman has something about her," mumbled Lamoneda, "I know her, she's Malvina; she doesn't remember me but you bet I recognise Malvina Canals i González. You bet I remember her, I remember everybody, I remember all those lovelies! My memory is good: too good. That's one of the things that led to my downfall, because nowadays only those who forget rise to the top. Yes, that lady is Malvina, but I was telling you about my tenant farmer, not about her" – and he went on to say that before the war his father had a different tenant farmer, a fellow with "evil ideas", to the extent that he had voted for the republicans in 1934. "Papa got rid of him and we did without; then the war came, they collectivised our land, Papa had to go into hiding in Barcelona; as for me, I expect you are aware that I had to flee in September 1936. I received my correspondence via the International Red Cross; in one of his last letters he told me he was starving to death in Barcelona, and that you couldn't buy bread on the black market for its weight in gold. It was in those difficult times that the new tenant farmer appeared; they had met in fifth-column circles. He was someone from our village who also happened to be hiding in Barcelona, but he had cash in hand because he was operating on the black market. He rented our land from Papa even though it was collectivised and he hadn't a clue when he would be able cultivate it, and into the bargain he paid him an advance of one hundred thousand pessetes for the rent, on top of the annual payment of ten thousand pessetes they'd agreed; he paid the advance in cash, in the presence of the notary who drew up the contract. Papa wrote to me enthusing about the man's generosity; I was quick to reply that he should watch out and check if the notes were genuine . . . Hey, that Malvina has really got something going for her!"

He had interrupted his flow to gawp.

"So then, were they genuine or weren't they?"

"What do you think?! I found them intact when I arrived; my father had died weeks before. A hundred spanking new thousand notes! Hot off the presses of the reds! The Bank of Spain told me that if I wanted to paper the walls of my flat with them, they could let me have as many sacks of them as I needed. I asked that the contract be cancelled; the Supreme Court upheld its validity. I had only one option: to get the new tenant farmer executed as a red. But he was quite the opposite! I am such an unlucky man."

The mysterious woman chose that moment to swing round on her stool and lean back on the bar, presenting us with a racy profile; simultaneously she crossed her legs and stared brazenly at Lamoneda.

"What a filly! And all ready to go! You are obviously out of it; a sexy filly like this Malvina does nothing for you; I, on the other hand . . . I am no Jesuit! Don't tell me about clerical hang-ups! Hang-ups have never been my forte, but getting it up . . ." At this he laughed idiotically as if to suggest he had been terribly witty. "You know, I'm a man in the fullest sense of the word, a *man*! That too has been my downfall . . . The new chief of police, this pinko liberal, this Mason in disguise, this commie, even thought I had got certain young ladies, like Malvina here, arrested as reds, when the only red thing about them was their dyed hair . . . Ahh, one day I must read you my novels. Stendhal is not a patch on me! And so what? When one is a man, it's not natural . . . if you only knew, I've always been partial to redheads . . . What's that? Do I still write novels? More than ever. I don't have anything else to do! They are better than Stendhal's, stylistically much better; my style would knock Eugeni d'Ors into a cocked hat. I'll read them to you one of these days, can you credit that they are still as unpublished as they were under the masonic Republic? Publishers continue to reject them; I informed on the lot of them, but now with this new chief of police . . . Hell, take a look at those legs! That girl knows they're fantastic so she's flaunting away . . . though they're hardly St

Pandulfa's!" – at which he burst out laughing idiotically yet again.

I said nothing and clearly he thought my look was disapproving because he switched to a different, more defensive tone: "You see, I'm no Jesuit, I detest hypocrisy! Why should I deceive you? Do you really want me to pretend that I prefer St Pandulfa to a filly like her?"

I had never heard of any St Pandulfa; from what he went on to recount, I deduced she was someone venerated locally, in his village and nowhere else. He muttered something or other about an uncle of his in the eighteenth century, the younger brother of his great-great-grandfather: "Not the Uncle Gallifa you knew, but an Uncle Lamoneda who was quite the opposite sort," a wealthy canon who'd gone to Rome and brought back a relic, a mummified St Pandulfa. "So that's why all the girls in our family from then until now have been called Pandulfa, though it's some time since we had any girls.

"Of course, the mummy is rather disgusting," he added, "but she works miracles. They built a crypt for her paid for by my uncle the canon; a crypt under the main altar in the parish church. They placed a glass urn on a black marble pedestal in the centre of the crypt; to save on marble the pedestal is hollow inside and the mummy is laid out as if it were asleep in the glass urn, so it is visible. You have to ask the sacristan for the key, because the crypt is always locked: and bolted and barred, you'll say, no doubt, as it contains that treasure, that cold meat. It's still there, don't ask me how; how is it possible that the church in my town, the crypt, and that hunk of St Pandulfa, weren't burned by the reds? Well, it was that arsehole of a tenant farmer my father was forced to get rid of because of his subversive ideas who made sure they were all safe and sound; he was mayor and defended the village like a hunting dog to keep out the flying anarchist patrols cleansing the country in requisitioned lorries. Even the men in the town guard opened fire on them. That was how he saved the priest's life and prevented the church being destroyed. It all goes to show what a dangerous red he was; how could he have stopped the anarchists from burning it and killing everyone if he hadn't been a red of the most powerful kind, a red of the worst stripe? He was even cynical and brazen enough to stay on in the village when all the others were fleeing in terror, and that's how we caught him."

The unknown dame had finally stood up with a sigh of resignation and sashayed out like a caravel; Lamoneda's eyes pursued her: "There really are some beauties around," he muttered, "but all they want is your wallet. I know perfectly well that if you offer this Malvina under a hundred pessetes she'll laugh in your face and say: 'Who do you think I am, handsome?'" And then he abruptly switched tack: "Do you remember the last time we met? It was in that church they were about to burn down, and you wanted to stop them! What a lovely – yet another fling I've missed for want of a wretched hundred pesseta note! I'm such an unlucky man!"

Malvina – if that really was her name – had started strutting up and down the pavement, toing and froing past the bar window, looking and smiling askance at the better-off passers-by. Lamoneda's eyes followed her up and down – her stilettos were so high and she flounced with such style! – while pursuing his rant. The human flow on the Ronda continued to stream past on the other side of the glass in what seemed an underwater seascape; among the shoals of anonymous, grey conger eels that girl with her gleaming red hair and stiletto heels was quite a goldfish. Time was also flowing by and the ghost's voice became increasingly monotonous; I missed the drift of what he was telling me: "How could we have defended the church if nobody had attacked it?" he said, perhaps referring to the old tenant farmer, but I had lost track. "Obviously he was a red, if not why was he so keen for them not to kill the priest or burn the church? They caught him and he got his just deserts; imagine, he spoke in Catalan all through the trial! Well, true enough he didn't know how to speak any other way as he'd never left the area; anyhow, it's not him but the other fellow, the new one, I should really have liquidated. I am such an unlucky man." Then he let rip against heavens knows who that had chosen not to help him – quite the contrary, in fact; it rose to a delirious tirade that was beyond me, I had no idea what he was talking about, he had swollen into a raging torrent and was now saying something or other about the anarchists, an individual I couldn't identify, but whom he reckoned was very important: "How come you've not heard of him? He's really famous!" – when I suddenly cottoned on: "Did you say Milmany?"

"Of course, the renowned Llibert Milmany, the potentate, the manager of Rexy Mura," and Lamoneda winked: "Did you ever crack the secrets of Rexy Mura? The same concoction makes men's hair grow and removes women's, you can go a long way with a fantastic recipe like that! Did you know he's the son of one of the most dangerous kinds of anarchist? How do I know him? Just imagine! I've known him for years . . . How come I know him? Don't make me laugh, Cruells; you're pulling such a face! Anyway I find it odd you have never heard about old Milmany's execution; obviously the press don't tend to mention these things, but there's never any shortage of rumours. They garrotted him not too long ago. You must know he'd been publishing a weekly in the red zone throughout the war in which he insinuated that the arsonists and murderers were quite possibly led by agents provocateurs. He was a very dim-witted old man, as you can see; so unlike Milmany his son . . . so different! The son was a slippery character; he'd grasped how you could get the most contrary results from the same concoction. He was a past master at the art of killing two sparrows with a single shot, a brilliant comrade! As for his father, ugh, he could hardly have been more dissimilar. Just imagine, he didn't want to leave Barcelona at the end of the war: 'Better to live in Catalunya than in foreign lands,' there was no way to get him out. And you must remember how my Uncle Gallifa didn't want to go into exile either? Llibert was longing to send him far away and forget him, because a swine like that can be very compromising and cause a lot of trouble; let's just say he was as interested in getting his father out of the country as I was my uncle. The old man, though, was very prestigious in the eyes of many Catalan workers; he was put forward for an important post in the new unions . . . He only had to switch his colours like so many others and overnight he would have been a somebody, practically a minister. He refused. They hinted he had to choose between a post or . . ."

Lamoneda gave a deep sigh: "His son is currently earning millions. The last time I tried to see him, a uniformed servant slammed the door in my face. And I can tell you I know all there is to know about his servant, every little detail! He's as fat as a gorilla, and that's why Llibert employs him as his bodyguard. He's a Gutiérrez who comes from Medellín; during the war he'd managed a collectivised enterprise, I think one that made pasta for soup – and now you see he is bodyguard to a millionaire, the great Milmany. There you have it: our brilliant comrade, with his millions, and me, in dire poverty. What a turn up for the books! That fool Soleràs had predicted it would come to that . . ."

He had said "that fool Soleràs" and I could hardly believe my ears: I was completely unaware Lamoneda had known him. What was I to make of this rambling ghost who kept on with his garbled spiel – and so monotonously, my God! – a mishmash of murky insights, lunatic insinuations, and incredible half-truths? However, when he said "that fool Soleràs" I gave a start and awoke from my drowsy state: "Soleràs? So you knew him as well?"

"Too right I knew him . . . ," and he looked at me suspiciously. "I know everybody, even though nobody knows me, or at least they pretend not to. Did I know him? You bet I did! From 1930! In those days he paid me the occasional visit at the chemist's on carrer Sant Pau; he'd had the cocaine habit for a while. He wanted to experiment. He soon got bored; he was a young man who soon got bored of everything, the fickle, inconstant type, with no will-power! He wasn't like me, when I set out on a chase I follow it to the very end. Did I know Soleràs? He was the person I knew best of all! Just imagine, we ended up in the same battalion in the last few months of the war. Did I know him? And why are you so interested in that Soleràs devil? Did you know him? What would you like to know about him? He disappeared at the tail-end of the war, and there's been no news of him ever since. You see, he tried out cocaine but soon got bored; he was fickle."

"You say he disappeared . . ."

"Well, there's been no news of him . . . agh," and the ghost looked at me askance. "So you'd like news of him? I'm amazed you knew him too; I don't recall him ever mentioning you."

"The last time you and I met, I didn't know him. I met him later, in the course of the war."

"Since you knew him, you'll remember he was a one-off. He often said: 'People always do the reverse of what people do'; he was always coming out with these shafts of wit. He was simply a fool. Why are you so interested in the fact that he disappeared? So many disappear in the course of a war . . . but wasn't it my uncle's disappearance that really interested you? My uncle! A kind of old Milmany! What a character! I'd told him repeatedly that they'd massacre priests, and Jesuits with even more reason: he refused to believe me. 'Who could possibly want to harm us that much?' he retorted. I could have shipped him off to Italy with a republican passport thanks to my relationship with the great Llibert; all to no avail. He said secret masses, and confessed, the whole caboodle. He even took the last sacraments to dying souls, can you believe, even if they were reds. The last time I saw him was in that attic, it was already September, just before I fled Barcelona. It was still stifling hot; the sweat was streaming down his face. I tried to persuade him for the last time. He looked at me so slyly: 'Flee? Like a coward? My boy, you ought to know that the worst that can happen to a monk is to turn out a nun . . .' All these Gallifes are hard nuts to crack, each in their own way; my maternal great-grandfather, my uncle's grandfather, was the Gallifa who fought in the Carlist wars. In 1837 he held out for six months in the Guilleries forests with a handful of men against a whole brigade of Maria Cristina's men."

"Dr Gallifa was no Carlist!"

"Nor a supporter of Maria Cristina, and who said he was? I wasn't referring to him, but to his grandfather, Commander Gallifa, from the Seven Years War. Every Gallifa has his own hobby horse, but they're basically all the same: stubborn as mules! You tell me if carrer l'Arc del Teatre was the right place for a father of the Society of Jesus to live in, where every doorway – every last one a dung heap! – had its lady of the night offering herself to the generally drunk passers-by. He prepared his own lunch every day, on the days he ate any; so where did he get the pittance he lived on? I garnered all this from a neighbour, an old woman who lived on the same staircase; it turned out that this sanctimonious old crone who lived up those stairs, clinging to the skirts of priests and friars, probably saw him and guessed he was a Jesuit: 'Dressed like a worker, but with that expression . . .' She was the kind with a flair for smelling out a reverend father of the Society of Jesus, whatever his disguise. In any case, my uncle, as you will remember, had one of those faces straight out of a painting; I mean, out of one of those gloomy paintings you find at antiquarians', or hanging in a corner of an old church, where you come across the ugly mugs of priests from bygone ages with bulging eyes that seem to be staring vacantly at the moon. He would have starved to death in that attic if his goody-goody neighbour hadn't taken him a packet of rationed vetch now and then. Only vetch, you know, because she'd twigged him."

"Twigged what?"

"I don't know if you remember how my uncle was addicted to snuff. Initially, she gave him a bit of everything she could get hold of, mainly rice, and during the odd week, bread; in a word, she shared her rations with him. She also had the key to the attic and one morning, when she thought he'd gone out, she went to give it a good clean; she caught him in the act, engrossed in his snuff taking! He had bartered his bread and rice for some tobacco powder; shamefacedly he mumbled: 'I can manage without bread, but not without this . . .' Subsequently, once I'd scurried out of Barcelona, I got no news of him for the rest of the war; in 1939, shortly after we made our entry, I visited that house on the Arc del Teatre. The old woman still lived there; she said my uncle vanished at the end of November 1936. She spoke of him as if he were a saint; she said she had pledged herself to him, that she'd dedicated novenas and other such hallowed acts to him, she told me the strangest stories, miracles, you know, stupid rubbish, nonsense, the most incredible crap. Hell, I'm no altar boy; I started shaving a long time ago, so don't give me that load of rubbish. We'd have been in a pretty pickle if even our relatives . . . fancy telling me that someone I know is a saint and works miracles! A saint? He let himself be caught in a rat trap, and that's a fact; in the end, it was his own fault. Who was forcing him to stay put in Barcelona? As far I'm concerned, if people act like imbeciles, what can I do? How am I to blame?"

The ghost broke off and added meekly: "Would you mind buying me another croissant?"

That was how I first heard the rumours about Dr Gallifa's supernatural doings, but it was some years after this conversation with Lamoneda that the inexplicable cure took place which so bewildered the disbelieving doctor – the same man who then became the fiercest proponent of the cause of his beatification. While Lamoneda soaked his second croissant in his second cup of malt, I remained silent.

"Now, if you like, I'll tell you about Soleràs."

He wiped his lips carefully on a paper serviette after finishing that second croissant and looked at me suspiciously: "By the way, how come you got to meet him?"

"I knew his aunt," I lied evasively. "I also met him during the war, as I said earlier, but I had little contact with him."

"Hmm, she was an old woman and a great devotee of St Philo-mena; but perhaps what you don't realise is that before he came over to our lines, he'd been a red. What a fool! He had deserted from a red brigade, bringing with him all kinds of maps and more or less confidential reports . . ."

"You can't be serious . . ."

"Oh yes I can. That was why he was held in high regard in spite of his eccentric ways; he was a lucky fool! The aunt you mentioned wasn't only a devotee of St Philomena, she was also a millionaire, and he was her only nephew! Although I finally came to suspect that the person who most influenced him wasn't that old aunt, but another lady, one who was neither old nor devout, quite the contrary . . ."

"A quite different kind of dame?"

"Absolutely, that dame was quite something else!" Lamoneda winked at me again. "It's a complex business I never did get to the bottom of. Apparently our side owed most of the information they had on one particular section of the Aragonese front to that woman, as they subsequently relied on Soleràs for reports on another nearby sector. I don't think I ever worked any of that out; I was involved in the secret services, but not in the army's – that depended on the General Staff, where we weren't allowed to poke our noses. It was really complex, I can tell you, and, besides, I'd rather not talk about that."

He gave me another suspicious glance, but evidently my expression reassured him because he went on: "All I do know is that with the scraps of information they gleaned here and there, almost by chance, the General Staff managed to reconstruct, by dint of extreme patience, as if they were solving a crossword, whole stretches of enemy lines. Apart from that, she must have been a very connected lady to wield so much influence: she was the one who got Soleràs out of the concentration camp. I expect you are only too well aware that they used to stick all deserters from republican lines into a camp on a temporary basis and it wasn't easy to escape; naturally, they were always highly suspicious. Such people might be spies, saboteurs, who knows what. They approached our lines shouting, "¡Nos pasamos! ¡Arriba España! ¡Franco, Franco, Franco!", but it could all be an act; we also sent some of ours to their front lines pretending they wanted to go over to their side. In fact, lots of ours went over to them and lots of theirs came over to us and because there was so much traffic it was easy to slot in the odd good secret agent. For example, almost all the Catalan soldiers that conscription had caught in Francoist territory went over to the reds: the fact that I was Catalan was one of the reasons why they never really trusted me. They couldn't believe a Catalan might be on their side! Because almost all the Catalans deserted one day or the next . . . But let's pick up our thread. So, thanks to the influence of a grand dame whose identity I never flushed out, Soleràs was able to leave that concentration camp after a very few weeks and, what's more, with a lieutenant's stars! That fool was so lucky! I was a mere adjutant and never promoted; they never promoted me, quite the opposite. The military and I have never got on; rather than promoting me, they often spoke of demoting me. Soleràs, on the other hand, always fell on his feet! Not only did they make him a lieutenant, they even sent him off to a 'dead front'. Talk about falling on your feet! They sent him there, as I eventually discovered, because our positions were right opposite those of the red brigade where he'd served; are you starting to understand things?"

Yes, I was . . . We had started to understand on that now distant day when Lluís, along with Trini and their severely ill son, had galloped off from Santa Espina in a cabriolet; Lamoneda had only torn away the last tatters of the veil obscuring that particular enigma; he had said nothing I had not already suspected.

"He had to organise to meet up with his old friends now and then in the villages in the deserted valley between the two front lines, and on the excuse that they were swapping goods he maintained a contact that was as unbroken as possible. I don't know if you're aware that these swapping arrangements were very common on the so-called dead fronts. We were short of clothing, most of all socks; they gave us socks and shirts made in Catalonia in exchange for coffee, tobacco, sugar, items we were well stocked with, because we got them from Andalusia, the Canary Islands, and Guinea. Soleràs honed his skills to the point of organising football matches on the threshing ground in one of the villages; thanks to all kinds of deviousness, the General Staff found out the exact positions of enemy lines and as a result could choose at the right moment the deadest sectors, the ones most lacking weapons and fortifications, the worst supplied with troops, the most unsuspecting and unlikely to imagine we might attack. Our offensive was devastating; the surprise element, one hundred per cent. The people who'd most contributed were promoted, so Soleràs was now a captain. During the last months of the war he was a captain acting as commander; I belonged to that brigade before he came to take charge. And that's how we met up again after so many years; we hadn't seen each other since 1930 during those last visits he made to the chemist's on carrer Sant Pau. The fool who always fell on his feet! If the war had gone on and he'd not been such a fool, he'd have ended up a colonel."

"Soleràs a colonel!"

"He knew how to fall on his feet but he remained a fool. I'd need a couple of weeks to tell you about all his tomfoolery. I'd been expelled from another battalion a couple of months earlier; the commander had got wind of something I was up to. The fellow was a monarchist, a supporter of Alfonso, and suspected that I was keeping an eye on him, that I never let him out of my sight. He harassed me in every way he could until he managed to persuade me to ask for a transfer to another battalion; that's right, I put in the request myself, but it was as if they had chucked me out because if I hadn't, that liberal in disguise, that pillar of free-masonry, would have fixed it so I was demoted as well. He'd sworn to do just that! He'd already put a dossier together with loads of statements made by captains and lieutenants from the fusiliers, an envious bunch who reckoned I behaved like a chicken in attacks and counterattacks. Me a chicken! I've got more spunk – and juicier – than the lot of them, but they always invent these stories about me, there are always envious bastards ready to bury me under a pile of slander. Anyway, it would take too long to go into all that – what can you expect of supporters of the liberal branch of the Bourbons? They all belong or had belonged to masonic lodges. Though at the end of the day none of this had any-thing to do with Soleràs; the fact is they moved me to a different battalion and that was how I came to be there when he was appointed commander. And chance led me to serve out the last months of the war under him, always as an officer in charge of pen-pushers. Don't think for one moment that working in the General Staff's offices was a bed of roses; Soleràs knew I hated the trenches and took advantage of it. He often had fun in the worst possible taste, cracking the lousiest, most hurtful jokes, particularly about Miranda the heiress."

That was the first mention of this new character who, as I gathered later, was an obsession of his. Naturally, I hadn't a clue who she was; he told me that before the war his father and Miranda's had decided to marry them off because their farms were adjacent.

"She didn't seem very enthusiastic, even though at the time we didn't know that Papa had mortgaged a large part of the recently acquired land, or that he had an illegitimate son. Nobody had a clue about any of that, and on the other hand she was well into her thirties, though still very lukewarm about the prospect of our marriage. She had pretensions because she'd been educated in France, at a boarding school run by the Dames Noires in Lyon, and had spent long periods in Paris; that's where she became acquainted with a lightweight dauber, a penniless bohemian who held exhibitions in Paris without ever selling a painting. I can never work out what women are after; in any case, her father made a big mistake when he sent her to be educated in that immoral country France . . . Soleràs knew the whole story, because I had told him; towards the end of the war I still assumed it was settled we would marry once it was over. Our parents had prepared everything down to the fine details, so how was I to know she would turn out so blind and obstinate? I just assumed we'd marry come the end of the war. It was in fact Soleràs who predicted the thing would turn out otherwise: 'Poor Lamoneda,' he said. 'You're a man who's misunderstood and women will never understand you.' He even added, 'They don't like marrying cuckolds.' 'That doesn't make any sense,' I retorted, 'how can you be cuckolded before you're even married?' 'Everything is possible in this world,' he replied, 'and women have incredible intuition, it's amazing what they can guess if they use their intuition. Everyone talks about female intuition! I'd bet my last cent on her having intuited that you will be a cuckold one day.' Yes, he liked making that kind of distasteful comment I found hard to stomach, but he was battalion commander and I had to take it on the chin if I didn't want to be removed from administrative duties and sent to the trenches. I put up with it and he went on and on about little Miranda. One day I decided to get my revenge by playing a joke on him; we often did that, awful practical jokes were our daily bread. I'd discovered he kept a woman's photo at the bottom of his suitcase (you will have worked out that I never missed seeing anything, not even what people kept well hidden in their suitcases); just imagine, it was a woman's photo, nothing out of the ordinary; I can't think what he saw in her. The truth is we all collected postcard pictures of film stars wearing next to nothing. They're so nice to look at. There were those platinum blondes with great legs, you know, such long legs; I don't know why film stars have such long legs, perhaps so they have more to show off. For a bit of mild amusement, in the odd idle moment, we'd draw a civil guard's moustache on the photos of stars belonging to other soldiers; stupid pranks, I agree, but we all played them. Well, you know, I had the bright idea I'd do the same to Soleràs' lady, who was no film star, though he kept her well out of sight; he caught me in the act. You should have seen him! He went raving mad! He grabbed me by the lapels, shook me up and down, and banged me against the wall. I mean, she was nothing very special; she wasn't blonde and didn't flaunt her legs; I'd have said she was simply a housewife who got by and was happy with her lot; I can't fathom what he saw in her. Her face was on the plump side, I can tell you, with smallish eyes. How shall I describe her? It's hard to describe a face that's so run-of-the-mill, and her clothes I'd say were the opposite of an actress'. I'd have said she was a teacher and the truth is I have no time for ladies who teach algebra rather than show off their legs . . . No, don't ever bring me a blue stocking, give me girls with sex appeal! But that was the kind of woman in the photo Soleràs had tucked away at the bottom of his case. I told you he's a real eccentric! Still, he was such a lucky fellow, always falling on his feet! In the last winter of the war . . ."

The ghost had said, "In the last winter of the war". My God, the last winter of the war was so balmy! Even in the middle of January we saw no ice or snow, not even on the peaks of the mountains; what remained of the Catalan brigades after the battle of the Ebro had been forced back north of the river; our battalion, led by a fellow called Picó, now promoted to commander, was once again reduced to a handful of men, as it had been after the debacle on the Aragonese front. We were wandering aimlessly once again, though now with an enemy at our heels that was always on the verge of cutting off our retreat. We lost our way and ended up on a small plateau of bare mountain on the top of Montsant; for as long as I live I shall never forget you, rocks of Montsant! It didn't seem possible – all this that was happening – in such balmy weather, under such a blue sky. We were into 1939 and had fetched up on that high plateau of bare rock, with the A-rabs camped at the foot of the mountains and in control of all the passes. We were penned in – finally. For the first time in his life, Picó's instincts had let him down: we had walked into a rat trap. A few days later, when the

A-rabs started to climb up every mountain path simultaneously, many of our lads tried to escape straight down the precipices. Montsant's precipices are vertical. Some made it; others . . . At night we could hear them moaning, sometimes almost howling, for hour after hour at the foot of those crags; people in the nearby farmhouses didn't dare go out to help them for fear of retaliation by the A-rabs. My God, what a relief it was when the howling ceased.

Somehow or other, Picó found the entrance to a deep hole that was so small you had to crawl in. He had only six men left; we survived for several days in that fantastic hideout, perhaps four or five, I can't be sure; we lost all notion of time in those dark depths. We couldn't see each other; our eyes never adapted to such pitch-black darkness. We clung to each other so as not to go astray in shadows we imagined to be vast and full of labyrinths and pits; there was plenty of water and we had a few crusts in our haversacks. When we'd eaten the last, we decided to emerge into the outside world.

It was a strangely warm night for the middle of January. How could the Milky Way twinkle so brightly over that plateau of bare rock? There was no moon, yet we were dazzled when we came out of that cave. The broad rock plateau was deserted; there wasn't a living soul, only silence. We later discovered that the front had made big advances in recent days to the north-east, towards Barcelona; quite unawares, we were now behind enemy lines. Someday perhaps I will recount how Picó led his band of six followers through occupied territory to rejoin the Catalan troops – just in time to fight alongside them in the final battles. We reached Col d'Ares, where there wasn't a single patch of snow in February, then on to the mountain ridge between Molló and Prats-de-Molló, between the two Catalonias, between France and Spain, where

Picó sat on a stone frontier marker and, turning to the south, tears in his eyes, muttered: "This is the end of culture."

Someday I will recount all that, and how the remnants of so many other devastated brigades kept reaching the ridge in a tremendous jumble of professional soldiers and columns of volunteers, nationalists and communists, anarchists and Christian Democrats, republicans and socialists, trades unionists and federalists, one huge unspeakable mess of brigades and divisions in disarray, mules and lorries, cannon and machine guns that had to be abandoned and now littered the ravines, and suddenly, arising from that almighty chaos, the powerful anthem of the "Virolai"[3] that we all chorused as we looked into the distance at so many villages, towns, and cities going up in smoke in the mist over the plains, a "Virolai" in the dying light of a February sunset, before continuing our march, now down towards the north, heading into exile.

And here is this ghost now taking me for one of theirs, unable to imagine I could have been anything else, his monotonous voice droning on: "We'll be in Barcelona before the month is out, we said. And we were happy, you could say. I already saw myself back in the Lamoneda household, enjoying the great life that awaited the man who would now be master – finally! My father having died not long since, I'd marry Miranda the heiress; tenant farmers and hands would toe the line, and we'd treat them like dirt. She hadn't yet married that dauber and, as my father's will hadn't been read – they were waiting for me to come – we remained in the dark about that mortgage malarkey and the illegitimate son he'd left as

3 The hymn in honour of La Moreneta, Our Lady of Monserrat, with lyrics by Jacint Verdaguer, priest and popular Catalan poet.

a souvenir. As for the rental contract, I then thought like an idiot that it would be the simplest thing to cancel as an anachronism from the time of the reds. How could we ever have imagined that the Supreme Court would still be dominated by Freemasons and liberals pronouncing on matters as if nothing had happened? I was heir to the Lamoneda estate and would make my appearance as the returning hero. They'd never promoted me during the war, but I *was* an adjutant; an adjutant is somebody, watch out, I'm not one you can fool around with! I've always lived on my illusions . . . I have no choice, I'm like that, an idealist! If I'm going to be sincere, the war was always too much for me; all I was interested in was the moment when I would stride into town in my riding boots, brandishing my whip; in an adjutant's uniform, ironed and spotless, a hero, complete with boots and whip" – and our hero stuck a finger up his nose – "That was why I was so annoyed when the General Staff called off the offensives."

"Called off the offensives?"

Silence followed.

"Soleràs had guessed why" – the ghost's droning voice resumed its monologue. "Yes, he was more clear-sighted than me. True, he was a fool, but he often anticipated things more clearly than the rest of us. You know, the war could have been over in May '37, when the anarchists rose up against the Catalan government and left sectors of the Aragonese front practically bereft of troops. But why rush to end it? The longer it lasted and the more the anarchists got up to their tricks in Barcelona, the more people would want us; the moment would come when they'd have had their fill of war and anarchists, and our triumphant entry would seem like a dream come true! So, dragging it out was worth our while, it really was!

Soleràs was the one who grasped why we were halting those offensives that could have led us into Barcelona in one fell swoop; in March '38, for example, when the front in Aragon had been punctured along hundreds of kilometres. Starvation and bombing raids meant Barcelona was hell, and long may it last was what we said! The longer the craziness went on, the crazier the welcome we'd get! It could have been prolonged for another two years if Hitler hadn't been in such a hurry; he needed to finish this baguette before beginning a much bigger one, a gigantic cottage loaf! So Soleràs had predicted – but because he only kept hinting at it, we all thought him a fool. And he could really act the fool . . . One night he called me aside; he often did, and we'd chat for hours on end. He and I were the only Catalans in the battalion, and that bonded us . . . as I said, there were hardly any Catalans, they had all deserted. We chatted for hours and I put up with all his sly digs as long as he let me linger comfortably in the office. You know, the trenches didn't appeal at all, and if I'd wanted to be a martyr I could have stayed in Barcelona. I could have stayed put if I'd felt like being a martyr like my blessed uncle . . . ," and the ghost chuckled. "So then Soleràs summoned me aside; for several days I'd been thinking he seemed more outlandish than usual, that he was more and more insulting and making nasty remarks about little Miranda, but I said to myself: 'Stick the knife in and say what you will, as long as you don't pack me off to the trenches, my shit-faced commander . . .' On the other hand, I could never have done what I had to do if I hadn't been in the office department; I'd done very risky business in much more important places, in the General Staff of Central Army Command, just imagine, but the envious, niggling backbiters got their way and I was gradually relegated to much slighter roles, until I was buried deep in the command of a battalion. Like the military generally, Soleràs wasn't aware of my special mission, and that was what it was all about – not ringing any alarm bells. It was such a well-run, dangerous undercover operation that we once earned congratulations from Himmler in person; Soleràs may have got a whiff, or else he didn't really get it, or pretended not to . . . or didn't care a fuck, which was perfectly possible, given what he was like. So over those last few days he'd been rubbing every kind of innuendo about little Miranda in my face; I thought he seemed on edge and peculiar, I mean, more peculiar than usual. He called me aside and led me out of the encampment. 'Lamoneda,' he said, 'you and I weren't born to be winners, that's obvious from our deepest instincts.' 'What deepest instincts?' 'The ones we always radiate; don't be under any illusion, winners have never radiated the deeper feelings that you and I do; you can't feel it, nobody can ever feel their own, and that's a real piece of luck.' He leant on my arm because he was tottering; he'd had too much to drink that night, he'd been hitting the bottle more and more recently. While he talked, he stared into my face and a puff of his breath came my way; it was so laden with alcohol it would have burst into flames if you'd put a match to it. His stare was defiant and reinforced by his bad breath: 'What I want to do,' he went on, 'and right in your face, is to show you I couldn't care a fuck.' I quickly glanced behind me; the pair of them were there . . ."

"The pair of them? What pair?"

The ghost shut up and looked suspicious; after a bit he gave me an evil scowl and asked gruffly: "Why are you so fascinated by Soleràs? At the end of the day he was simply a fool. His bizarre behaviour was starting to bore me; we'd already had the business over Ibrahim. That night he came out with a stream of idiocies: 'You must understand, Lamoneda,' he said, 'you and I may be a couple of morons, I won't deny that, but we hail from over there . . . Didn't you say you'd read the whole of Stendhal from beginning to end? There's a passage in Stendhal that sums up your lot wonderfully . . .' He'd often refer in his mad way to 'your lot', as though he hadn't changed sides, as if he'd forgotten he was now in this camp. 'Here you have it, Stendhal *dixit*: *une rage sauvage les animait, surtout ils n'entendaient pas un mot de cette belle langue du Midi, et leur fureur en était redoublée; ils croyaient gagner le ciel en tuant des Provençaux . . .*' 'I've not killed any Provençals, you're crazy,' I retorted. 'What! Did you skip over that passage? Well, it's in *De l'amour*. I thought you swore by *De l'amour*! When all's said and done, one Provençal more or less . . . a dead cat can also be a tasty morsel . . . The only relations one can choose, one's wife or one's cat.' 'What the hell's a dead cat got to do with Stendhal?' 'Nothing at all, only that at the time it was all about the Albigenses, doesn't that name conjure anything up? You're like that dyed-in-the-wool Minister of Education from Paris who on a visit to Avignon was shown the papal castle but reacted in consternation saying "If the popes had ever lived in Avignon, I'd have heard about it." Conversely, when cats go on a crusade, something that happens unfailingly in the month of January . . . Oh hell, you know I've forgotten what I was talking about. Did you never hear that moonlight concert of miaows? You bet, it's a cats-only crusade. If we take things to an extreme, apart from one's wife and one's cat one can choose a child via the judicial fiction they call adoption. But a cat? A cat will never in a lifetime renege on its hearth, its country! Not in a month of Sundays! We kept finding them in those villages in the deserted valley, in the middle of no man's land, every cat in its favourite corner, faithful to a shelter that everyone else had betrayed. Sometimes, after nightfall, when we went into one of those abandoned houses, in the darkness, at the back of the kitchen, next to the extinguished hearth, we'd see the green flames of their eyes . . . kitties are a thousand times superior to me or you!' 'Soleràs, really, I don't think you're trying to . . .' 'One can never make off with someone else's cat; we've been able to manoeuvre our way around women, made off with someone else's wife through the judicial fiction we term a divorce, just as we appropriate someone else's child by adopting it, but there's no way you can do that with a cat! No way! It's impossible to adopt another man's cat! It will always escape and go back to its house . . . Kitties are a thousand times superior to the lot of us! Kitties and aunties; yes, aunties. Aunties are phenomenally loyal too. Have you noticed that the only adoption recognised in law is a child's? Like the only divorce is between husband and wife? There's no way you can adopt or divorce an auntie! It's impossible to adopt someone else's aunt or divorce one's own! An aunt is for life, like a cat. I lived with mine until the war started and, Lamoneda, I'd like to tell you I'd not change mine for all the aunties in China; each to his own!' So, Cruells, you can see the endless tripe Soleràs could spout once he got going, and better still when he wasn't spewing out against my little Miranda: 'I don't know why I imagine,' he'd say, 'that your little Miranda must be a fantastically shapely lass.' 'She is,' I'd reply, 'especially her legs . . .' 'That's what I suspected: wonderful legs. If the marriage comes off, you just see how friends will throng to the Lamoneda ancestral house.' 'Friends, I don't have any.' 'You will have, don't worry on that count; with legs like hers . . .' He was always coming out with innuendo and wisecracks, heavy shafts of wit that he aimed at me, and I harboured my own suspicions, you know, because there'd been that dubious business over Captain Ibrahim . . . I didn't want him to push me into the mire with his devilish tricks. He thought he could do whatever he wanted and I was fed up with him."

"Captain Ibrahim . . ." I asked. "Was there really a Captain Ibrahim?"

"You really are mighty curious, aren't you? Perhaps you can imagine . . ."

"What do you expect me to imagine if I know nothing about any Ibrahim? On the other hand, I did know Soleràs, but only vaguely." I lied again. "I got to know him by chance and really had little contact with him. The only person I did get to know was his aunt, because of some would-be miracle by St Philomena, and that was it. I think I've already told you about that."

He sighed, seeming reassured by my words, and said: "Would you mind buying me another croissant?"

"We were a long way from the encampment . . ." – he began to drone when he resumed his monologue – ". . . when Soleràs said: 'Lamoneda, everyone's now talking about the horrors of Spain, the whole universe is pointing a finger in our direction; you just wait a bit, and all this will seem very small beer. You know, I've lived in Germany, and I know what they're like: wait and see, the place is full of the most civilised people in the world, they'll work wonders! Make note of my prophecy, Lamoneda, and remember it when it comes to pass.' Soleràs had a mania for making prophecies, he prophesied left, right, and centre for no rhyme or reason. He'd come out with the stupidest predictions . . . Nonetheless, he did guess that right, yes, he foretold the war's final end on account of that other fellow being in a hurry. That's when he made the crack about the bread: 'He wants to finish this baguette before starting on another and that's why he's on our back, and what a hunk of bread that will be, a humongous cottage loaf! They'll work wonders! Our shenanigans will seem like a joyride! A lachrymose novel in comparison!' And he predicted we would soon be entering Barcelona. 'But get this straight,' he added, 'this imminent triumphant entry changes all my plans completely. Don't expect me to be part of any triumphant entry into Barcelona!' 'What do you mean?' 'That you shouldn't count on me!' he shouted angrily. 'And you'd be much better not joining in that glorious farce . . . how can you and I make an entry like arrogant conquerors? It would be like cuckolding your own father. You'll say that's a can of worms, so what's this here? To every man his can of worms . . . yours and mine are there, not here . . . If I'd known your lot would win, there was no way I'd have changed sides.' 'Hang me if I understand you, Soleràs,' I said bad-temperedly. 'Lamoneda,' he went on, 'you can only think about your little Miranda and basically you're just a . . .' 'A what?' 'Oh, nothing, just a lecher; don't be offended. Just a lecher. Bah, we mustn't fall out over something so petty; we all are, it's emblazoned on our foreheads. In comparison, peace is of no matter; lots of insects lose their skin to get a bit of it, and they're so happy! And that skin isn't ours, others wore it before us; organic matter never changes, we simply pass it on to others – plants, animals, humans. If I eat a cut of beef, the beef changes into Soleràs; the same cut eaten by you would change into Lamoneda. In troglodyte times, that's what impelled honest working people to turn to cannibalism, because it's really wonderful to think that if I eat you, what was once Lamoneda will turn into Soleràs. The materialists can tell you all about that! Matter is always the same, clothing we pass on from one to another, stuff that's been passed down for aeons, for millions of centuries.' 'That's your opinion, Soleràs,' I added, 'you're off your head.' 'I'm referring to the material,' he continued, 'not the manufacture, which is somewhat subtler. The manufacture is more personal, derives from the family. For example, in terms of manufacture, I'm a copy of my great-great-grandfather, about whom I know nothing. They don't let us choose the manufacture, only the cloth; we have to slip on predetermined clothes, whether we like it or hate it.' 'I reckon you've got a screw loose.' 'We transmit a parental form to our children; this power to transmit our form goes to our heads, and rightly so; for a moment we are almost godlike! But our power is limited to the transmission of a form, simply a form; no mind nor matter! Simply a form, a ghost, you could say. People don't realise and blessed are they because if someone did cotton on, they'd end up with migraine! By dint of wrestling with all this, one comes to sense that we are but forms, evanescent ghosts. The water we drink has been drunk thousands of times, no, millions of times before, from the beginning of Precambrian days, by billions of plants, animals, men, and women, and I do know what I'm talking about, I was mad about geology for a while. If you make an effort of the imagination, you feel unbearably nauseous: water is always the same, the immense ocean has been drunk and pissed out a thousand times! Lamoneda, my friend, you simply drink what I piss.'"

That was the ghost's cue to break off and ask me the time, because he didn't have a watch. I then realised to my astonishment that we'd been there three hours – three hours during which he'd droned endlessly on and on at me.

"He was off his rocker," he went on, "a pity it's so late, I could have told you so many more of his crazy ideas. He kept coming out with this rubbish without head or tail. 'So much fuss over so little,' he told me, 'so much fuss, and a small change in the way we reproduce could rubbish all the literature that's been written over the last three thousand years. What if there'd been three sexes and not two . . . You can laugh, Lamoneda, isn't it odd how all morons split their sides at the idea of a third sex? Well, it's no laughing matter; if we reproduce via two sexes, it's only a contingent state of affairs, by no means one that's necessary; fissiparity, that still exists at the lowest levels of living species, might have continued at the highest and then . . . goodbye to little Miranda's legs; goodbye to Stendhal; goodbye to *De l'amour*, goodbye. Why doesn't fissiparity make you laugh, you morons? It is fantastic how the idea of a third sex makes you so happy and yet you find fissiparity irritating . . . what's one got over the other? They are ways to reproduce, but let's resume our thread, as you will recall, it was dead cats.' 'Dead cats again?' 'Didn't I tell you how, at the right time and place, they can make a really tasty dish? We were talking about dead cats, adoption, divorce, and such nonsense.' He reiterated that several times: 'Adoption, divorce, a load of dead cats, a load of nonsense!' 'But why nonsense?' 'Sweet greenish stuff and nonsense, very fine, sugar-coated shit.' I'm simply relaying his words to you verbatim: *very fine, sugar-coated shit.* I'd begun to realise that he had what they call a complex, what you might call a running sore that translated into a kind of obsession against adoption and divorce; he went ballistic when he talked about them, which was often. Was he perhaps the son of a divorced couple, adopted by somebody else? That struck me more than once, but I never got to the bottom of it. His diatribe went on and on: 'Nursery rhymes to make us think that storks bring us children, how is it possible for somebody else's child to be your child, somebody else's wife to be your wife? As if that . . . as if . . . as if one could escape one's own obscenity! One's own, maybe, but other people's? The other's ghost will always intercede . . . fissiparity rather than that any day!'"

Lamoneda winked at me again and fingered the button in the middle of my soutane: "You know, I'm only quoting what he said word for word: 'How can one be with another man's wife? Can't you see the other's ghost will always be around?' He was mad. You know, I am the opposite of Soleràs when it comes to women; I'm always hungry for it and get a hard on, hmm; as far as I'm concerned, provided a female's got a good pair of . . . Hmm . . . Even if she's slept around before . . . with Nebuchadnezzar in person! Provided she's got . . . Hmm . . . But I was fed up with that lunatic; I'd already got far too involved with his madcap pranks in the Captain Ibrahim business. Ugh, what a nasty mess that was."

"So a Captain Ibrahim did exist?"

"He didn't exist any longer; he had existed once. To be precise, this Ibrahim was the dead cat, the edible morsel he talked about."

"Precisely this Ibrahim . . . ?"

He looked at me askance, suspiciously again, as if trying to size up how much he should tell me about all that; he started chuckling again: "Bah, that was war. What would be the point of bringing all that back? After all, Soleràs was basically a fool, a fool, nothing more. He's not worth bothering about. He went off, and that's that."

"Went off where?"

"Well, off to the trenches facing us. Luckily, I'd taken the precaution of getting those two – men I could trust – to follow me at a distance; he'd not noticed, they followed us discreetly and I . . . didn't let them out of my sight . . . Hmm . . . but why stir up all that past history? What's the point? Let's let Soleràs be; I'm sick to death of him."

"You say he went off . . ."

"I'm sick to death of all that, let's forget past history. That's enough of Soleràs! He went off to the reds' encampment and that was the last I heard of him. Not another word about him! What's the time?"

I told him what time it was and he sounded surprised it was so late.

"I must be going. I can't waste any more time. They're expecting me at the courtroom."

"I wasn't aware you were a lawyer."

"Nor a chemist!" he sighed. "But I have to make a statement. That's how I earn a few pessetes."

"Doing what . . . ?"

"Nothing grand, a pittance. It was different before the war; there weren't many of us and we managed. Now it's a waste of time! Too much competition! And very little in the way of solidarity! There are snitches who queer our pitch and drive down prices, who will say anything people want for twenty-five pessetes."

He stood up and winked at me, again mischievously: "I don't know why," and stooped down to whisper in my ear, "but I get the impression that you are disillusioned. We the disillusioned should meet up more often. Give me your address."

I lied to him, said I'd got nowhere to live for the time being, that I was playing it by ear, waiting to find out which living I was going to be allocated.

"Just like me," he replied, "and just what I'd thought. I've also been living hand to mouth over the last few months. But I've still got that *garçonnière* I had before the war, if you remember? You occasionally visited me there, and I read you some choice passages from my novels. Now that rents have been frozen, it's incredibly cheap and that's why I keep it on. I've done it up like an artist," and he winked again. "If you come someday, we can have a long chat. We must meet up. The disillusioned of this world should start organising . . ."

As I was all ready to try to fob him off, he added, to seduce me: "Well, if you come, I promise I'll tell you more about Soleràs. I've even hung on to a notebook that once belonged to him . . ."

And with that parting shot he slipped off in the direction of the goldfish bowl, turning to wink at me.

He reminded me of the daydream I had that day at the front, the day when Picó blew up the bridge and all those lorries, the time I stared into the red sunset; the ghost slipped away, winking at me, faded beyond the window and disappeared into the distance. He had fled Barcelona in September, Dr Gallifa hadn't disappeared until November, so the dates didn't tally and my daydream was wrong; yet all the same . . . did his ghostly presence at least exist? Could he be an essence with no real existence, I mean, a symbol? One that lingered in the air like the sweet smell of festering carrion.

II

I had only stayed in a French concentration camp for a few weeks; what could I do so far from my country? I asked to be allowed to return; they held me for nine months in another camp. At the time these camps were all the rage from the Algarve to Kamchatka. I was unable to return to Barcelona until a year after the war, and then I completed my studies there. After that, my memories become hazy; however, I do remember quite precisely the time of year and weather when something specific happened; for example, when I had that unexpected encounter in the bar on the Ronda de Sant Pau, it was a day late in December, a scabby, damp day I remember only too well, but what year was it – 1942, 1943? I'd have preferred never to recall it, it was too distressing; everything it involved was so turbid and ambiguous. What was he doing, what had he done, in whose pay was he, what was he planning? Was he just deranged, perhaps by his abuse of cocaine, which meant he went off on imaginary trips that made no sense, simply wanting to give others an enigmatic view of himself, one he thought worthy of a novel? That was more or less what Dr Gallifa had always suspected of his nephew; if there was one reason driving me to see him again, it was to find out more about his uncle and Soleràs, though repulsion was the feeling he'd really inspired in me.

As for his uncle, shortly after that ghostly meeting in the bar on the Ronda, I managed to locate the anarchist's widow. She had left her flat on carrer de l'Arc del Teatre a few weeks after the end of the war, so she was no longer living in it by the time I was able to return to Barcelona; she had left without telling her neighbours where she was going and locating her seemed like yet another of the many wild goose chases from that period. My efforts to track her down had led nowhere. And then, three years later, out of the blue, she wrote to Dr Gallifa's brother showing signs of life; he in turn informed me.

She is dead now; she died not long ago. At the time – 1943? 1944? – when I met her, she was a woman in her sixties who still did housework. Her name was Alberta and she had decided to live with her niece so as not to be so lonely. If she hadn't shown signs of life in all that time, she told me, it was because she didn't feel like seeing anyone. What she'd been forced to see during and after the war had left her feeling that she was no longer part of this world. She now felt she'd come to, and wanted to be in touch – she was extremely keen in this respect – to tell us all she knew about Dr Gallifa, mainly some peculiar happenings related to him that had come to pass after he disappeared.

The little flat on Hostafrancs where she and her niece lived was, of course, a very humble affair, though welcoming neverthe-less; the niece, probably in her forties, was as convinced of the reality of those incidents as Alberta herself. I was rather sceptical for the moment about the so-called miracles and more interested in what his final days in Barcelona had been like.

One evening late in November 1936 a complete stranger had visited the attic; Alberta took Dr Gallifa to one side and told him: "Don't trust strangers." "Someone who's dying sent her to see me," he retorted. "And what if it's a trap? Don't do anything silly, all kinds of things are happening . . ." "As long as I've got a pinch of snuff," he joked, "my strength comes back for a while." Because he was really very exhausted.

"After saying that, he went to the lavatory. There was only one on each floor and it was occupied; he was forced to wait. The poor fellow had to go all the time, recently; I think it was that rubbish snuff that was giving him the runs, especially as he ate almost nothing but worm-eaten vetch. If I gave him bread or rice, he bartered it for snuff . . . He was pitiful, so old and on his last legs. That unknown woman waited for him downstairs in the doorway. The streets were in darkness because the sirens had blasted, you had to grope your way along those narrow backstreets in our neighbourhood if there was no moon. From the lobby I watched him move away into the distance arm in arm with that stranger; he did that so as not to arouse suspicion. They were persecuting priests more than ever towards the end of November . . ."

He walked through the dense shadows on the arm of a strange woman like an aged client of the knocking shops on the carrer de l'Arc del Teatre. His last words to Alberta sounded very odd: "Tell everyone to forgive my bad sermons," she said he told her when bidding farewell in the doorway. He was eighty at the time. That was the last anybody heard of him.

According to Alberta, various uncanny happenings started from then on, sudden cures of the terminally sick and other mysterious favours gained by people who had known him and prayed for him to intercede on their behalf. She pledged herself to him nightly. At the time, the so-called supernatural incidents she recounted weren't so extraordinary that they couldn't have been put down to chance, and I was unimpressed, or perhaps just sceptical. As for pledging myself, I had already done that and told

her so; Alberta was very happy to hear it, because she was frightened, she told me, that it might be a sin to pray to someone when
you weren't even sure whether he was dead or alive.

The X-ray business didn't come until years later, around 1950. A
sister-in-law of the niece was suffering from a cancerous tumour
and when her doctor gave her only months to live Alberta suggested
she should pray to Dr Gallifa; the tumour that had been so visible
on previous X-rays suddenly disappeared. The incredulous doctor
was stunned; he was the most impatient of the lot and took the
X-rays to the Curia. He didn't understand why I was so hesitant
in the matter of the cause of his beatification. We'll go there, my
God, I thought, we'll go there; we won't hide the light under a
bushel; we'll make our statements as witnesses, but what will
that doctor think of us who was once a non-believer and is now
bowled over by what is beyond understanding? And all that red
tape and bureaucracy to declare a saint? This miracle will be lost
in an ocean of forms, O poor miracle . . .

And surprise, surprise, that was where I saw Lamoneda for a
second time when I went to the Curia to make a statement.

All Dr Gallifa's relatives had arrived to provide their statements;
all his friends and relations, everybody who had known him, had
been summoned to say what they knew.

And there he was, among them, with the cynical expression of
a crook who believes in nothing. What could he declare? What had
he come to do? Given he couldn't believe in any kind of miracle,
or refused to believe them, why was he wasting his time listening
to statements made by a distant aunt or a nebulous cousin, clinging to family bonds that had vanished in a fog of genealogy?
Lamoneda latched on to the most vapid reasons for an excuse to

be asked to make fresh statements; he hooked on to whatever he could, concocted the most amazing stories, and wanted to shine by recounting supernatural happenings. Yes, sad though it is to say, he invented miracles, the most horrendous miracles, to attract the attention of people, to catch in flight a slice of that prodigious cake, glory – the glory that, for him, meant making it into the newspapers.

We met up in that bishop's parlour I knew so well and visited so often at the time; a vast parlour furnished by the ugliest styles from the end of the previous century, gigantic sofas and armchairs dripping in fancy cord, buried in a dense, tepid half-darkness that smelt vaguely of camphor. While they waited endlessly, the family members scrutinised one another on the sly as if in a great sizing-up operation, and whispered, and rattled on. The entry of the archbishop[4] suddenly imposed silence. He appeared unannounced, out of nowhere, through a small door which had been papered like the wall. He observed us with the gaze that was typical of him, of somebody who understands nothing but lives in the hope that one day he will. Years later a stroke struck him brutally down; sick and poorly, he was no longer the colonel-archbishop – a military colonel – who had arrived with so much energy and so little understanding shortly after the end of the war. He died a few months before I began writing these lines; on the last few occasions when I saw him, his waxen skin and frozen smile had already given him that lethal air; sickness, old age, and disillusion had changed him profoundly. In that last phase, when by his side, you could smell the wan odour of his imminent

4 A clear reference to Bishop Mondrego, imposed in 1939 by the victors.

death agony; I was shocked to see him again in my memories as he was then, around 1950, the shepherd who didn't understand his flock.

He would suddenly appear, unheralded and silent, on the threshold of that little secret door, and listen for a second until we noticed his presence and shut up. Then he would say – always speaking in Spanish – "Well, I say, did somebody forbid you to speak in Spanish?" Years after, struck down by apoplexy or Grace, old and frail, he had worn himself out fighting obscure, stubborn battles in defence of his flock, trying to undo the wrongdoing he himself had wrought when his ignorance of the diocese that had been bestowed on him was total; in that era he had continually found it inconceivable that anyone in the world could speak in a manner different from his, unless out of pure pig-headedness. It took a quarter of a century for Grace, with the help of apoplexy, to shake his convictions; as I soon began to grasp by dint of my dealings with him, he was as nice as pie, though incredibly stubborn and dim-witted; we, his flock, initially assumed him to be a wolf, when he was but a donkey.

My Lord, he was as nice as pie, but thick as two planks. O Lord, you sometimes send us saints who are simpletons when our world needs clear-sighted saints like Dr Gallifa! I understood him only years later and then I loved him; suddenly I understood him, as if my eyes had been opened to what I had taken to be the mysterious depths of iniquity but that were merely the mysteries of provincialism. I know – some thirty years later – that I am only now grasping this, but I realise from the testimonies of people I completely trust that, at the start, when His Excellency stepped out to stroll around the Gothic quarter with some of his staff, he would come to a halt when a group of children walked by on their way to school. His Excellency stopped to listen, and his expression became more and more bewildered until he was forced to exclaim: "So young and already speaking Catalan!"

These were no mysterious depths of iniquity but the humbler mysteries of a Portuguese backwoodsman. What I am about to relate will perhaps give you an even better idea of the man; I myself witnessed these things. It was long after I had returned from the Caribbean, when His Excellency, having taken a paternal interest in me, often summoned me to his palace to provide him with companionship. He had to go out, once, and we went into the courtyard; moving to get in the car, we found his chauffeur was having trouble starting the engine; it wouldn't fire and he swore rather coarsely. "Don't say that, my man," said His Excellency, "rather say: 'Please help, my Lord.'" The engine immediately started to chug. Then His Excellency exclaimed: "Holy Mother, if I'd not seen it, I wouldn't have believed it!"

When I came back from the Caribbean, and he embraced and welcomed me back to his diocese, I saw tears in his eyes, little peasant eyes that had never seen the sea before he was appointed bishop and I heard him mutter as he clasped me: "But, my son, what would it cost you to preach in Spanish? Do you think we are devils?" That was when I suddenly understood: he wasn't a bad man, but just extremely dim, to a degree that was incredible in a bishop of one of the most complex, densely populated dioceses in the world.

In that era he still retained all the ideas he had brought with him, and that was the way he tried to frame the statements of witnesses. As far as he was concerned, Dr Gallifa must have been a "martyr of

the Crusade", a "hero of the national cause". He looked flabber-
gasted when everyone without exception, including Lamoneda,
said that wasn't at all the case, that Dr Gallifa never showed any
interest in politics, robustly refused to flee the "red zone", and
had continued to administer the sacraments in secret to anyone
whatsoever. "To reds as well?" he exclaimed, taken aback. "Even
though they were excommunicated?" His surprise peaked when
he grasped – and it took him ages – something he found inconceivable: "Are you trying to tell me that Father Gallifa didn't speak
proper Christian?" He found the idea that Dr Gallifa might not
have spoken like a character out of *Gente bien* so unlikely that even
Lamoneda burst out laughing.[5]

As for me, years and years of disillusionment had made me
extremely cantankerous; I'd turned into a prickly little beast who
felt increasingly penned in. Over time my aversion towards certain
individuals had spread like a skin blemish that turns malignant
and eventually cancerous after too much scratching. My Lord,
what a monster I harboured within myself; I, who had never seen
evil anywhere, now saw it everywhere. The worst of the post-war
time was what I carried within, if only somebody could have
brought back the dark storms from when I was twenty, those often-
dry storms that suddenly dissolved in a downpour of tears!

Auntie Llúcia . . . believed around 1950 that she had been
impoverished of her own free will, evangelically. The collapse of the
pesseta, together with the fact that rents and revenue had been

5 *Gente bien* was a popular play by Santiago Ruisiñol which ridiculed the
Catalan nouveaux riches who tried to replace Catalan with Spanish even in every-
day family conversations. From the Middle Ages "to speak Christian" meant to
speak Spanish, as opposed to Arabic or Hebrew then, or Catalan here.

frozen, had reduced the purchasing power of her income – which was nominally the same – by a tenth, or even more; she wouldn't accept the evidence, and finding herself in the same situation as so many elderly people who lived on fixed incomes she thought it was her almsgiving that had reduced her to penury.

I had stopped visiting her; she occasionally visited me in the mountain village where I had established myself as a rural priest after returning from the Caribbean. She would drive up in the usual big black saloon car with her aged, uniformed chauffeur; the things of this world being quite relative, the evangelical state of poverty in which she believed she lived didn't stop her from holding on to her car and chauffeur. She no longer worried about the dearth of vocations, which she took for granted had disappeared along with the Republic, precisely when the really acute problem was of so many rural parishes having been left unattended. She had now dedicated herself to other edifying good work, the Internal Missions, the I.M.s. Accompanied by elderly spinsters like herself, she would take off to the shanty towns now sprouting around Barcelona; they went there to preach Catholic doctrine, though the forte of those confirmed spinsters was inculcating in the women in those hovels advice as to the proper behaviour of married women in society.

When she came to see me, she would sometimes arrive with such a flush of excitement that she delivered a sermon or two, as if she had forgotten she was in a rectory. I admit the wonky table, the chair with its burst straw seat, and the mattress on the floor could have been mistaken for the furniture of a hovel. We rural priests had never before been so poverty-stricken. Eventually, as soon as I could, I got rid of that mattress – and now I own a bed like anyone else – so as not to shock people who might have concluded I was trying to act at being a saint. I got rid of it reluctantly because I loved that mattress; I slept so well on it! Just like in the war . . . After an exhausting Sunday (four scattered mountain parishes meant many hours on the road), as I slipped between the cotton blankets of the sort we had then, I loved to hear the straw in the mattress crack and the mice scurry, until the noise transported me back to those hours of intense peace you can only experience in war; as on that night, the night I recall so often, at the very end of autumn in 1938, two or three months before the end, that cold, rainy night when we had to take up a strongly entrenched position almost on the top of a bare mountain. We were going to have to advance along the steepest of slopes without artillery or tanks to prepare the ground, across five hundred metres without a single blade of vegetation: we had been reduced to suicidal forms of combat. Picó suggested a "scientific climbing plan", as he put it; "with a minimal scrap of culture, on the basis of small groups that would climb in staggered turns, protecting one another with their fire, all protected by a curtain of machine-gun fire"; "Forget that nonsense, Picó," the oldest of the captains interrupted, "we'll advance all together, blindly, like a bunch of illiterate fools, as we've done so often already! You take enemy trenches by dint of the cognac you swig." We advanced in pitch dark, through the rain, and I brought up the rear with the stretcher-bearers; each officer and soldier carried a flask full of coffee and cognac – almost as much cognac as coffee – that we all downed in single gulps before throwing ourselves into an attack; I felt more disgusted than terrified. Picó was the only one who refused his ration of alcohol. He crawled in front of the deployed battalion like everyone else; at that very moment a brigade messenger arrived with a counter-order; the general offensive had been called off at the last moment. We found animal pens with straw in the small valley we retreated to; what a long and delicious sleep, what peace in that soft, warm straw mixed up with sheep and goat turds, what a lovely goat smell, how comforting still to be alive . . . ! What good company the rain brought, pitter-pattering on the pen's ill-fitting roof tiles, what good company we found in that goat stench and the rough blankets that rubbed our cheeks like a grandmother's gnarled hand . . .

But what does Auntie Llúcia know about any of that? What does she know about the wonderful peace one can only find in the heart of war, as in the heart of poverty? I would even say I was pleased to register the disgust in her eyes at the sight of my mattress on the floor; she scolded me in an annoyingly unctuous tone and encouraged me "to change my style of life", and stop being a "rebel".

"You can do so much ill! It's so shocking!"

She was never still; she looked at her watch every five minutes; she always had things to do, was always in a rush to go back. Though now nearly eighty, she was just like I remembered her at fifty in my earliest memories. She had been mummified once and for all; she *was* a mummy, but a mummy that suffered from attacks of frantic activity. She would get up, go to the rickety corner cupboard where I kept the few books I owned, and survey the spines. She had already glanced over them many times, each time with a start: "Are you *really* reading that?" She would give me an infinitely pitying look. You would have thought she mistook me for somebody else, and perhaps suspected I belonged to the Communist Party; then she started meaningfully and insistently to tell me about lots of very strange things that she believed were happening in Russia: young Red Army lieutenants were raping ninety-year-old women (I even suspected she was under the unconscious illusion that she too could still be raped), something that, on the other hand, didn't fit with another aspect of her prejudice, the unbridled lasciviousness that turned Russian women from the age of eleven or twelve into insatiable nymphomaniacs, the most bottomless pits in the whole universe. She declared she knew such things on very good authority, and I expect she probably got it from some nunnish little magazine, because the truth is all kinds of things got into print over those years . . .

When the first man-made satellite was sent into space years later and created such an impact internationally, Auntie couldn't believe it: Russia was simply home to the hordes, "red hordes", so it was as incredible for such a feat to have been engineered by the Russians as for it to have been by the cannibals of New Guinea. Later on, after more triumphs in outer space, I couldn't deny myself the pleasure of introducing them mischievously into the conversation when she visited me; one day I told her I wouldn't be surprised if the Russians sent an astronaut to the moon or even to Mars or Venus. She looked at me pityingly: "You're the only one in the family who takes an interest in that silly astronomy business."

The family! That was the idol she worshipped, as ever, and the reason she had so taken against me. In her eyes I could only be a traitor, a traitor to the hallowed family I had abandoned after the war. And anyway, who was her family? What exactly was left of it? Monsenyor Pinell de Bray had died a few years ago; I had deserted her; what relatives remained? Of course, she had succeeded in reconstructing one for herself – she had sought out another nephew to fill the gap I had left. She had found a fellow who was barely twenty, a Raül de Valldemil, a nephew twice removed (the son of a cousin-in-law) from a bankrupted aristocratic branch of the family – bankrupted after the First World War as a result of over-risky speculation in German marks. My auntie thought she had discovered in this poor nephew with a grand name (grand, I mean, in her eyes), the very essence of her rose-tinted idea of our family, an idea derived from some naive, nebulous sort of "Christian chivalry" she must have found in the books she'd read as a thirteen- or fourteen-year-old boarder in a convent, which had marked her for life. This Raül de Valldemil was as tall, svelte, fair-haired, and blue-eyed as his novelettish name anticipated and my auntie immediately associated him with her edifying good works, as she had previously done with me. In my presence she always praised him to the skies, told me of that "child's" angelic innocence – she did really believe he was a "child" – a nineteen-year-old child! – and was much moved by the affection Raül had shown towards her. That all led to the founding of the "Home for Christian Upbringing", the H.C.U., one of her most wonderfully bright ideas. With her mania to be always doing something or other, to be organising or directing, around 1952 or 1953 she gathered together in her Sarrià mansion a group of thirty or so girls from the shanty towns, aged twelve to sixteen, with a view to educating them to be proper mothers: "I want to make proper mothers out of them," she would say, an aim one soon achieved with unexpected ease, though, naturally, it wasn't my auntie's doing.

She was in despair: "They are incorrigible, complete animals . . ." An even more painful blow awaited her: Raül declared he was willing to marry the girl. "But what business is this of yours?"

"Auntie, do you think she has conceived by the grace of the Holy Spirit . . . ?" I know, which is even worse, that she tried to dissuade him. I prefer to think she did so with the same lack of awareness with which she tried to dissuade me from becoming "a common or garden priest". From then on Raül paid me several visits; we had hardly met previously. He wanted to find an ally in me against them. I confess that his stubborn decision to marry that girl – the daughter of gypsies from Granada – made me appreciate him; I encouraged him as energetically as I could to do what he believed to be his duty, bypassing Auntie and the entire universe if necessary.

I even welcomed into the rectory that fourteen-year-old girl that my auntie had thrown onto the street – four months pregnant and all – so she wouldn't have to go back to the hovel in Somorrostro where her father, mother, grandmother, and thirteen siblings were crammed. I also confess I had high hopes for him and her; if my auntie invented sentimental chivalresque fictions, I invented equally sentimental ones of a proletarian variety. In reality, Raül was a rather superficial sort; the marriage failed; the girl ran off with a gypsy grocery-store assistant with the blackest of side whiskers, leaving her baby, of course, with Raül.

His place at my auntie's side was occupied by another nephew, a distant one, and I had no idea how she had found him; I was totally unaware of his existence. This fellow finally did appear to be a "genuine saint": "A genuine saint," said Auntie, "even though he was educated in a state school." This was because he was a poor, not bankrupted, relation – something quite different, in fact: he was the grandson of a cousin-in-law from another branch of the family that had no connection to the Valldemils: a cousin who had married badly – a lowly bank clerk who never rose through the ranks. No sooner had Auntie involved him in her good works than this pearl of a nephew started to prepare a vast, definitive monograph on the heroic virtues of that Marchioness of Valldemil, Raül's grandmother and Auntie's aunt, who had apparently been a kind of *fin de siècle* Auntie Llúcia; that exemplary youth didn't forget to illustrate his voluminous study with a nigh-on complete genealogical tree, where one could see that the "holy marchioness" was the big sister of Auntie's grandmother. There could be no doubt now that this young man, who was so young, pious, and erudite, would inherit the considerable pile that, despite the continuous collapse of the pesseta and freezing of revenues, was still his patrimony.

And it was because of my auntie that I came to hate the city outskirts. I looked at her and saw myself reflected there; surely my restlessness was but a mirror image of hers, a family tic? I began to imagine I was simply disturbed, useless, and lacking the necessary grace; I saw my dearth of grace in Auntie's and in our joint lack of achievement. Because good works without faith are as dead as faith without good works; good works require a grace that God alone can bestow, because all grace is Grace as all love is Love and all glory is Glory and nothing outside God can be grace, love, or glory; and whoever has grace attains Grace. However, my auntie and I quite unconsciously tended to preach to others a religion that is ours, and if it is ours, it is false, because it can only be true if it is God's and God belongs to everyone. "You shall love your neighbour", that is, the person next to you at this moment in time, who by chance sat next to you in the bus or metro, who by chance served next to you in the same battalion or the same brigade.

You weren't told: "You will correct him, you will mould him as you think fit", but rather "you shall love him: you shall love him as he is".

But what if you can't love him as he is? Then flee, seek out solitude, live without neighbours. Love him or leave him. If neighbourliness annoys you, if you are incapable of love, if you are powerless, conceal your powerlessness and shame in solitude. God will take pity on you if you admit to your powerlessness.

He can be charitable towards the cowardly and powerless who confess to their cowardice and powerlessness! I have taken refuge in a corner of a mountain because I am like that, am cowardly and powerless; I must seek God far from others, as I don't have the courage to seek Him among them, because what I have seen men do from 1917, the year when I was born, is horrendous, so horrendous! Our century is horrendous, an endless nightmare, an ocean of blood, wars and revolutions, *jours de gloire* that are trumpeted, and what follows, all that ever follows, is endless butchery, that and nothing else.

So much butchery over so many years, so much never-ending butchery from the Algarve to Kamchatka; how they conceal it from us, what a silence has cloaked Europe from 1939; we have lived for years and years under a thick layer of ice. Sometimes a rumour drifts through the air, like an imperceptible wind that barely bends a blade of grass and leaves no trace, you never know if you have heard or dreamt it! And the vast majority continued their lives as if they knew nothing, while Hitler and Stalin ruled and all those little Hitlers and Stalins flourished . . . the vast majority . . . Aunt Llúcia looked at me as if I were mad. "And how could that be possible in this day and age? The papers would report it . . ." And she would even add sarcastically: "You've always been subject to bouts of sleepwalking . . ." Gas chambers worked to full capacity, crematory ovens raised their columns of smoke like the temples of a new religion, concentration camps spread, anticipating the kind of "future for humanity" they were preparing for us, and they kept on executing and hanging, hanging and executing, and the vast majority went on living their lives as if they knew nothing, frivolously, without a care in the world, as if all that didn't affect them one iota; people wanted to live their lives, come what may! Perhaps people, like nature, are indifferent to catastrophes; perhaps that is how it has to be, nature is indifferent and couldn't care less so it can build afresh after every flood and earthquake; perhaps the masses have to be frivolous so the world can survive in eras like ours.

That is how it is, and there is only that, do not seek anything else.

And one floats like a ghost above those hungry, frivolous masses who worship the latest Moloch, be he called Hitler or Stalin, little Hitler or little Stalin, and one can only curl up in one's den like a cornered animal if one wants to refuse to witness that incomprehensible spectacle. One clings to the bitter consolation that one is a loser, that one has nothing in common with the winners of this world – especially with a species that is perhaps even worse: of those who lick their feet. The only consolation left to me thirty years later, with my life wasted, is that I am a loser among the winners.

Now when the time comes, I have arranged everything I need in order to die in a home for priests and the elderly; I have organised it so my eyes will go to a bank of cornea implants. O Lord, I forgot I still had these eyes; I thought I owned nothing in this world; I really am my auntie's nephew! Two miserable, myopic eyes; I felt ashamed to go and offer them to Dr B.[6] He was the one who told me that even myopic eyes have their uses. Can be useful to someone, can serve some purpose; perhaps someone will recover their sight thanks to my miserable eyes: now that is a real consolation, you know, my passage across this earth won't have been completely in vain.

Because my life really has been more futile than my auntie's; I am a much less worthy priest than she thinks.

I lived two weeks in hell. Like a somnambulist. Like the one I am.

When the bishop banned me from preaching, I disobeyed; then he effectively relieved me of my duties; I couldn't say mass until a new dispensation was issued, I was even banned from wearing the soutane. My aunt found out: it was the mud of dishonour in her eyes. In the eyes of others, it was the halo of martyrdom. They were wrong. I was no martyr: I acted basely.

I lost my faith.

At the end of the war, or more precisely when I left the concentration camp, she had scrupulously made available to me my parental inheritance (I had come of age as the war ground to a halt), which was still worth something at the time. I still kept that in 1949. Not being able to function as a priest barely changed my material situation, because I was wealthy.

I lost my faith. One morning I woke up and had none. I woke up, and there and then I no longer had my faith, which I had always possessed and which had never been a problem or caused me to

6 Dr Barraquer, the renowned ophthalmologist.

doubt. I woke up without faith, as I could have woken up without my wallet, stolen by a burglar. However, my wallet was there, and in fact swollen to bursting. I simply felt a void inside, a sense of shock; I had gone to sleep the previous evening praying as usual and, lo and behold, I now woke up without my faith. I had lost it while I slept; which of my dreams had led me to lose it? I simply couldn't remember the horrible dream in the course of which it had been axed!

Because that axing turned me into another man; I looked at myself in the mirror and grimaced in disgust at what I saw and didn't recognise.

"At last look at yourself as you really are," I told the reflection I didn't recognise, and everything seemed one gigantic leg-pull, a boundless carnival, a gross farce, from an ultra-microscopic virus to the most distant galaxies. "All those galaxies," I kept telling myself, "what is the point of all those galaxies? All identical, billions of galaxies, uniformly distributed in interminable space, how monotonous, how lacking in imagination!" I grimaced at the mirror because I was thinking both of the galaxies that now seemed so stupid in their incomprehensible monotony and of the new bishops, and I asked myself: And what if they were the ones that were right? Why shouldn't the Church be like everything else, a blow-out for those on the make and torture for the meek and mild? Jesus was meek and mild and Caiaphas was on the make – that sums up the whole of the Scriptures! Except that Caiaphas, precisely because he was on the make, centuries later has exclusively assumed the representation of Jesus, poor Jesus. My soutane had fallen on the ground by the foot of the bed; the sight of it made me feel sick. I winked at myself, at the image reflected:

"They have stolen my faith, but left me my wallet," and thought I looked uglier than ever.

That night I embarked on a somnambulist's pilgrimage.

I barely knew where I wanted to go or what I wanted; something like my shadow kept following me. No, it wasn't a sense of shame; it was much worse than that. I scraped against the walls of houses, I sought out the narrowest, darkest, most serpentine backstreets. Not knowing what I was looking for, I surrendered to pot luck. I felt I was being followed by that other presence; a cold breeze clipped the back of my neck.

I was witnessing all this for the first time. Touched by the hand of night, those slums opened up to my eyes as if by magic, like an overripe melon in which grubs have dug out a labyrinth of passageways. Through the early December mist dives appeared like flickering eyes, cut-price hells where I was sometimes hit in the face by a rush of dank breath from a bedroom that has never been aired. Everything about that night-time vision of the port area shocked me; some of those dens glowed with a dark purple light and seemed so lugubrious; from afar, through the haze, they seemed to be watching me like the glowering eyes of a panther in the black depths of a jungle, and strident chords from dance combos helped create the illusion of an equivocal Amazonia, though the air was cold and the night damp in Barcelona's lower reaches. It drizzled and at times a heavy downpour soaked everything, giving off the stench of a drenched dog. For the first time in my life I watched the wary to and fro of mature, even elderly men, a grim sight to bring tears to your eyes, shamefaced men and shameless women. My shocked eyes encountered long lines of skinny women, half-naked despite the biting cold; the dark purple glare illuminated them bizarrely, never quite salvaging them from the gloom. I even thought I could see in the dark like a panther, and as I walked past I breathed in their vile, tepid perfumes – the cheapest, you can be sure! – and their raucous laughter sent shivers down my spine, like when you scratch glass with your nail.

Some rowdy groups had formed in front of those garish doors. They smoked and chatted and I drifted off into a reverie, imagining what each of their lives might be like; perhaps, I told myself, they are like the galaxies, billions of galaxies uniformly scattered across the universe with no rhyme or reason, all basically the same; billions of identical items, galaxies of prostitutes, all uniformly spread across an endless void, and what a void, what stupidity, and then that other stupidity – time – another unending void! Time and space, what a couple: a pair of nincompoops lacking all sense! But other, more solitary women stood on the steps of dingy doorways half-open like a wolf's maw, and these looked older, taller and skinnier than the others, even shivering more; they shrank into their shawls, stood still, each on her own doorstep, and I spotted one, apparently the tallest and skinniest of the lot, more solitary than any, more set apart, and on a street corner, not on a doorstep. I hadn't noticed her at first, there were so many of them who looked alike, hundreds and thousands of large birds without wings, large, sickly, and feverish, unable to stand the light of day; I didn't notice her until I had walked past her time and again, and she hadn't stirred or looked at me. She couldn't see me. She stood there like a sentinel on duty, her eyes staring into the darkness, seeing nothing, not even blinking. Seemingly magnified by staring into such emptiness, her eyes were bright and surprisingly beautiful. As she stood on the sharp-angled corner of two backstreets and faced the wet wind gusting in from the port, her thin, shabby clothes clinging to her body, I thought for a second she was one of those wooden figureheads that years ago you'd find on the prow of a frigate. You might have said she endured there like the sentinel of a defeated army that had never surrendered, that she was doing her austere duty in defiance of the night, the rainy wind, and fate – that sordid, old comrade.

And I felt a burning desire to hurl myself down an endless abyss, as we sometimes do in dreams, hurtling terminally down a kaleidoscopic abyss, a cold wind constantly on the back of my neck and an inner voice tyrannically ordering me to do what I had in mind when I ran away from home; I needed to see it through to the end and I did so, as if it was the vilest of tasks, the most unpleasant of duties, as the cold wind of night hit my neck.

That wretched woman had just ridiculed me with her mocking contempt: "Is it really the first time? You're a big boy now, you know!" I was well into my thirties, nevertheless I lived with her for two weeks. Yes, I *wanted* to live with her and she couldn't make head or tail of that. The first two days her pimp was discreet enough to show no signs of life; on the third day he turned up, amazed I hadn't scarpered. And I couldn't have plumbed more disgusting depths when I told him he could stay with us; at the end of the day I couldn't care less; nothing mattered any more. "The more, the merrier," I said, and I could have sobbed my heart out. I also gave him money and it was terrible how they both wasted it on trifling things, but I gave them whatever they asked for. The fellow, no youngster – it was obvious he was into his late fifties – was swarthy and wore jet-black side-whiskers, and neither he nor she spared me their mocking glances. I was a fool in their eyes, and worse, an idiot from some unknown, incomprehensible species. She was no longer the silent statue I had espied on the corner of those two backstreets: she chatted away and gave me headaches. Her garrulous flow overwhelmed me; I would have given anything to be elsewhere, but I had to live with her; that cold wind gripped me by the neck whenever I hesitated. I was being watched; I couldn't possibly flee! That invisible presence was following me and breathing down my neck to remind me it was there, that it could see me and read my thoughts; I had to obey and see that vile task through to the bitter end.

And she recounted an endless stream of stories about film stars, she was a cornucopia on the subject: she knew every man and woman, every detail of their divorces and marriages, and was appalled by my ignorance when I confessed I didn't even know their names! That was from day one; from the third I also had to put up with her pimp and his dog. Yes, her pimp had come back with his dog, about which I shall have more to say. We only had one room for the foursome, her, the pimp, the dog, and me; one room with a single small window looking over an inner yard that was dark and narrow as a well, which wafted our way the most incredible smells, and songs spewed out full tilt by radios, and the sound of water from lavatories near and far – as you might listen to the bells near and far for evening Angelus on a tranquil, rural dusk, the bells of villages and hamlets scattered out of sight: lo and behold *our* Angelus bells were so many lavatories near and far. She showed particular tender loving care for his dog; I can picture her now, sitting on one side of the half-collapsed sofa that acted as our bed, the dog on her lap, catching one flea after another with the patience of a saint, squashing them between the nails of her index finger and thumb; I feel I can hear the sound of each crushed flea . . . and there was the day when that animal came in from the street with a fat tick –what a palaver! What drama! – until a neighbour showed her the trick for dealing with ticks, a drop of egg white poured on the parasite detaches it from the skin.

She and her pimp often chattered away as if I weren't there, just as they might have chuntered in front of his dog; I was all at sea in the middle of their random and incomprehensible exchanges. I sat and gaped, as if absent, not budging from the tiny corner where I had bedded down. One evening, much to my astonishment, they began to argue about the existence of God. She had gone that day to the basilica in plaça del Pi to take a candle for St Pancras, of whom she was a great devotee; he made fun of her, he made fun of that big saint to whom the devout prayed for good health and work. She was angry and told him to leave her in peace, that taking candles to St Pancras did nobody any harm: "And if you don't believe in St Pancras or God, you tell me who made the world, people – or dogs for that matter?"

"Of course, I can tell you," he rasped without a moment's hesitation. "It was Columbus, that fellow on the monument at the end of the Ramblas, and then they killed him, which is what always happens."

Then, lo and behold, one evening our erudite pimp turned up with a girl who had nowhere to sleep; at least that was what he said. There was a nasty scene. The prostitute riposted that she had brought me in and that I was supporting her; she bellowed that I was "very different" because I was a "gentleman" who gave both of them money. He started shouting that he was the man in charge, he wore the trousers, splicing his rage with outrageous obscenities, while the newcomer kept quiet and huddled in a corner like someone waiting for a storm to blow over. In the end she slept on the floor with the pimp, while the mistress of the house, the dog, and I shared the sofa. A couple of days later the pimp told us he had found a room somewhere else and then he upped and left with his new girl.

So we were left alone for a few days, and one morning something strange happened. She went shopping, taking the dog with her, and I was alone in the bedroom. I sat alone on the corner of the sofa. I suddenly felt I wasn't simply alone in that room, but alone in the whole universe. I had become frighteningly alienated from everything, from the sofa to that room imprisoning me within its four filthy walls, to the window overlooking that pit as it might have contemplated the absolute cold and emptiness of space and time beyond the galaxies. I had become alienated from the absurd, the downright absurd! I felt utterly cold and empty. Within me I sensed only an absolute cold, absolute emptiness, absolute darkness. I existed, since I still felt I existed, but I *was* no longer. I was nobody; I was empty. I felt mummified; I experienced myself from the outside, as if I had become external to myself and was gazing at myself from the outside.

And that was unbearable.

I seemed nailed to that sofa; my eyes were wide open, staring at a spot in the wall, a little hole left by a hook that had disappeared God knows when and that black spot was everything! I seemed frozen there, my eyes glued to the small black dot, thinking I could stay like that for the whole of eternity. I was an object; a peculiar, meaningless object that might stay in that room for ever, sitting on that settee, motionless, eyes glued to a tiny orifice left by an old hook. "They will summon death, and death will not come." I wished I had had the strength to get up, grab the knife I could see on the table, and make an incision in my arm, and at least feel something that could bring me back to myself. Impossible. I had frozen.

She found me exactly like that. She shouted at me and I heard her speak but I couldn't reply. I was there, but far away. I heard her as a dead man hears the living shuffle around his coffin.

She shook me but I didn't move. Alarmed, she went to fetch her pimp from the other woman's house and they both shook me and I heard her say: "If this guy dies here, we'll be in real trouble," and I thought how wonderful it would be to die if I could, but I couldn't, I couldn't die, because I could do nothing.

Until I burst out sobbing; sobbing that erupted as suddenly as that previous state had overwhelmed me. I sobbed, and between sobs I moaned in a series of subdued howls – I could hear myself – and couldn't stop sobbing and they looked at me, disconcerted, and I heard her say: "This fellow is mad; I'd always suspected as much." But I was wonderfully happy sobbing, whimpering and howling, and that passionate flow of tears lasted a whole hour – that's what they told me afterwards – an hour of non-stop crying, motionless, saying nothing, my eyes still glued to the hole left by a hook.

From that day on they exploited me more than ever; they never stopped asking me for money and making barefaced fun of me; they didn't care a damn. The dog, which up to that point had slept on the eiderdown by our feet, now decided to sleep between her and me, under the sheet; she made me cater to her every whim because she now knew for sure that I was a fool loaded with money.

Until one day, before dawn, I beat it barefoot, after giving Bob a meatball so he wouldn't bark because he would be too busy eating. I had carefully prepared it the previous night; I had taken a piece of meat from the fridge (she had purchased a fridge with my money, that fridge which was all we needed to pack out a room where we couldn't budge an inch); I minced it meticulously like an expert chef, at night, when she and her pimp were in the cinema on the corner. I'd mixed in some white powder, a powder white and fine that I'd bought in the morning at a grocer's while she was shopping in the square. I just had to do it: Bob had to kick the bucket once and for all, and with him my fortnight in hell. I'd leave them a dead dog as a memento.

I jumped over the pimp, who lay snoring on the floor, put my shoes on outside on the landing, and felt the iron in my soul. How I exulted! Finally I felt something, even if it was only iron in the soul. I roamed the neighbourhood; I no longer knew what else there was left for me to do in this world, where to head or what to look for. But I was free, that invisible presence was no longer following me, I no longer felt its cold breath on my neck. I wandered down strange backstreets, gawping at dingy shop windows that displayed the most heterogeneous rubbish from sordid shipwrecks: umbrellas, parasols, Chinese vases, urinals, Russian coffee pots, laxatives, rubber gloves, grey top hats, gramophones with horns, radios with whiskers; my eyes ranged from those motley objects to paving stones soaked in horse piss, stones covered in green or reddish moss, a green that had never seen the sun, and golden brown patches left by piles of manure that had been flattened by the wheels of a lorry; there were still horse-driven carriages at the time in Barcelona – twenty years ago! And it's as if I can see them now, those large horses pulling those unsightly carriages to and from

El Born. And the river of poverty streamed endlessly by; old women in rags, some drunk, skeletal, bare-legged girls shivering with cold, hunched workers, their toothless mouths sucking on fag-ends they had picked up off the ground. Who will ever speak of the dreariness of fag-ends sucked as you might suck your last illusions dry, dreariness without end, year after year, the hunger, misery, and despair of those years when radios spewed out triumphant speeches and commemorations, one victory parade followed by another, who will ever speak of all that? And there was I, a defrocked priest who had spent a fortnight shacked up with the most shagged-out strumpet imaginable, and in my bitterness I wanted the news of my fall to reach the ears of Auntie Llúcia so she would know what her beloved nephew was really like: a defrocked priest shacked up with his tart, the most puke-provoking thing there could be for her finicky little nose! And I could see Auntie Llúcia, and I could see Monsenyor; I could see him and others of that ilk – who weren't *in partibus*, but in livings – on top of army lorries decked out like carnival floats . . . I still possess magazines from those days; perhaps if I didn't have those photos that were already beginning to yellow I would think it had all been a nightmare – they were all giving the Heil Hitler salute – but here I was wandering aimlessly with iron in my soul when I noticed a poor woman, one who was still young, sitting on the shabbiest, dirtiest doorstep; she was shivering from the cold in a large woollen shawl that was wrapped around her and swaddling a child suckling at her breast. All I could see of the boy was one eye, she had wrapped him up so tightly, but his eye, that single eye, an eye belonging to a new-born baby, was so thoughtful and so clear-sighted it made your hair stand on end.

It stared at me lucidly, sharply, with such gentle resignation and benign reproach, and an older man stood behind the woman and child, his hair greying – was he the child's father or grandfather? He stood erect behind the woman crouching on the doorstep and held his hand out over her head, silently asking passers-by for alms. And I suddenly took that hand, placed my wallet on it and fled in terror, because all of a sudden I'd seen the date on a calendar in the next-door grocer's – I'd lost track of time over the last fortnight.

It was December 25.

That was when I saw him. He was walking in front of me; I couldn't see his face. He was tottering badly, though he walked at an even pace and never actually fell, an old worker hunched by his eighty-odd years. I saw his back bent by age and exhaustion; his rope sandals left prints as if it had snowed when it hadn't. Then on the corner I saw the name of the street, l'Arc del Teatre, and I started to whimper.

But he had disappeared; only his footprints remained before me; I followed them and was soon on my knees opposite the confessional in Santa Madrona.

I want to be one of Yours, my Lord; meek and mild, one among the millions who are, were, and will be like that, because those on the make belong to the Other and the Other horrifies me. We have to decide, there is no other choice: You or Nothingness. Those on the make opt for Nothingness and that is what I too had wanted; I had sucked on it like a bitter fag-end plucked from the middle of the street, but I want to be one of Yours, like Dr Gallifa, the old man, back bent under the burden of atrocity, anonymous among the anonymous, a loser among losers, his lips never spelling out the atrocity. Because You cried out to those "worn down by exhaustion", the infinite army of the defeated in this world. Lord, I want to be one of the defeated, a failure, because those on the make disgust me.

In other times, at the beginning of each mass we hailed You as "the God who brings cheer to our youth" and those were mysterious, luminous words because, however strange it seems, that is what You desire, that we stay forever young, even when weighed down by eighty years, because the spirit of poverty is the spirit of youth, youth that ignores everything that isn't the ideal, and the only way to remain young is to dedicate body and soul entirely to You; if not, one adapts to the ways of this world. Only a person who has devoted himself to You can enter, when the time comes, the old people's home with the same eager, cheerful curiosity with which he previously entered primary school, boarding school, university, and the army; the cheerful, happy-go-lucky curiosity with which we marched off to war in 1936! Everything is an adventure, everything brings joy to the eyes of the young; if only one could bite the last baguette of life as hungrily as the first!

Let those on the make squabble over this world like dogs warring over a bone on a rubbish tip; let them kneel and worship Deceit on their knees, that is their god; let them run after Nothingness and Vainglory, after Vainglory, my Lord, that is no less grotesque for being so spattered in blood.

How often have we heard over the centuries that *le jour de gloire* is nigh, that it has come – and it has always, but always, turned into a savage massacre. I ought to hate war, I know what it's like, and yet at that time I still occasionally dreamt I was back with Lluís, Soleràs, and everybody else, and in my dreams we were always advancing through reeds on the banks of a huge river pursued by a vast army bristling with guns, preceded by an ants' nest of tanks, and protected by a swarm of planes we pressed forward along a broad, hazy river that was perhaps the river of our one million dead . . . And in those dreams I was no longer an innocuous medical adjutant, but an infantry captain always leading my company in attacks on enemy trenches. My dreams were guilt-ridden. They were criminal. As ever! Because war is horrific and, in spite of everything, my heart was so swollen with rancour, I could only dream of war.

The fact was I envied Soleràs and all those who had died in the war, who died before they reached thirty and did not betray their youth, who had refused to grow old, who would never know the anguish of ageing, and who did not collapse at the feet of the Deceit that today lords it over the world.

There is only one path to avoid betraying your youth, apart from an early death: it is a narrow path, and so narrow you cannot walk it on the arm of a woman. You must walk alone.

It would be so nice . . . on the arm of a woman, as I had dreamt in a moment of madness! That path is narrow and you must walk alone.

Trini . . . and finally it is legal! That's how a mother must be. A mother's dreams must be filled with deep cupboards whose warm darkness conceals all kinds of goodies for her children, the softest blankets, the coolest sheets and lightest clothes; my dreams, my very own, my dreams in other times were worse than guilt-ridden, they were stupid. She is doing her duty, she owes herself to her children and to her cupboards and comfortable house, a house as welcoming as a grandmother, and all this . . . all this costs money. A mother must fear poverty; the spirit of poverty, eternal youth, insouciance, are only possible within celibacy.

If anyone travelling the roads of this world finds a family that is both indigent and happy – and they do exist, because this world is as broad and varied as it is dark and incomprehensible – they should know it has a name and it is the name of heaven upon earth, the name of Nazareth.

But I am simply a failure; if only I could learn to be one with a full awareness, with complete humility, sincerity, and acceptance of my failure! Because, after all, happy the man who feels he is a failure and accepts it without rancour; acceptance of one's own failure is the only possible success. And the face of success can be really ugly, I have seen so many winners in this world bloated by self-satisfaction! I have seen the dead who have had to be dragged from their niches, a priest in the slums has to witness so many burials, ugh, and gravediggers are completely unmoved as they take one out and replace it with another, so many die every day in a city like Barcelona! There would be no room for them if we preserved all the corpses. If a million die every twenty years, the city of the dead grows more quickly than the city of the living, because the dead do not die, and they cast old bones into the common grave, that huge grave where every winner will end up one day or the next, however grand the burial or funeral mass with a hundred choristers. We, the living, are a drop in the ocean compared to the millions and millions of deceased that have accumulated from the beginning of time; as if we lived on top of a mountain of bones! The dead would have submerged this world a long time ago if, happily, they had not dissolved into imperceptible dust.

The winners of this world, the victorious, the self-satisfied, can force their slaves to construct a breathtaking string of pyramids, imposing Escorials, fabulous valleys of the dead, but nothing will prevent Cheops, Khafra, and Menkaure from turning into dust one day, and nothing *but* dust, *pulvis es et in pulverem reverteris*. Hence the obsession with the success of victory, of triumphing, the rush to be inebriated on success before going to join the Himalaya of bones that has accumulated from the beginning!

But, Lord, this idea conceived by a benighted neurotic, this Himalaya of bones whitening at the bottom of the history of humanity can never cross my mind without making me feel yet again my hottest, most guilt-ridden desires ...

Yet again I see those fine red tresses, rustling like a flag in the cold morning wind in the Aragonese sierra; her green eyes ... We were there, Ramonet, she, and I, at the foot of a precipice silhouetted black against the snow, an almost vertical precipice the snow could not clothe, strangely bare amid a universe carpeted by that spongy whiteness. The sun was glorious, the cold, biting; we could hear, but not see, because enemy planes were flying too high on their way to Terol. Occasionally they were perceptible like specks of dust crossing a sunbeam; how distant that battle seemed, seen from our peaceful haven in Santa Espina! We lived on our dead front like so many frogs slumbering under fallen leaves; three months of inaction had made us forget we were still at war, that our turn might come when we were least expecting it.

We had walked out that morning because the sun was radiant and I was struggling to digest what she had told us in one of our interminable conversations about lime escarpments on the long benches almost surrounding the hearth: the rocky strata, sometimes several hundred metres thick, that make up so many of our mountains had been formed at the bottom of an ancient sea by the accumulation of small creatures' shells over millions of centuries. I had never been a blind bit interested in geology until then and was totally ignorant; I now realise that all and sundry know about the formation of limestone rocks, but right then I thought it was incredible. She had brought a small hammer and levered off small chips of rock she made me examine under a magnifying glass: I could see a whole lot of shells that were invisible to the naked eye, of snails or cockles, of all kinds of microscopic beasties: "They make up almost the entire precipice," she told me, and as she and I looked through the magnifying glass, I breathed in the perfume from her hair that was brushing against my cheek. I was amazed to discover that the rocky crust we felt to be so solid underfoot was indeed merely dust left by myriad lives; and I thought: *Il triomfo della Morte*, but at the foot of that strangely bare, brown precipice, her perfume was the victory of life: her thick woollen jersey clung to her svelte body, the wind rustled her hair like a flag and, half-mocking, half-wistful, her green eyes disturbed me as nothing had ever disturbed me before on this desolate land.

How many years have passed since then? Thirty! My Lord! I too have just made it to fifty like an idiot; there comes a moment when, humongous idiots that we are, we reach this watershed in life and suddenly realise we are no longer who we were, that we are other people now. Our youth has gone! Once the threshold of fifty is crossed and the road begins to slope downwards, who is so stubborn as to dare lay claim to youth? Nonetheless . . . nonetheless, when I see her again in my memories or dreams, my heart beats as fiercely as it did then! When its loud thuds took my speech and almost my breath away, and my hands trembled and my face was on fire . . . when I would have liked to bellow: "It was Dr Gallifa!" but the words wouldn't come, like one of those nightmares when we want to scream and an invisible hand is strangling us and stops all sound from surfacing.

It *was* Dr Gallifa! The eighty-year-old Jesuit she had met and been so impressed by – but how could I tell her? How could I tell her I had read those letters on the sly? And, lo and behold, the campaign for his beatification, off the agenda for so many years, has now reopened as the result of a fresh miracle and I must go and make another statement. But I will not say I saw him on that other Christmas day, you can be sure; no, I will not say he appeared before me and silently guided me across the Paral·lel to the confessional in Santa Madrona. I shall keep that to myself; nobody but me will ever know. Anyway, who is bothered about this story of mine?

III

*Que l'échec soit lié à la structure du moi, cela ne
signifierait-il pas que l'homme ne se suffit pas à lui-même
et qu'il doit être achevé par un autre?*

Jean Lacroix, *L'échec*

Unless, unless the lot of them, Lluís, Trini, and everyone else have got it right. Yes, Lluís and Trini; I heard them, they are of the same opinion as that pen-pusher in the bishop's office: "I'm afraid he's become completely neurotic," Lluís said; I heard him perfectly. I was about to open the door to the "palace" suite and stopped when I heard them . . . Yes, I stopped to listen behind the door as I did in Santa Espina. "It's a miracle," replied Trini's voice, "that these poor priests aren't all neurotic now . . ."

It was the same word I had overheard days earlier in the bishop's office! I had had to go up to His Excellency's parlour, where I had been summoned so he could question me about a number of irregularities; he had apparently been tipped off by a parishioner of mine, I don't know who, though I suspect, of course, that it was the most sanctimonious of them. As I walked through the offices by the entrance to the Curia, on the ground floor, I heard voices behind a closed door and thought I heard my name. I pricked up my ears: "Neurotic?" said one, "all these mountain priests are." "Do you know," asked the other, "that this wretched mossèn Cruells fought the entire war with the reds, and was a volunteer from the first day to the last? He's a real basket case!"

They were the two priests who worked in the Curia offices; I recognised their voices and thought it was like wartime, it was *always* like wartime; there are always two worlds, a lice-ridden one in the trenches and another for those sitting pretty at the rear. I thought how those two had never been mountain priests! And their voices assumed the pitying inflections we soutane wearers are so expert at, and you could hear them giving thanks to Heaven they weren't like me. From that day on I loved my bishop even more, so dim-witted, but so good, and so misunderstood in Barcelona at the time; he really belonged to our kind, to the trenches sort! If only the ones opposite . . . If only we could eventually come to accept that in every war all lice-ridden fighters belong to the same breed . . .

But, Lord, what if it were true that I was now a neurotic? "The poor Catalan priests," Trini's voice said, "it's a miracle they all aren't now." I heard her. I listened behind the door, like in Santa Espina, as I always did!

Neurotic . . . and why not? Why should I not be neurotic? Who could have prevented it? In any case, I feel at peace, I have arranged everything so I can go into the home for old, poverty-stricken priests when the time comes, if I do ever reach old age; it is all arranged, so the only valuable thing I own, my eyes, my myopic eyes, will be of use to somebody else when I don't need them. O Lord, the inconceivable is now happening, things that could happen anywhere; the realm of crime is the universe, where silence reigns; You have given us mouths to speak with, eyes to see with, and ears to hear with, but they steal our mouths, our eyes, our ears, they will not let us speak or see or hear. Lord, how can one not become neurotic? Who can prevent it? Neurotic? I could be an awful lot worse! Yes, much worse than anything the two pen-pushers at the Curia could imagine; long ago those sitting pretty at the rear thought we, the lice-ridden at the front, were neurotic. If I were as neurotic as they say, I wouldn't love Lluís, I would hate him! And yet, whenever he comes to Barcelona, we hug each other, and tears inevitably come to my eyes, I haven't felt anything but happy on those occasions! And the hours I've spent with him and Trini have passed so quickly and I have felt so happy, the happiest in years and years. O Lord, ever since the war!

More tanned than ever, with the white temples of a sporty fifty-year-old, Lluís is as tall as ever, though fatter now; baldness is expanding his receding hairline. Whenever he gives me a hug, he squeezes my back in the protective manner of one who is a winner. They had just arrived in Barcelona – to spend a few days there – in 1958 and had informed me by telegram, and I couldn't run fast enough to the palace to see them. I had never set foot in one of these palaces and luckily I had taken the telegram with me or I wouldn't have been let in. A character stands outside the palace entrance who looks as if he has been disguised as an admiral or field marshal out of an operetta, in an extravagant top hat, what a topper, red and gold like his livery, and a huge umbrella that is also red and gold; as I soon understood, to my amazement, the character in question who subjected me to a brutal interrogation stands at the palace entrance so he can bark at you if he smells that you don't belong to the race of his gods, or bow and scrape if you do. In the latter case, though only a few drops of rain are falling, he will even accompany you with that huge umbrella as if you were the Holy Sacrament he was carrying under a canopy.

My rustic priest's clodhoppers sank into the thick carpet as if it were red-hot snow and I could not stop my thoughts wandering back to the concentration camp where they had sunk into the shit and the slime. That had been at the foot of the French Pyrenees. In the rampant disorder of the defeated army crossing the frontier, farmers' mules had evidently got mixed up with army mules, and all this rushed back to me as I advanced bewildered across a carpet which was so sumptuous, soft and red. I glimpsed vast lounges and sophisticated ladies who seemed buried in the depths of armchairs that were too big and deep for figures that were so tall and thin, who smoked and looked bored out of their minds as they crossed their legs; how bored they were, how unhappy they seemed, how long-legged they were! And brutalised by boredom and filthy from concentration-camp shit, soldiers wheeled in circles around them, served as a distraction in the absence of anything better. Among those ladies who smoked and were bored idled a few men of the species that one only meets in such palaces, the species of man who looks to be forty-five, always forty-five to the day, and is always turning over in his head the most crucial and complex of business deals. The soldiers were shouting like people at a football or boxing match, they were shouting to hurry the mules along, the spectacle was simply shocking, until red with indignation as I had never seen him before, Picó erupted: "It was shameful how we allowed ourselves to be given a hiding by the fascists, at least we could have a little culture!" And that was going through my mind as I crossed those lounges bewildered, as they all stared, men who were eternally forty-five and women who were eternally bored to death, staring at me in alarm, as I walked among them. The truth is my greenish soutane, shiny at the elbows and knees, must have irked them! I imagine what they were thinking because on another day I had stopped and listened to what Lluís and Trini were saying about me after I had said my goodbyes, and Lluís told Trini: "Poor Cruells already looks the part of the pauper."

I would have got lost on the upstairs floor if the palace's manager had not personally guided me along those corridors, in the knowledge that I was a friend of Lluís'; that palace's corridors were long and broad, the parquet polished, the carpet thick and red; I could feel my rustic priest's clodhoppers leaving footprints from the shit of the concentration camp, that ocean of shit from the Algarve to Kamchatka! What a huge ocean, what a *mare tenebrosum*! As I walked by, I glimpsed a bathroom through an open door – absurdly extravagant, like a regal salon with a W.C. in the middle like a throne; it even had aquariums built into its black marble walls where exotic fish glinted mysteriously in the chiaroscuro. It was profound and mysterious like the crypt of a secret cult that used a W.C. for an altar, and I could feel the sadness coursing through my body because luxurious excess is as sad as the depths of poverty, even sadder. Poverty... bah, what does that matter to me? If it weren't for my neurosis... and I was reminded of a former chef in a grand hotel who took confession with me in the days when I was a priest living among hovels, of when he told me how in his time as a chef he used to drop a big gob of spit in the *bisque de langoustes* before handing it to the *maître d'hôtel* to serve to the gods of this world. It was in those years, the "hungry years", and one day the *maître d'* caught him at it and that was why they sacked him.

Yes, I love Lluís; I feel so happy to be near him whenever he comes to Barcelona – he has come more and more frequently after that first visit – but it is because of the wartime Lluís, who lived on so vividly in my memories, that I find the latest Lluís . . . this other Lluís, disconcerting, like someone whose innermost life we were privy to in another era, but no longer, now he possesses no such thing, in respect of others or himself. Ever since these people have been allowed back, many venture to spend a few weeks in Barcelona, and all seem ashamed of their status as losers, the only one this world has ever given God! As if they wanted to camouflage their failure beneath success, they come and try to shock us by scattering fistfuls of dollars around; the hapless creatures are so ingenuous.

His brother had died two or three years after the end of the war – the Ramon who once influenced him so much. I never did meet him, though we exchanged correspondence briefly from when I left the concentration camp until his death, but after he died I did visit the St John of God's home once or twice where he had lived surrounded by beings who were barely human. Three of them had survived him. If anyone mentions "Brother Ramon" in their presence, they let out hoarse, inarticulate cries; one of them loses his tether, grunts and bawls loudly and streams of slaver dribble from his lips. Just another way of crying . . .

Ramon died in 1942 from anthrax in his nostrils, a fact that inspired Auntie Llúcia to produce one of her memorable phrases: "From anthrax! But didn't you say he was a saint!?"

And . . . Trini?

Trini, no beauty at twenty, is one at fifty.

IV

I had not seen him since those meetings at the Curia on the occasion of Dr Gallifa's beatification. He had again given me the address of his *garçonnière*, insisting I pay him a visit, but the revulsion he evoked was too strong. Then there had been my conflicts with the archbishop, my suspension *a divinis*, my fall from grace, my repentance, my sojourn of almost two years in the Caribbean; it is a long story to tell and one I probably never will tell. They sent me there as a kind of penance; once I returned, I no longer wanted to be a slum priest. I asked for a rural parish and chose the most mountainous of the livings available.

I travelled to Barcelona now and then because the archbishop often wanted to see me. There was one bus down in the morning and one back up in the evening, and I was forced to stay in the city for most of the day. So I happened to be there on that day: was it 1952, 1953, or perhaps 1954? The years are a blur in my memory, and how could it be otherwise if they were all alike in that dark, endless tunnel. The fact is something incredible happened, and even twenty years later nobody knows how it could have been organised, if in fact it had been: a general strike in Barcelona. I certainly wasn't in the know and, as I said, I was there on other business; I suddenly noticed that buses were empty, shops were closed, and that the masses, who should have been in their factories, workshops, or offices, were crammed into the city centre. They walked in silence; the only sound was the tramping of thousands of feet; what a silence a crowd can create! There were no slogans or placards; there was no need. And there I walked up and down carrer Pelayo, mingling in that crowd, and the only sound to be heard was the tramp of anonymous shoes on worn pavements occasionally interrupted by the clanking iron of the trams they insisted on circulating with only the police as passengers. I walked up and down fascinated by a spectacle that was so unusual at the time, the great city on strike, and then, lo and behold, I thought I recognised a familiar face among the thousands floating in that silent river.

It was an old man's face, though strangely at the same time it was Lamoneda's.

I instinctively slipped into the crowd; when I thought I had lost sight of him, I felt him squeeze my arm: "I do believe you were trying to avoid me," he muttered. "But we are old comrades. We've got so much to talk about . . ."

His voice whined.

"In fact," he went on, "we're close to my *garçonnière*; do you remember it's on the carrer Tallers? Yes, it's the same one I rented before the war and now the rent is really low. I'm on duty, but no matter, they won't notice. Let's go up and chat for a few hours. I've already done four hours patrolling this street."

He squeezed my arm and pulled me along, elbowing his way through the crowd. The "*garçonnière*", as he called it, was a lumber room at the top of a nineteenth-century building; to get into the lift you had to slip a coin into a slit in the door's brass handle and then the ancient contraption started to sway and climb, as noisy as it was slow.

"Look, I've done it up all artistically," he said as we walked in. "Oriental style, rather than arty," and he winked when he said "oriental style", as if the very idea of the Orient was in itself risqué. We were in rather a small room, with a mound of cushions on the floor and a very low ottoman, not backed against the wall but positioned in the centre of the room. Everything was shabby and covered in dust but the most startling feature of that "*garçonnière à l'orientale*" were the mirrors. Every wall had one, as did the ceiling; wherever the mirrors reflected the wall, you saw the paper, flaking or mouldy from the damp; everything seemed impregnated with damp that must have seeped through from the roof terrace directly above the flat; impregnated by countless years of damp and dust, everything was so filthy and threadbare, so cold and dismal it made you want to weep, though he seemed oblivious. He pointed to an incense burner next to the ottoman and winked again, as if it were the spiciest oriental item in the universe.

"The inspector won't notice I'm not there," he repeated as he warily shut the door. "Everyone deserves a rest from time to time; I felt exhausted after four hours of walking up and down!"

He lit the incense burner in my honour; I don't know what on earth he was burning but it spread an acrid, somewhat irritating smell around: now that the ghost had managed to lure me into his den, how would I ever slip away . . . He poured me a glass of Pernod; there was a half-empty bottle open on a low table. While we drank, he commented on the mirrors, the disposition of which I had found so striking, "a really ingenious idea," he said, "when you're lying on the ottoman, you can see yourself reflected from every angle." As the only window was shuttered up, he had switched on the electric light; the noise of the crowds walking silently along carrer Tallers and carrer Pelayo barely reached us. We were so isolated from the outside I felt anxious and desperately needed to open that window.

"What are you doing?" he asked. "It's better to be barred and bolted in. But if you prefer it that way . . ."

Once I had opened the window, I found it allowed a view so high up you could see the dome of the church in the old military hospital close by on the other side of the street, and roofs and yet more roofs extending to the port. The noise of the crowds tramping along now reached us quite clearly, together with fresh air from outside. While I looked out of the window, seated on the ottoman, he chattered on: "You can't imagine the fantastic orgies that have been reflected in these mirrors . . . I've lived it up to the hilt, I'm no Jesuit like you! Do you see the Arab chest on that tripod? That's where I keep my collection of amazing photos . . . I'll show them to you later. I keep them there with my manuscripts; this is where I come and write on days when I feel inspired. If publishers weren't such a reactionary, stupid bunch, they'd have grasped how successful my complete works could have been, particularly if illustrated with the right photos."

Earlier, when we'd met in that café, he had told me about a notebook of Soleràs' and mentioned it again when we met years later in the Curia. However intrigued I had been by such a note-book, the loathing aroused by the mere idea of his *garçonnière* had proved much stronger; yet now I had landed there as if caught in a gin trap. And now I was . . .

"Yes," he replied, "I did mention that, you've got a good memory. I keep a lot of old papers in this chest, together with my manuscripts and photos! Papers concerning individuals who'd pay their weight in gold to get their hands on them . . . for example,

I have a number of items that relate to the renowned Llibert Milmany! The only thing I don't have there is that notebook, and I don't for the simple reason that it never existed. It never existed because Soleràs never wrote anything apart from an article in *El Mirador* entitled 'The rebellion of the youth'; the one he told me about once. His whole output, do you see, amounts to four pages of print; mine, on the other hand, my complete works, would run to seven or eight volumes as thick as the Espasa Encyclopedia."

"In that case," I asked, "why did you persuade me to come up here? I'm off, as I can see this is a complete waste of time."

"Oh, come, come," he replied, "the Soleràs notebook does exist, but I keep it here" – he tapped his forehead – "he had no need to write a notebook because everything he said was recorded here as if on tape. I have a spectacular memory; everything is recorded here for ever; memory is the principal tool in our line of business. I can tell you there's probably not another one like mine in the whole universe, modesty apart. Himmler hallucinated when he heard me recall things!"

He mentioned that again as one of his most glorious memories and started churning over the injustices he had experienced at the hands of envious colleagues, how back-stabbers had plotted and planned a series of little obstacles so he would lose the important post he had held at some point; they had now let him back in, but at a much lower grade.

"I was an underling, you know, yet at the time he reserved his most enthusiastic congratulations for me. He realised I was a genius! But this country has never appreciated talent. I could tell you, for example, every word uttered by passers-by on carrer Pelayo, and could do so in one year or twenty years' time! However, talented men in this neck of the woods . . . end up in dire poverty! So you see how easy I'd find it to recite from memory this or that harangue that Soleràs declaimed (because he really did seem to declaim) on this or that occasion, but why do we always have to talk about Soleràs, who was nothing but a fool? Besides, didn't you say you hardly knew him? I'm surprised you're always asking for the latest news about a figure of such little interest when there is so much else in this world. So much else worthy of note! Take my collection, for example, my collection of photographs: I can assure you – though I shouldn't perhaps be the one to say so, but begone false modesty – that it is unique in the world."

Naturally – he then showed them to me – they were simply pornographic. They made me want to vomit. I pushed away his album. It was crammed with monstrous, unspeakable photographs that shocked me; he, in turn, was astonished by my absolute reluctance to flick through his filth: "They are unique! Photography is another indispensable skill in our trade. Far be it from me to say so, but I am one of the most intelligent photographers in Europe; a pity you are so obsessed with talking about Soleràs, I could tell you so many other interesting things . . . I once earned a mint as a private detective by providing a millionaire with photographic evidence of his wife's infidelity, you wouldn't believe the ingenuity it required to take them! I gave the millionaire the negatives and told him I hadn't kept any copies; he paid me splendidly! Naturally, I've kept all the copies in this album. What do you reckon? You still want me to talk about Soleràs? You're fixated . . . How come you know him as well? Yes, I remember now, you told me: you'd got to meet his aunt because of St Philomena's miracle. Right, well I've known him from 1930, when he worked in that chemist's on carrer Sant Pau.

"You've told me all about that," I interjected.

"What else do you want to know? He always bored me to tears and I simply tolerated him, you might say. What choice did I have? He started talking about the reverend fathers of the Society of Jesus and made no sense at all: 'Lamoneda, you must remember,' he said, 'that when you were a little boy and went to the Jesuits, the reverend fathers put you on your guard against the temptations that, according to them, you'd be faced with when you were a bit older. And you, admit it, waited impatiently for those temptations to come, though never in order to resist them . . .' 'Naturally,' I replied, 'resisting them would have been really stupid!' 'Naturally,' he continued, 'it would be a pity to resist a temptation when we were lucky enough to experience one, but, admit it, no such fucking temptations have ever come your way that were as hot as those you imagined.' 'They will in due course,' I retorted, 'I'm still a young man,' – I had yet to hit fifty at the time – 'You can sit and wait,' was his rejoinder, 'you still haven't grasped that the only worthwhile temptations are those that will never come your way.'"

He refilled the two glasses with Pernod, quaffed his in one gulp, and stretched out on the ottoman; he lay there, prostrate, staring at the ceiling mirror: "'Poor Lamoneda,' Soleràs would say, 'You're simply another Stendhal. My aunt, on the other hand, is not at all like Stendhal, though she does come from Grenoble; if I'd told her, say, that I liked Nati, she'd have simply told me to marry her.' 'Who is this Nati? The one in that photo?' You know, Soleràs kept the photo of a woman at the bottom of his suitcase, perhaps I've mentioned that already? 'Don't be an idiot, Lamoneda,' he replied angrily, 'the woman in the photo is the exact opposite; like me, I'm the exact opposite, I am always the exact opposite!' 'The exact opposite of what, exactly?' 'Of everything! Of Ibrahim, for example; I am, as you know, strictly *non potable*.' You see, Cruells, he could say the most stupid things."

When he looked up at the ceiling his face was again that old man's face which had so shocked me on carrer Pelayo; how could it be an unknown old man's and Lamoneda's? I silently started to calculate his age; I then remembered how in the course of our conversation in the bar on the Ronda he had told me he'd just made it to fifty "like an idiot". How many years had gone by since then? Ten, eleven, twelve? At the very most he might be sixty or sixty-two, but caught between two lights, the electric bulb that was still lit and reflected in the ceiling mirror and the crepuscular light entering through the half-open window, for a second his face seemed that of a ninety-year-old.

That mixture of dim brightness from the naked bulb hanging from the ceiling and urban twilight from the window gave our conversation an unreal, even insalubrious air, with him supine on his ottoman and me standing by the window, looking out and feeling stifled by the stale air inside. And as I mentally calculated Lamoneda's age, he unnerved me by whispering: "Are you worrying about how old I am?"

It was the first time I had caught him guessing what I was thinking, as if he was able read my eyes or mind – yet he wasn't looking at me. He was looking at the ceiling.

"Are you worried about how old I am?" he repeated. "Alright, I'm past sixty, why should I hide that from you? It's nothing to be ashamed about. Sixty *is* nothing; everything has changed, the world is progressing. Nowadays, everyone is sixty."

And then he revealed an item of news that did really take me aback: he was married. Yes, he had married just over a year ago. "Once I'd made it to sixty," he said, "I thought it was time to settle down: I thought that if I didn't take the plunge once and for all, some fools might say I was on the shelf. Right, I was keeping this as a surprise for you: I *am* married. You don't believe me? I know you don't, nobody ever does. That's why I always carry my marriage certificate on me."

Without getting up from the ottoman he took a creased bit of paper from his inside jacket pocket. It really was a certificate of civil marriage (it specified that the religious one had already taken place) between Rodolf Lamoneda i Gallifa, sixty-one years of age, and Malvina Canals i Gonzàlez, thirty-four years of age, both single, born Spanish nationals resident in Barcelona.

"That convinced you?" he grunted, putting it away.

"Malvina Canals i Gonzàlez . . . I can't think why, but that name rings a bell."

"It's *that* woman," he replied, "and you know her. She's the only one you do know. The one who came in and had a croissant with a cup of malt in the café where we were chatting. Of course, you remember her. That time, on the Ronda de Sant Pau."

"The redhead?"

"That's her; the very same. You know, I brought her to live with me here, though transformed into Senyora Lamoneda. You'd think she'd have been grateful, wouldn't you? Not a bit. She was unable to rise to the occasion. I'd had all kinds of high hopes, but nothing doing. I should add that at the time I was riding high and in a position to give her a slice of the good life. I'd discovered a gold mine that poured ore out non-stop. Malvina thought I was wealthy and I was careful not to disabuse her. Why disabuse her before time, the poor thing? Disillusion would come quickly enough; as we know, in matters of marriage, all is disappointment. You should have seen poor Malvina, she was so chuffed that she'd hooked an old tycoon, because she did think she had hooked me and that made her so happy. So happy and so chuffed, the poor dear! It was so easy to let her think that, it's worth making them happy when it's so easy, don't you agree? One day I caught a snatch of conversation between her and a friend from her days on the Ronda de Sant Pau: 'Yes, I've married an old fogey,' said Malvina, 'and don't think I just had to whistle to bring him to heel, the crock was as slippery as an eel. He's rolling in it. As you know too well, Greta' – the other woman is or at least likes to be known as Greta – 'in our line we get too many poor young fellows, old 'uns loaded with loot like him are thin on the ground.' That was at the beginning – what we might call our honeymoon period. I'd been telling her we'd be moving, that this *garçonnière* was a temporary abode while we looked for a place on the passeig de Gràcia or, even better, a mansion on Reina Elisenda. And why not? I could promise her anything that came into my head, and she believed every word. And why not if she saw me turn up day in day out waving a wad of thousand notes that would turn anybody's head? I even let her think I'd take her to the Liceu, with me in a tuxedo and her in an evening gown, and that, spruced up like that, I'd introduce her to the widowed *Vescontessa* de Rocaverd; you may know I'm a distant relative of hers. The detail of the *vizcondesa* – Malvina says it in Spanish – sent her into seventh heaven, would you credit it? It turns out she'd recently seen a Spanish film where one appeared, just imagine! How come this Rocaverd is related to me? Well, she is right enough, her father and my mother were first cousins; suffice it to say that I once tried to go and see her, and not only did she not receive me, she even instructed her maid to tell me never to set foot on her doorstep again. But I had this hunch that if my cousin – since cousins we are – saw me in a tuxedo in a box at the Liceu with a most elegant Malvina in an evening gown . . . yes, my friend, don't doubt that for a minute, at her most elegant, Malvina could have swept all before her! Do you think the Rocaverd widow wouldn't ever have swallowed the idea that Malvina was my legitimate wife? 'Well, my dear cousin,' I'd have retorted, 'she is with all the i's dotted and t's crossed,' and saying that, I'd have waved this marriage certificate under her nose. That's why I always carry it on me; 'Be Prepared' is my motto. I'd have shown it to my cousin and all those toffee-nosed ladies and gents who doubted it so they'd see that when I do something, I do it in style. Married by the church *and* the town hall! Signed papers beat hearsay any day! I always carried the certificates just in case and Malvina would only have had to flaunt herself, for my thousand notes always did the business wonderfully. Know what, instead of being grateful and acting her part, know what she did? She made the most of the time I wasn't in my *garçonnière* to invite her crowd of friends round, and they whooshed up here like so many flies the second I turned the corner! I couldn't be here all the time, I'd lots of work to do, loads of it at the time. Those thousand notes didn't just rain down! I had the bright idea of locking the door with my key, which gave me a few weeks of peace and quiet, until I discovered that one of her little friends was a handyman. I couldn't afford to waste my time on tomfoolery; I was too busy and important; I was earning wads of thousand notes with the sweat of my brow, right? I was a man of standing and found it intolerable that a band of no-hope chancers should be making a fool of me so blithely, taking advantage of the fact that one of their crew had made a fake key (because the handyman was also an altruist and let others use it). When one has attained a prestigious position through one's own efforts, one has a duty to ensure that respect is duly shown – they had a nerve! I had to go to the office every day; it was no laughing matter. I'll tell you the whole story, it's now all water under the bridge: I had discovered that a certain shoe manufacturer, who'd toiled to keep his little factory open in the '40s, was now raking it in hand over fist exporting shoes, even to the United States, just imagine! Well, this man had been a member of a Masonic Lodge when he was young and I knew all about it. If I'd left him alone during the '40s, it was because it was all he could do to keep afloat; the only joy I'd have got then would have been to have had him dispatched to the Camp de la Bóta.[7] What's that? Just for belonging to a Lodge? That's how things were in the early years, or have you forgotten? True enough he'd only gone to the Lodge for a few weeks and long before war broke out, when he was seventeen or eighteen, but the fact remained that he had been a member and I had proof. When I turned up and showed him my party card and my proof, he went pale, as if he'd seen a ghost; I ought to add that an elder brother of his had ended up in the Camp de la Bóta in 1940 for the very same reason. He immediately agreed to the deal I proposed: I'd spend a few hours in his office every day to check on his business' outgoings and income and would collect a percentage of the difference every month. We'd done that in many such cases

7 The Camp de la Bóta was located on the Barcelona coastline and was one of the many prison camps which mushroomed in the 1940s. Almost 2,000 prisoners of war were executed there. The Forum Park was built over the site.

in the early post-war years and I assured him it was still common practice, though the truth is that it had all changed by that time. Nothing was like it was at the start. If they had caught me in the act, they'd have come down on me like a ton of bricks. The heroic struggle in those first few years, the struggle against the nineteenth-century liberal bourgeoisie and international Jewish-Masonic plutocracy, had collapsed: the imperial and proletarian idealism that had inspired us in the good old days was past history. Why should they let us persecute the black Freemasonry if the white variety had already started organising so it could quietly push us to one side? However, this fellow knew nothing about any of that; he was scared stiff by our terribly devious tactics and in fact he believed everything was as it used to be. He thought that a man like me, with his party card, was still all-powerful when it came to someone like himself with past connections to that leather apron, set square, and plumb line malarkey. He assumed he was totally at my mercy and coughed up without a whimper. He was grateful to get away with only thousand notes! One day, quite timidly, he suggested that perhaps I didn't need to spend so many hours by his side in the office; I'd given Malvina to believe I was a partner in that shoe company and that this gentleman and I ran the show. The fact that I spent a few hours in the office every day made me seem important in Malvina's eyes, which was one of the reasons I liked to go there; on the other hand, I had more and more proof that she was profiting from my absence to welcome in all kinds of elements, including characters one might simply describe as the dregs, and I'm not exaggerating. So I was in the position of having to carry out two checking operations simultaneously, the ins and outs at the factory and Malvina's, and that was impossible. I decided it was more urgent to exert control over Malvina, and, as the shoe manufacturer insisted I didn't need to put myself out at the factory – he even said that working so much might be bad for my health – he and I finally decided it would be enough for me to show my face at the end of each month. I'd go on the last day of the month and he would hand me a wad of notes: he was a man I could trust. He assured me he was religiously paying me the percentage we'd agreed on the difference between his outgoings and income – and I believed him. I believed him in good faith: that good faith which has always been my downfall! And the last time I paid him a visit the chief of police was sitting there next to the shoe-maker in the armchair that had always been mine, waiting for me with a smile that froze the blood in my veins. The shoe-maker had finally worked out that I was operating on my own and had had the bright idea of rushing off to reveal all to the new chief of police, who wasn't one of ours, telling him all about the Lodge and his brother who'd been executed! I'd have been taken to the cleaners without my party card, which – though it hardly behoves me to say so, and modesty apart – was one of the first to be issued; without my glorious, heroic record as an outstanding pioneer party member, I'd have been in a real fix. They didn't touch me in the end, but my gold mine had dried up for ever; in compensation, so I wouldn't starve to death, they gave me the post I have now, at the bottom of the pile. Dire poverty! When Malvina realised that the outlook had changed, that at the end of the month I got a bundle of hundreds, rather than thousands, if I was lucky, she laughed contemptuously in my face: 'I've always suspected,' she said, 'that you are a clown; so you're an impoverished plutocrat now, are you? Well, good riddance! There's plenty of youngsters around. No need to court disaster! Just as well I've not entirely wasted my time: I'm pleased to say I've given you such huge horns you won't get into the cathedral, not even through the front entrance.' The stupid wench said that; she obviously thought I didn't know. That I didn't know! She took me for a fool! There are so many idiots . . ."

"So why don't we talk about Soleràs?" I asked, taking advantage of a pause, after he had sighed deeply.

"Soleràs? Yet again? You've got Soleràs on your noggin! That bastard Soleràs! I can't even remember where we'd got to with him, perhaps when he said that he was *non potable*? Yes, those were his words: he was *non potable*. 'I'm completely *non potable*,' the fool told me. Yes, that was just the point we'd reached, and he even added: 'Oh, I'm not that fantastically *non potable* . . . You wouldn't believe me even if I swore to it, and that, in fact, is why – because you will never believe me – that I'm so keen to tell you all. I've always liked telling others what I think they'll find hardest to understand! So here's what I want to tell you right now: I'm quite incapable of cuckolding anyone, even my best friend.' He liked to come out with these shafts of wit, you know, wisecracks you couldn't make head or tail of; he'd always sling these thunderbolts out to shock others. 'Not even my best friend, however incredible that may seem! The reason is plain enough; I'm far too imaginative. I can always imagine myself in the other person's shoes; I have the liveliest imagination in this regard. You, for example, Lamoneda, I find it so easy to imagine you married to little Miranda . . .' 'Don't start on that again,' I interjected, 'be so good as to leave my fiancée out of it.' Because at the time she and I were still engaged. 'So you're threatening me now, are you?' he asked. 'You know, Lamoneda, you're only a ghost.'"

"It's odd he should say that," I ventured.

"Why is it odd? Why on earth is it odd that Soleràs should call me a ghost, if he was always coming out with such bilge? Just as he had always predicted that if I got married I would be the most magnificent cuckold on display in Barcelona for many a year – even on the whole plain of Llobregat; he once used those very words to annoy me. So you can imagine that when all this eruption took place over Malvina – and it would be never-ending if I were to tell you all the tricks Malvina Canals i Gonzàlez got up to – I remembered Soleràs and his predictions. According to him, I was born when Venus and Mars coincided under the sign of Taurus, which he said was a nasty astrological moment in time; people born under that combination of stars, said Soleràs, should never marry. He'd come out with all that, you know, though I reckon he knew sod all about astrology; he would invent all that without batting an eyelid simply to annoy me. Yes, he did say: 'Bah, you're just a ghost.' That was the first time he'd said that; then it became a phrase he liked to repeat."

Lamoneda suddenly broke off and asked me in a strangely whining voice: "Cruells, would you mind switching that light off. The bulb is shining right in my eyes and giving me a headache."

We were plunged into a crepuscular darkness that deepened by the minute and in that gloom I listened to him prattle on, lolling back on the ottoman, as he had done in that exchange in the café, as he would again in the much deeper shadows of yet another den.

"'You're just a ghost, like everybody else,' he told me, 'except you're a ghost that belongs to a rare species, the solitary cuckold species.' 'What on earth do you mean? How can a solitary man be a cuckold?' 'Oh, of course they can! They don't have a wife, never have had, and maybe never will have, unless they're past sixty, and a strumpet gets her hooks into them' – yes, he predicted what happened to me, incredible though it sounds – 'and their heads bow under the weight of so many horns. It is rather a rare species, I grant you, but it does exist and you are an example, the most perfect I've found so far, and a finely rounded model!' You see he wasn't short of vicious things to say about me, though I had no choice but to grin and bear it; not only so he didn't dispatch me to the trenches, which I didn't fancy one bit, but also so I could carry through my trickiest mission to date. He suspected nothing, not a thing, no more than anybody else did, even though he thought he was so perceptive; in any case, if he did, he never let on. I'll tell you I did once suspect he had an inkling and I even felt that, all things being equal, he didn't give a fuck. Once, for example, he told me: 'Lamoneda, you're a first-rate talent, a Himmler, but this country doesn't appreciate talent; the envious will always stab you in the back.'"

The rumble from the striking city reached us in waves through the window and it was like the hum in the hive before the bees begin to swarm; I had completely forgotten the world outside, having been so engrossed by his voice, which had grown increasingly monotonous in the descending gloom: "He often started talking about his aunt as if *she* were a fascinating topic of conversation. 'She's the best of all possible aunts,' he'd say, 'she would have stunned Leibniz. Yes, the best of all! Now, I feel I can say that. If I'd told her I liked Nati, she'd have replied: Well, marry her. As simple as that! You must recognise that nobody has an aunt quite like mine. Do you think I say that to sound important? You must be thinking, how could a millionaire aunt let her nephew marry the daughter of sharecroppers? A worthless country girl who couldn't even read! Well, my auntie is like that. You'd never understand her; you could never have an aunt like mine. She's a big supporter of the Oratory and the Jesuits. I mean – no more than any other auntie! I'd even go so far as to say that she is more understanding and indulgent than most when it comes to poor folk who haven't enjoyed a Jesuit education. One day she said, for example: "Mr So-and-so is a very decent chap, even though he was educated by the Escolapians." You'd not find so many who were so tolerant! Granted, she is on the side of the Jesuits, but even closer to the Oratory, though she's yet to organise a charity tombola or mount an alms-collecting table – she's an exceptional auntie! Not many aunties like her are left, and I don't say that to boost myself; so St Philomena sometimes appears to her? Granted, I can't deny it, but so what? In the end she doesn't appear very often, only once in a while; that's quite restrained, nothing outlandish. And you can be sure of this: if she had ever suspected I liked Nati more than the notary's daughter, she would have simply said: "Well, my boy, you marry Nati rather than the notary's daughter." I tell you, she really *is* like that! Conversely, if you knew how she'd hate the idea of you wedding little Miranda . . . Hmm, what a whiff of scorching . . . a whiff of singed horns . . . a cornucopia of horns that would make the planet quake!' His mania for mentioning my fiancée, forever insulting her, really got on my nerves. He was always needling. He'd reiterate: 'You're just another Stendhal' (because I'd read him a choice extract from my novels, and, though a fool, he was intelligent and knew what he was talking about and was forced to recognise that they reminded him of Stendhal, though they were better); 'you're just another Stendhal,' he insisted, 'such a refined, tolerant, understanding man; a pity wives hardly appreciate that capacity for tolerance in a husband. True enough, as if to compensate, his friends appreciate it hugely.' 'I don't have friends,' I'd reply, 'nor any wish to have any.' 'You'll have more than enough when you've married little Miranda, your house will be packed with them!' In the end I listened to him like someone listening to the rain's pitter-patter; I took no notice of the tasteless innuendo he directed my way. However, then there was that business over Captain Ibrahim. He went too far."

"So who was this Ibrahim?"

"An A-rab who commanded a platoon of regulars. During the battle of the Ebro his platoon was next to our battalion and we visited it from our battalion and vice versa, on days when all was quiet. As you know, the Ebro cost a thousand dead a day and lasted four months, but there were tranquil days and we made the most of them to relax. Hey, it's a bit of alright in this *garçonnière* of mine, isn't it? A genuine artist's den, *à l'orientale* ..."

He had sat up and was looking around, pleased by the sight of that "artist's den" which he felt was so oriental and was now almost completely in darkness, and that was when he noticed I'd finally sat down in a corner, on one of the cushions scattered around the room, and asked me to forgive him for not having a chair to offer me. He started telling me how, when he was inspired and working on one of his novels, he would do so standing erect on his Arab chest, breaking off now and then to pace up and down his *garçonnière*, reciting what he had just penned, "to ensure," he told me, "that it has the necessary 'eurythmy', to use Eugeni d'Ors' admirable phrase. I shouldn't say this," he continued, "but, modesty apart,

I've not only surpassed Stendhal, but d'Ors and everyone else."

"So why don't you tell me more about Soleràs?" I persisted.

"Ugh," he replied, lolling back on the ottoman; he sighed, then after a long silence, continued in this vein: "Damned if I understand why you're so interested in that fool Soleràs! Anyway, our battalion commander had set up in an old farmhouse that had been hit by bombing raids, though the vat was still intact. It was a tub as deep as a cistern, full of red wine that was gaining in body. We were lucky to be in an area reputed for its wine, practically the Priorat. We organised our drinking sessions on the lid of the vat, next to the open trapdoor; all we had to do was lower a bucket on a rope; it was like drawing water from a well. We drank out of the bucket and had fun sloshing our faces and chests with wine that was almost as black as ink. It warmed us up and restored our good spirits; the smell of the wine drowned out the smell of the dead. Ibrahim was a big man, around thirty, a mestizo, if not a negro, and his lips were perpetually slavering. He was a hero, you know – he'd taken countless villages leading his platoon, bayonet to the fore. I don't know how Godfrey de Bouillon behaved on his crusades, all I can say is that I don't believe you can fight wars with puff pastries. Ibrahim was a character overflowing with energy; he often came to dinner with us, invited by Soleràs; Soleràs amused himself by getting him to tell us stories. He urged him to speak up and recount his feats with the bayonet and with . . . but, hey, why are you looking at me like that?"

I wasn't, I was staring at the window, a square of light in the pitch black, and, conversely, when he said that, he was staring into space. He asked: "Why do you stare at me without looking me in the face?" but neither was he looking at me. Could he see my reflection in his mirrors?

"War is war, and you can't fight it with puff pastries! Ibrahim came to have dinner with us almost every evening and we'd chat long into the night in the bright glow from an oil lamp that attracted all the mosquitoes, because we were close to the river marshes. By that time the machine guns and mortars had been silent for a good while; peace and quiet reigned along the whole front. Each time we dropped the bucket into the vat, it unleashed reverberations that echoed under our feet; now and then, in the peace and quiet, we heard the big howitzers shelling from ten to twelve kilometres behind the lines. We'd sometimes hear a shell whistling over our heads, like the wind blowing through a pine forest; it would explode in front of us, in the middle of the enemy lines. Soleràs encouraged the A-rab to drink, urging him to recount his exploits, and that's exactly what the A-rab did, laughing and flashing incisors as strong and yellow as a dog's. Soleràs killed himself laughing too, but there was always something fake about his laughter, as if it was cracked – it sounded like the cackle of a mother hen. The 15.5 cm howitzers whistled overhead and seemed to deepen the nocturnal peace and quiet even further; as for Ibrahim, he laughed so boisterously he once pissed himself in his riding trousers. Ibrahim was spirited, tough, a real character! His accent sometimes made him difficult to follow; his squat nose emitted a sort of whinny, but his way of telling this or that picaresque anecdote was so funny, so damned funny. He was especially funny when he put on a woman's voice and manner to imitate whatever they tried to do when they were kicking and punching; he made the racy detail even spicier! You know how you must give these A-rabs plenty of rope; they have their own ways and traditions of waging war; you simply had to let them pursue things in the manner of their own hallowed traditions. Soleràs liked to tank him up so he'd talk; he'd be sent into ecstasy by his prowess. After we took Gandesa, he'd led his platoon in the most audacious attacks, it was rumoured they'd promote Ibrahim to commander. He was a general in the making! But then Ibrahim . . . Ibrahim disappeared . . . our wonderful Ibrahim."

Lamoneda sighed woefully.

"He had come to have supper with us and left just before dawn. He never reached his platoon, and that last night he'd told us the raciest of tales, sounding as racy as could be in that guttural voice of his that sometimes cracked. He'd recounted how in an isolated farmhouse, in the strip of Aragon bordering on Catalonia, he'd found a young girl in mourning who was probably under fourteen; a young girl who only spoke Catalan, as is often the case with country women in these areas. It was as if they *were* Catalans, said Ibrahim, and you know the orders we were under: no holds barred. The young girl bit and scratched, at one point she managed to slip away from him and grab a pig-slaughtering knife and came within a whisker of making a capon of him – oh, Ibrahim was wickedly funny telling the spicy detail! This is what he related on that last night, and it was the last we ever saw of him."

"In an isolated farmhouse, in the strip bordering on Catalonia . . ." I muttered.

He wasn't listening; he just went on: "After Ibrahim disappeared, Soleràs drank more than ever: 'Don't you find,' he'd ask his guests, 'that this wine gets more full-bodied by the day? It is amazing how it gains in body and bouquet as the weeks go by.' A colonel from the legal unit was put in charge of the investigation of his disappearance; he came to question us and Soleràs invited him to a glass: 'Wine from our own harvest,' he said, 'an exceptional year: please be so good as to judge for yourself, given that you're a judge.' The bucket went down and up, triggering, as it hit the liquid surface, subterranean reverberations that got deeper and deeper as the level diminished and the vat emptied out. 'It's strange,' Soleràs told the investigating colonel, 'they always come after me when things disappear. With the reds, it was tins of milk; they almost executed me over a few tins of El Pagès milk. You must know how the reds only need the slightest excuse to execute you. Here it's not about tins of milk, but A-rab captains . . .' And he laughed with that mother-hen cackle of his as he watched the colonel knocking back the wine; with his white moustache and pink cheeks he looked like a lord from a bygone era. 'My Lord,' said Soleràs, 'My Lord Investigating Colonel, what is your opinion of ectoplasms? As regards dead cats . . . My Lord, would you deny the existence of dead cats? They make highly *potable* potted meat, I can assure you!' The colonel smiled contentedly; he liked to be called My Lord because he was an Anglophile; a monarchist champion of Alfonso, more liberal than that whore Maria Cristina – the army was full of them! People of that ilk, together with the clergy-wergy, have been our ruin: white Freemasons and black Freemasons! We've been shipwrecked in an ocean of holy water and shame-faced liberalism . . . On the other hand, he wasn't proper military, but a civil magistrate militarised by the needs of war; he laughed complacently when he heard himself being addressed as My Lord, laughed with a wine-stained face and understood not a blind word of Soleràs' incoherent blather. 'Highly *potable*; judge for yourself, My Lord, as you've come to help us! Wine from our own harvest; an extraordinary harvest, better than Sauternes 1902!' The heavy artillery was still firing those big shells northwards; now and then we'd hear them whistle overhead as if a light wind were blowing high in the sky. By now it was very late into the night. The colonel from the legal unit went off pickled as a newt, his snow-white moustache dribbling red wine, delighted to have met the renowned Soleràs. Yes, Soleràs was renowned throughout the army contingent because of his excesses and oddball remarks. They fought for the honour of being his friend; nobody understood a word of what he said, but they pretended he was profound and ironic and that way they too became reputed as intelligent and erudite. Characters like the investigating colonel felt duty bound to sound like an egghead and Soleràs provided them with an opportunity. As far as I was concerned, I was happy at that point; the battle of the Ebro was costing a thousand lives a day, but, far from the trenches and next to that bottomless vat, I was happy like someone between threadbare sheets who can hear it raining cats and dogs from his bed, cosy as a mouse nesting inside a cheese. Everybody acted up like eggheads, ironic clever clogs, listening to Soleràs' witticisms, yet they never took a peep . . . that bottomless vat was no such thing. There *was* a dead cat inside."

"A dead cat?"

"For sure, and it wasn't that bottomless! None of those eggheads, none of those bright sparks, whether part of the investigating body or not, had taken a look inside. One morning Soleràs, who usually spent the day in the trenches, stayed back in the farmhouse doing jobs for the high command: he and I were by ourselves. As I said, a table and chairs were set on top of the vat lid where the trapdoor was always open; the trapdoor had hinges, like a shutter, and if you gave it a kick, it slammed down tight. Soleràs eventually kicked the lid open and, as the din echoed round, he exclaimed: 'We're such drunkards! It sounds emptier than a tomb.' I grabbed the bucket and threw it inside; when I pulled the rope up, I saw a fez on the hook that was still bright red despite its weeks-long soaking in that dark wine. I grabbed it as it dripped wine and stared in amazement! I couldn't believe my eyes! A wan, pale Soleràs now stared at me, but said nothing. Suddenly he seized the fez from me, threw it back into the vat, and kicked the lid shut. It banged to with such an echo! Just like the belly of a double bass; the walls vibrated . . . From then on, it was forbidden to drink that tipple! By order of Commander Soleràs! I was the only one in on the secret; I could destroy him. But he didn't care a fuck about me, he didn't care a fuck about anything. And I was sick to my back teeth of him. I didn't want him involving me in any more idiotic nonsense."

We heard the church clock in the old military hospital strike seven; Lamoneda interrupted himself to count the chimes. I said: "Do you remember that time in the café on the Ronda when you told me about the two trustworthy individuals who followed you when Soleràs led you out of the encampment?"

"Seven o'clock, oh dear," he replied. "I should be on my way back to carrer Pelayo. You've got a good memory. Yes, I did mention that in the café; your memory serves you well, but mine is even better. In effect, Soleràs kept leading me further and further away, though it wasn't during the battle of the Ebro, but later. Months later, in the middle of the Plain of Urgell, a few months before Barcelona was taken. He dragged me towards the enemy trenches in the middle of the night, and as he began to pull too hard I sounded the alert. They were two clerks working for the battalion's general staff, two rank-and-file soldiers who nobody would have ever suspected of being anything else; even Soleràs, clever as he thought he was, and even as battalion commander, didn't have a clue. They were on our side, but the genuine article – like me! No fans of Albion or Alfonso, or the clergy-wergy . . . rock-hard idealists! From day one! We kept discreet tabs on our officers, especially people like Soleràs, who had come over to our lines. It was a well-organised, hugely tactful operation; apart from those of us involved, nobody suspected it existed. When Solerás told me to accompany him on that night-time stroll, I alerted my two men: 'Follow us at a distance, make sure he doesn't see you. I don't know what's buzzing round his head tonight . . .' I knew them well; they'd worked under my orders in Barcelona. They followed us stealthily like wolves and Solerás didn't catch on; he was so short-sighted . . . and, that night he was drunk out of his mind. I'd never seen him so pissed. There was a cold wind, by now it was early January, 1939, although it had been a mild winter; it was one in the morning. There was a full moon, the men were sleeping and we couldn't see a single patch of snow on the entire undulating Plain of Urgell that vanished into the distance. Our men slept out in the open with a fire burning in the centre of each bivouac. These were the last weeks of the war in Catalonia; the moment we stepped on Catalan soil, we had decreed the suppression of autonomy and pursued a scorched earth policy. We could see the fires lit by our army as they occupied the ridges across the undulating terrain and outlined the position of our front; we could see hundreds, perhaps thousands, as far as the eye could see. The reds, on the other hand, didn't dare light any because at the first spark our artillery would lambast them with shells; all we could see was the pitch-black night in front of us. Solerás moved forward: 'Do you see that darkness,' he said, 'they are the external shadows . . . That's where teeth are chattering. They are the defeated, the eternally defeated; the sons of darkness . . . or who knows, perhaps the crucified? Who will ever know! Be that as it may, they are *my* people.' He walked on, dragging me behind him. I felt uneasy; that madman might do anything. 'Where are you taking me?' 'Believe me, Lamoneda; it would be shameful. You and I wouldn't be conquerors *comme il faut*. Look at the shape we're in . . .' 'Don't you worry about my shape.' Then, just fancy, he came out with this bilge: 'You can only think about what women have between their legs, but, you know, you ought to think about something else now and then, at least to ring the changes. You only think of little Miranda and live in hopes of moulding her as you want; you don't understand that every individual woman has a statute of autonomy stuck in her head and in the end they do exactly what they want.' 'Little Miranda and the statute of autonomy aren't connected, that's a crazy invention of yours,' I replied. 'Perhaps you'll get to marry her, brute force works wonders, nobody would dare deny that! But nobody, not even God in his heaven (are you listening, not even God in his heaven!), will stop her crowning you with the most magnificent, ornate horns ever seen on this earth. I've said how not even God in his heaven can do a thing, and I will repeat that. I don't know if you have ever heard of free will.'

'"So it's free will now, is it?' He was dragging me towards a pine wood that lay between our positions and the enemy; I refused to follow him any further. 'Where do you think you are going? Can't you see the others will catch us?' 'The others? The others don't exist! Only the ego exists; beyond the ego there is only a phantasmagoria.' 'When they fire a round of mortars our way you'll see if it's only a phantasmagoria.' 'Lamoneda, don't let's argue over such a piddling trifle; a round of mortars? The only worthwhile thing now is to change sides.' 'Change sides? What do you mean?' 'Go over to the others; always go over to the others.' 'But didn't you just say the others don't exist?' 'Exactly right. Hey, one goes over to them because they don't exist; the worst of it is that once one has gone over, they start to exist again. That's why I've spent my life going over, forever going over to the other side. Like poaching someone else's wife, for example, if she's attractive, that is! But when she threatens to turn into your wife . . . In fact, a war would be as intolerable as a bed where you could never change sides, if one could never go over to the other side now and then. A little variety, O Lord! A period with the reds, one with the fascists, and then back to the reds while there's still time; it's so tedious when it's always the same.' I glanced behind me; they were both still there. That fool ranted on: 'Lamoneda, I believe we should do the decent thing now and end this war in the only elegant way a war can end, that is, by losing.' 'You can't be serious now . . .' 'Now is exactly the ideal moment, beyond our dreams; now there is no doubt who is going to lose.' He went on to say many, many other things; he was inspired that night, he'd drunk more than usual: 'What's your opinion of the serenity one finds in the classics?' he asked at one juncture. 'The classics?' '*Larvam argenteam abtulit servus*, I suppose you're familiar with Petronius.' 'Of course.' 'What about Horace? No Horace, admit it. We quote Horace but we read Petronius; ah well, *c'est la vie*. Nobody reads poor Quintus Horatius Flaccus, and yet he was the Baudelaire of Antiquity! Poor little Horace, little dead kitten, I'm the only person in the world who still reads you! And if I were to tell you, Lamoneda, that he was a splendid poet, if I were to tell you, you wouldn't believe me.' He started reciting whole poems by Horace:

> *Eheu fugaces, Postume, Postume,*
> *labuntur anni . . .*

"'Poor little Horace,' he went on, 'my dearly beloved dead little kitty, you died a death far too long ago for anyone to be still reading you. That's why so many people speak of the serenity of the classics; they find them so serene because they've not even seen their covers. The classics are so serene because nobody reads them! You tell me, how was Horace any more serene than Baudelaire? Come on, morons of this world, tell me once and for all! Morons of this world, unite! Your hour of triumph is nigh!' He then told me a thousand other bits of nonsense, *potable* potted meat, trams, ectoplasm, and dead cats yet again: 'In Egypt they've found mummies of cats as tightly bound as Tutankhamen's.' 'Listen, Soleràs, if you've brought me out here to experience the serenity of night and tell me about Tutankhamen . . .' 'Lamoneda, you reckon I'm off my head when in fact I'm trying to get you to understand things that are too simple for you ever to grasp. They're so simple! It's the simple things imbeciles understand the least. If I were to tell you quite simply that I don't want her ever to think – when on one, probably very distant day or other, she receives news of me – that if I deserted at this precise moment it was because you were winning . . . I'd look ridiculous in her eyes! And quite right too. Perhaps I'd be etched on her memory with the modest proportions of a Eugeni d'Ors, like so many. Well, in her eyes, I want to be some- one who is unique for the whole of eternity, someone who never ever did anything like anybody else. So, you see, it *is* all very simple:

what I'm worried about right now is not bequeathing a memory of yours truly, that is too ridiculous; I'm not bothered whether she and I ever meet again in this world, but when she thinks of me I want her . . .' 'You mean the woman in that photo? And to think we wanted to give her a big moustache.' 'Don't bring that up, it would really be better not to. Your piggy chops . . .' He pulled my arm but I wriggled free. 'Don't call me a pig, I've told you that time and again; you must see I'm tired of it. You should know that . . . *I* know where Ibrahim is!' 'You do? Bah, poor little dead kitty, nobody but God knows where he is right at this minute. And, Lamoneda, you aren't God, as far as I know.' 'We'd only have to dredge that vat,' I retorted. He ignored my words and came out with quite something else: 'Listen, Lamoneda, I've spent my whole life pretending the opposite of what I felt, but right now I'm beginning to feel an imperious need to tell you, and you alone, the whole truth. And why you exactly? Maybe it's because you are such a pig.' 'Don't start on that again; I'd only have to dredge the vat to . . .' 'Dredge it then, what do you expect to find? The treasures of Golkonda? *Nelumbos* from the north? That load of nonsense Rubén Darío comes out with? I don't know what I'd give to find out what the hell *nelumbos* from the north look like. Don't raise your hopes: inside that vat is only one dead cat, Ibrahim. That Ibrahim was a pig; you're certainly one as well, but he was too large a specimen. Yes, far too large, the fat porker! It's alright for us to be little piglets, but never that size, believe me, Lamoneda, we shouldn't exaggerate. That bastard Ibrahim took it too far. Excess was his ruination. I'm amazed how I couldn't resist the temptation to blast him from behind with that worm-eaten beam which lay forgotten in a corner, when he knelt to let the bucket down. He fell into the vat without a single miaow. I'm amazed . . . while you . . . you're almost as piggish as he is, and yet how come I've never given you the same treatment? You really are a cowardly piglet, a little bug. I've always had a horror of squashed bugs; green, sticky stuff runs out of their insides and that gives me the willies. Disgust has no frontiers, it's another infinity.'"

Night had fallen and the droning voice of Lamoneda, still slouching on the ottoman, continued to rehearse all this in a dark haze, as fifteen years later he embarked on another endless rant in a different dark haze; he went on and on, oblivious of my presence: "'You, Soleràs,' I retorted, 'are as piggy as anybody; I've seen you reading the highest octane novels.' '*The Horns of Roland*? Well, if I start a novel, and the hero hasn't been cuckolded by page three, I throw it away; I don't like authors who can't get to the point. I'm a piglet or sublime, depending on the phase of the moon, because it does no harm to be a touch sublime now and then. A little variety, O Lord! To play the piglet all the time is tedious. It would also be wrong to be sublime all the while.' And he started talking about that economics professor, the one who had taught him as a law student: 'He was sublime, always sublime, perhaps not overly so, but sublime enough; you only had to hear the emphatic, soulful way he uttered names like Ricardo, Adam Smith, Stuart Mill and, above all, Sismondi; when he said Sismondi, his voice trembled like Llibert Milmany's. Oh, what a tragic hero's tremolo he would use to spell out the law of supply and demand! And the bronze law of wages! And cyclical crises! It was so sublime we were up to our back teeth with them!' Then he started on about his aunt again: 'You see, I'd never dared to tell my auntie that Nati's legs were more interesting than the stalactites. I was twelve years old and had yet to read Dostoyevsky; contrary to legend, I was never so precocious. At the time I was still on Bossuet's *Funeral Orations*, but soon enough . . . will you believe me if I say that basically I've always been a polite, good-hearted boy? A fiendishly ingenuous boy, capable of reading the whole of Bossuet, of swallowing any story, even stories about ectoplasms and such nonsense – that are no less incredible in any case than other stories, like the one about the Oedipus Complex or the tale of the future happiness of humanity the dictatorship of the proletariat has in store. I swallowed all these stories one after another; I was capable of giving a Christian burial to every dead cat I found squashed in the middle of the street; I was capable of anything. But our Political Economy professor thought he was as sublime as Othello; from the heights of his dais his fiery gaze swept across our benches until it came to rest on a corner of the ceiling. He'd worked at it: that was the profile he wanted to present for the benefit of our female colleagues, who always positioned themselves at the top of the tier in the opposite corner. Some were gorgeous, one in Canon Law stood out especially, pale and fair like Desdemona; he thought he was Othello, but pale Desdemona, steeped in Canon Law rather than Political Economy, couldn't have cared less. That cretin thought his profile was straight off a Roman medallion; he didn't grasp you can't be both Othello and Brutus. Desdemona, who was pale, though not silly, didn't give a damn; conversely, she didn't care for me either, but none, not a single one, ever cared for me. Without exception they all repeated in turn that they could talk to me like a brother! And it was like that from the tender age of twelve . . . First of all it was Nati, oh, Nati of the dark legs, and bright, flirtatious gaze! She was twelve like me; you see, she was a little country girl, the kind Ibrahim adored. And now we've mentioned Ibrahim, why would you want to dredge up the vat? Why would you want to betray me to that examining colonel, who behaved like a perfect gentleman? Don't you see that it would upset My Lord if you forced him to put me in the dock? Just agree that Ibrahim is a most *potable* morsel: ever since he's been swimming there, the wine's been more full-bodied than ever, it's taken on a bouquet nothing could rival! Why be so keen on salvaging him? Let him be, my friend; he's doing no harm.' Then, after saying 'he's doing no harm', he went straight into the problem of evil; it wasn't the first time he'd rattled on about that particular subject: 'Logically, there should never be anything but evil,' he said, 'and in fact, that's what all you morons think though you're quite unaware of it. That's why you say so pedantically: think evil and you will not err. You know, you morons can be so pedantic! If you were only moronic, I might tolerate you, but you're so pedantic. You managed to invent the word *malice*, but that alone. Your imagination can't get beyond that. Every language in the world has that word but passed up on the other which is equally basic – *goodice* – and, you know, no language has ever been able to create that word! The truth is languages make a people and the only kind of knowledge that honest, hard-working people understand is knowledge of evil. Knowledge of good? They don't even suspect it exists. Poor apostle St Paul, how you wasted your time advising us to be innocent when it came to evil, and cunning when it came to good; that would be *goodice* and, you know, no-one's ever managed to invent that word. They don't miss it or even remotely suspect it is necessary, everybody aspires to be more malicious than the next man, to manage to see evil on all sides, even in places where

nobody else can see it! But see good? What would be the point?
And in fact they are right; in fact there should only be evil, in the
same way that there should only be absolute darkness, absolute
cold, in a word, nothingness. Nothingness is the only thing that
isn't enigmatic. Imagine nothingness, stir your imagination for
once: absolute nothingness, a total void, what am I saying, *the*
void. Not even space will exist! And yet there'll be a tram in the
middle of the void. Just imagine, I beg you: a tram in the middle of
the void. To be more precise, if you like, let's posit that it is one
of the first electric trams, from the end of the last century; when
you and I were kids, they were still circulating along the streets
of Barcelona, glorious survivors of the wars in Cuba and the
Philippines. Fantastic trams from the last century! Trams that
promenaded the ladies of the time, with their trailing skirts and
little sleeves, and those bustles nestling behind; ah, such ladies,
such trams! Will those days, those trams ever return? Take a look
then at absolute nothingness, but with one of those trams stuck
right in the middle, a tram and nothing else! Do you realise the
philosophical issues that raises? It's scary! How would they debate
their essence and existence? The mystery wouldn't reside in
nothingness, but in the tram: who could have placed it there? But,
my God, what am I saying! What meaning could *in the middle*
have, if we are talking about nothingness? Nothingness has no
middle since it has no frontiers; could it perhaps have a posterior?
Could the tram be located atop the posterior of nothingness like
the bustles of those ladies from the belle époque? Inscrutable
mysteries! But let's cut to the chase: the tram would be there all
alone, steadying itself over the void by virtue of inertia, given that
fields of gravity wouldn't exist any more; a tram and its trolley

wheel, oh such a long, vigorous trolley wheel, a trolley wheel solemnly standing alone, and swaying melancholically for the whole of eternity, without hope, in the heart of the void and time without end . . . What's that you say? You don't like trams? Well, let's make it a dead cat; we won't argue over a trifle. Whatever you place there, the crux stays the same. Nothing should exist and yet it is undeniable that something does exist! Whatever you do, something will exist. *Eppur si muove*. Nothingness beats a retreat, fucked: therein lies the mystery.' 'I can't see any mystery,' I said, 'things exist simply because they have to, for heaven's sake. Why is that a mystery? Where is the mystery?' 'Where? Who will ever know? Who will ever know where this mystery is that's everywhere? Why, for example, at the moment of truth, when I was finally going to possess the woman I desired, the only one I really ever desired, did I scarper? Why did I make a run for it when I was about to get what I'd so passionately desired all my life? What force intervenes at moments like this? Our virtue? Don't make me laugh! Please don't; that would cap it all! If we took that route, we would end up with the self-confidence of a moronic self-made man, virtue doesn't reside within us, we are not self-made men; by ourselves, we are nothing but shit! Virtue comes to us from outside, but from where? What if I were to tell you that I saw these words written in fire across the firmament: *Thou shalt not covet another man's wife* . . . and if I were tell you I saw them with these eyes, you wouldn't believe me! Well, I saw those letters of fire: they went from west to east, and in the full light of day . . . I modestly admit that I've come out with a lot of shit in my time; each turd as big as a house, I will admit to that, but I would at least hope you'd believe this: I did see letters of fire across the firmament . . . A hallucination? You know, so what? That's how virtue comes our way; it comes from outside, when we least expect it, like a hallucination, when it most bugs us; it comes to anger us, to stop us doing what we want to do, to block our path when we least want it. I took dreadful steps to seduce her; what aren't we capable of when we desire a woman with all our instincts and our soul . . . And I fled! I know you understand none of this, and that's why I'm telling you; if I thought for a moment that you'd understand, I would shut up immediately. You're a bright spark and set on making the most of the least opportunity, and you'd think you'd behaved like an imbecile if . . .' 'Naturally,' I responded. 'Naturally,' he retorted, 'well, should I tell you everything I dared do to Nati throughout that summer, the last we spent at my auntie's farmhouse? Nati was our tenant farmer's daughter and they let us play together because they thought we were still children; we were both twelve. It was towards the end of that stay, a wonderful late afternoon towards the end of September and we were playing by ourselves on the threshing floor, not very far from the house. There were three new haystacks from the last harvest and the floor was covered with warm, freshly scattered hay. Nati lay down at the foot of one of the haystacks, her hands behind her neck, looking up at the sky, wanting to catch the first star, she said. We often played at who would "catch" the first. Every day she wore a sort of Turkish slipper that soon fell off, and, as she'd crossed her legs and was swinging her foot, a slipper did fall. I grabbed her swinging foot, which was very brown on top and very pink on the sole, I started tickling her and she rolled around laughing. As the haystack was in the way, the people in the house could hear our laughter but couldn't see what we were doing. Anyway, that was *all* we were doing; I tickled the sole of her foot and she rolled around laughing. That went on until she gave me a slap to stop me tickling. My great erotic adventure of that summer was over! What's really peculiar is that I've never had another, so now I've told you about my biggest bit of derring-do with a woman. I mean, of course, with a non-professional, don't start rooting for my beatification on account of my virginity! If you only knew how often I've remembered that tiny, quivering foot over the years, so dark on top, so pink underneath, if only you knew how I can still feel it wriggling between my hands like a bird trying to escape and how exciting that fresh warm straw was! If only you knew . . . But I expect my little story has only disappointed you.' 'Naturally,' I answered. While he went on about such trifling things, he continued to drag me through that forest towards enemy lines and started up again about good and evil, heaven and hell; he was loony. 'Mystery belongs to heaven,' he said, 'mystery is good! Hell is just incredibly vulgar, ridiculous, and makes no sense at all; I mean to say, almost. Note that I say *almost*; it is amazing how people ignore that *almost*, a small detail, and yet it is this *almost* that . . . oh, we'd be sunk in slime up to the roots of our hair, if it weren't for this almost! But this almost exists and thanks to it we can save our eyes, and only our eyes, and look in the air.' 'Yes,' I replied in a bad temper, 'what you are saying is common knowledge; if you raise your eyes and look up, you will see the moon and the stars. If you've brought me out of the encampment to communicate such sensational insights . . . if you'd said if you look up and spot a good-looking wench on a balcony, you can see her garters . . .' 'No, it's not as easy as you think,' he retorted, 'you sometimes raise your eyes, and you can't see stars or garters. Nothing but the absurd on all sides! An endless void, an endless darkness, the total cold physicists talk about, and perhaps what's the most terribly absurd of all, endless stars and more stars, galaxies and more galaxies and all identical, millions and millions of monotonous, stupid galaxies, hell! So when a moron like you lifts his head and looks in the air, you see a hell that is much more horrendous than the earth itself. And yet . . . *eppur si muove*! There is something else; something that surrounds us, that we can breathe, and yet what is that if not the desire for glory goading us on? What is glory? An empty word? Is there glory that isn't vainglory? Yes, this is often all there is, words and more words, sound and fury and nothing else, but occasionally, at the oddest moment, we hear it for what it is: fullness of meaning, the anti-absurd. There is nothing else, only that, and that's why we seek it out, something that is redolent with meaning! That stands by itself, and is absolute! Our mistake is that we seek it out in this life, not that it's impossible to find, though we could only withstand it for a split second: it would annihilate us. If it doesn't, it's because it evaporates, or else is transformed into something monotonous and finally becomes absurd. That tiny foot, so brown on top, so pink underneath, so quivering, so full of glory; yes, it was, but could I devote my life to tickling it? It was glorious provided it lasted a mere second and was never repeated. Glory in this world becomes tedium if it lasts more than a second. A second . . . that second . . . if only it could halt. Halt, second! But if it halts, it lasts and ceases to be eternity and becomes time once again. It should halt, but not last. Lamoneda, I wonder if you have heard of the *Cactus solerassus* . . . ?' 'Now it's cacti, is it?' 'It lives a thousand years to blossom for a second. But I have never blossomed, I have never known my moment of glory. Now, when I was about on the brink, when I had finally seduced that woman (and I don't mean Nati, you moron) when I only had to take that last step for her to be mine, I said Bah, and scarpered.' 'But didn't you say it was because you'd seen letters of fire . . .' 'Forget it, my friend, don't quibble. Letters of fire, did you say?' 'That's what you said just a moment ago.' 'I don't remember, you know,' he said, 'but no matter. I said Bah, and I vanished! The fact is that that moment scared me; suddenly, when I had it right there, I felt totally terrified. Because that moment is a breath of eternity, and eternity *is* scary.' And then Soleràs began to recite something or other in Italian; he was completely out of his mind; on the other hand, I know barely any Italian."

From my shadowy corner I began to mutter slowly:

> *Quando leggemmo il disiato riso*
> *esser basciato da cotanto amante,*
> *questi, che mai da me non fia diviso,*
> *la bocca mi basciò tutto tremante . . .*

"What's that you're mumbling?" Lamoneda asked. "Your rosary prayers?"

Yes, he said that: your rosary prayers, as he'd say fifteen years later in the darkness of that other den, using the very same words: Your rosary prayers? The very same words, and then he immediately resumed his tedious drone: "'Lamoneda, you don't understand,' said Soleràs, 'you're stuck inside time like a fish in water, unable to grasp that there is anything else. But how free is the air you can breathe outside! The pendulum stops: eternity. The still pendulum is so silent, what a silence! A stifling silence . . . Now we are out of the water: limitless free air without. Time no longer exists, the moment has stopped, but which moment? The moment of glory or of the absurd?' Then I interrupted him: 'You're mad as a hatter, Soleràs.' 'Like my aunt,' he said, 'my aunt is too, it runs in the family. And so what? Maybe you and the rest don't think you are a pack of loonies . . . At least my aunt had something unique about her; the world's going from bad to worse, it gets more vulgar by the day, very soon there won't be any aunts to whom St Philomena appears! Very soon aunts will bore the pants off you with lectures about the planned economy, the nationalisation of the banks, the class superstructure, and the alienation of wage-earners; that's what aunts will talk about in the future! And the world will feel nostalgic for those good old days when aunties talked to us about Jesuit fathers and the Oratory fathers, but by that time it will be too late to languish in nostalgia. Today nephews tend to be Marxists; tomorrow it will be the turn of aunties. The day will come when aunties will believe in Marx with the same good faith that they once believed in the appearances of St Philomena. Class struggles? Why shouldn't there be aunt and nephew struggles? Wouldn't that be as good an explanation of history as any? We could say the whole of history has been but a struggle between aunties and nephews; we could also say it has been nothing but a pile of shit. Much ado about nothing, a puzzle, the meaning of which we will never fathom – because we will only ever have a few of the pieces that, in any case, don't fit together. All that rubbish, the feudal revolution, the bourgeois revolution, the proletarian revolution . . . a load of baloney! It's none of that; there are only passions. And evil passions at that. Instead of nobility, put pride; instead of bourgeoisie, put avarice; instead of proletariat, put envy. They want to make us believe that there was a bourgeois revolution against the feudal nobility, that the bourgeoisie set fire to castles.

Lamoneda, do you think a bourgeois ever existed who was capable of setting fire to a castle? No, my friend, they don't set them on fire, they restore them. More Gothic, more feudal than ever!' 'Naturally,' I rejoined. 'Naturally, the bourgeoisie . . . think how some will spend their whole lives manufacturing the same thing and never tire of doing so! And yet there are still people who wish those self-sacrificing folk ill! What a world! But a new revolution is being planned, nephews against aunties; a new passion is peering above the parapet of history and it goes by the name of lechery. Everybody is preparing to cast off their complexes! Nephews of All Aunties, Unite!' 'You know, Soleràs, you've got a screw loose . . . !' Turning his hands into a megaphone, in the loudest possible voice, as if he wanted the red trenches to hear: 'Nephews of All Aunties, Unite!' Then he rattled on, as if nothing had happened: 'As far as I am concerned, I don't want to know; I am fed up with history. You can keep on with it, if you like; I'm fed up to the back teeth. Let the seven deadly sins squabble away; I've lost all interest. And do you think if I were born again, if I had to start life all over again, that I would repeat the same tomfoolery? I have often asked myself that question and I'm sure I never would, not the same old deal! I'd think up a new deal. A little variety, O Lord, or we'll die of boredom . . . Even that Ibrahim exaggerated! In good faith he had certainly cast off all complexes and hang-ups! I served with the reds for a year and a half, as you know; I've seen them embrace the same things, more or less the same topsy-turvy things as around here; exactly the same, although I won't deny that they have some remarkable specialities that are unknown in these parts, like disinterring mummified friars and nuns. That is an indication of real imagination; I would like that fuddy-duddy Marx to tell me why the proletariat digs up mummies – in what way disinterred mummies serve the interests of the proletarian class? Conversely, what I've never seen or heard there, and may Heaven bear witness to this, is . . . That is, I wouldn't want to lie, I do know of one case. Once, in a village, occupied by an anarchist column, there was a girl with mental problems, a poor stupid soul who could only express herself by grunting, who wandered around the encampment in search of leftovers from the field kitchen; one night, a guard abused her. The column committee – you should know that anarchist columns, as a matter of principle, have no commanders or officers, but committees that reach agreements by voting – the column committee voted unanimously to execute the guard. That's the only story I know of that sort. God in Heaven, bear witness to that!' I growled sarcastically: 'If you want me to believe they are a load of cherubim . . .' 'Don't be a fool, they're not cherubim, but nevertheless, Ibrahim did go too far. On the other hand, it is very strange that we, I mean, all of us, can only insult God like a bunch of monkeys; very strange indeed. Like a set of distorting mirrors. Our pride, a ridiculous reflection of His Glory; our greed, His Providence; our lechery, His Love . . . We are obscene monkeys. The seven deadly sins never change; a pathetic paucity of imagination! But if we lost all interest in the seven deadly sins, how would we ever amuse ourselves? With pure reason? Pure reason was crucified once and for all in this world, and not by brute force, as some idle souls believe, but by brute reason. Poor brute force, in fact, just washed its hands . . . It's the predictable scenario: foreigners wanting to interfere in matters they don't understand; it's always foreigners, hordes of foreign flies poking their noses in stuff they don't understand and then washing their hands. Yes, they wash their hands but the deed is done. Jesus is crucified. Foreigners! They are to blame, and nobody else!' 'To blame for what?' 'For everything! What can you expect of people who adore bull fighting?' Suddenly he started shouting: 'Take the photo, I don't want it any more!' and he gave it to me; he carried it, I think with the intention of taking it with him, but he had clearly had a change of heart. And gave it to me! 'Paint a big moustache on her, I've had my fill of her!' He gave it to me, as you've seen; I keep it in that Arab chest, with the others, and my manuscripts. Not that it is at all out of the ordinary, but I like to hang on to everything. One never knows, you'll see; you never know what you might make out of it. Right now it would be a chore to find it amongst everything else; one day, I'll patiently search it out and show it to you. You'll see it's nothing special; I don't know what Soleràs saw in her. I'd bet anything she was a married woman; there's a dedication on the back of the photo which leaves no room for doubt, and that any husband would find very upsetting. Why did he give it to me? How should I know? I only know he gave it to me as he shouted at the top of his voice: 'I've had my fill of her!' He only did and said outrageous things. I'd never really been interested in his stories – what could be blander than his carryings on with Nati? You know, all very lightweight . . . On the other hand, my novels are quite something else. My characters have real class, are brilliant diplomats, duchesses with incredibly suggestive names like Atalanta . . . Now I'm trying to weld them all together; I'm working on a unique, top-notch novel that will be a supreme synthesis. It will be my masterpiece, the culmination of my life, an epic of heroic, imperial youth! A lunatic labour that will take me years . . ."

V

Some years passed after that conversation with Lamoneda in his *garçonnière* before Lluís and Trini made their first post-war visit to Barcelona. The years are all a blur in my memory: my God, so many years, so many so alike in that pitch-black, endless tunnel . . . how do you distinguish between them? I often had to go down to the city because the archbishop wanted to see me; he had become very affectionate in a quite fatherly way, and I, who had not known my father at all and my mother very little – she died when I was four – was becoming increasingly neurotic, and came to love him like a son; yes, like a son, but a bad son. Like one whose father is an illiterate yokel, whose father is a half-wit only spewing out nonsense, and rather than hide it behind a merciful veil the bad son enjoys stirring it up and harbours nothing but contempt for him in his heart of hearts. He truly provoked a peculiar mix of filial love and contempt that was beyond my control; it was stronger than I was.

Barely a week passed when he didn't insist I come down from my mountains to be with him awhile; as there was only one bus that left early and returned in the late evening, I had to spend the whole day in the city. I liked to aimlessly roam its streets and backstreets full of memories of my now distant youth. I especially liked to visit the shanty towns where I'd been a priest; we are all so keen to revisit the places where we have suffered. I took the metro and then the bus to the end of the line and walked along those wide, muddy streets so like untarmacked main roads; at the time there were only a few scattered houses, surprisingly tall, narrow edifices that made the desolate suburbs even more desolate. There were few cars those days, and I walked slowly along roads on wintry twilights that began so early (the bus back to my village does not leave till around eight). There was such desolation on those eerie roadways that were too broad and mostly unfinished, lit by scant electric bulbs on the top of lofty, unadorned posts, gloomier than any gallows and looking down on you like the eyes of the infirm who have lost all hope at the back of a huge hospital ward, casting an unnerving pallor which had melded the twilight with the light from those puny bulbs; it all had an ersatz, nasty taste, like stewed tea at the bottom of a teapot. That was a taste of the void, because at such times my life was like a cup of cold, forgotten, stewed tea; I had once lived and died hungry and thirsty, now I neither lived nor died because I was no longer hungry or thirsty. I would walk back lonelier and more forsaken than a mangy dog and in the faint glimmer of those winter twilights I walked past the occasional group of passers-by, immigrant day-labourers from the south of Spain – so many had arrived since the war! – returning from work, spades or picks over their shoulders, on their way to huts half-hidden among the reed beds along the river. The moment they saw my soutane, some of them pointed me out with a wink and raised a horizontal hand to their necks as if to chop it off; that is how those wretches greeted us when they bumped into us in dark, deserted places and sometimes we heard one of them, generally the oldest and most weather-beaten, say: "When they lift the ban on priest-hunting . . ." How I would have liked to forget the ocean of hatred that surrounded us, the horrors over so many years, to forget that and have only eyes for the beauty of this world, of *this* world, my Lord, that is Yours, despite everything.

There is a poignant beauty that pierces so deeply on autumn evenings, at the end of a quiet day, when the sun has set and the night sky begins to appear. I often went far from the village along a deep track that ran between osiers to a hill with a hermitage on top, next to a tall cypress. At twilight the hermitage and the cypress stood out against the vertiginous abyss of the sky and I would sit on one of the hermitage's three steps and surrender myself to the profound sadness that was mine and that beauty's: an ineffable melancholy before the beauty of the universe. *Lachryma rerum.* Why do things cry? Why does atrocity laugh? I answered myself: the world's beauty heralds a Creator, its sadness proclaims Him crucified, atrocity with its laughter betrays itself as executioner – but these thoughts never spared me the state of stupor and apathy into which I sank.

Sadness everywhere, sadness in the eyes of the animals – the large animals slowly trudging along country tracks back to the village, as night fell . . . The chimes of the Angelus dropped like stones in a placid lake and I trembled because I should have been the one ringing them, I should have been in the church for evening prayers, while instead the sacristan was ringing the bells as I roamed those deserted heaths far from the village. The waves of sound expanded and gradually died; the mules and oxen listened and ruminated, and the tall cypress listened as thoughtfully as an ox and Lord, You know how I was capable of love, life, and courage in other times; I had friends and comrades, hopes and ideals, and felt at home with them; I loved a woman . . . Now, You have withered my heart, You have made me powerless, burnt out and sterile, and You know why, You who make and unmake us.

And what nostalgia I now feel for that war, the only time I had lived! The waves of air unleashed by the Angelus bells reminded me of that other air stirred by the howls of distant mortar; that vibration in the air so like the breeze on the top of pine branches in a vast forest, when shells whizzed over our heads in a harmonious parabolic curve – because we saw them when they reached the climax of their flight and began to slow down – all that flooded back together with the smell of green wood that burned poorly but was often all we had to protect ourselves against the cold, and here and now I felt nostalgic for all that, for the uncertainties of life wandering through woods and across steppes, for the bitter scent of green-wood fires in the heart of the night, for the uncertain glory of war . . . Lord, my guilty heart longs for that war and that woman.

And my guilty heart still longs for my lost youth; I know I will never experience life like that again! Here I am in my fifties, my entire youth lost in this endless tunnel . . . Could it have been otherwise? Every part of me replies that it could; I was only fourteen in that "spring that was so spring-like", that "spring as perhaps there would be no other in this world", when the whole of our country emerged from a long, long winter to breathe the scent of thyme blossom. I was only fourteen but I will always remember that marvellous aroma of resurrection and hope. At other times I think, no, each and every life cannot and could not have been any more than a shipwreck – which is all there has ever been – and that everybody secretly mourns their vanished youth. And that we pass on our laments from generation to generation like Adam's piercing scream when he lost Paradise. Which is all there has ever been: boundless, ineffable beauty. Lost in the beauty of the universe like a child in a wood; ugly little monsters immersed in an ocean of beauty. Beyond Sirius, beyond the galaxies, distances away that defy the imagination, a limitless beauty that forever looks down on us, opaque, cold, and alien. And echo after echo perpetuates the piercing scream of the first man to lose his youth, a chilling wail that comes from the depths of time.

Seen from the outside, how strong those trees now seem, careening in their fifties, but the termites have already eaten away their hearts. They are like ceibas, those huge silk trees in the wilds of the Caribbean; they all looked so sturdy, only the almost imperceptibly pale leaves marked out the ones with a termite nest inside. Like those men who came to confess, in the days when, a priest in the poor city outskirts, I gave those lecture courses the archbishop was to ban; they came to weep, rather than confess. Men you would have thought still in the prime of life . . . like the giant ceiba a gust of wind unexpectedly blows to the ground because a hidden termite nest has been gnawing away for years and years. A storm assaulting the senses, so beautiful to the hopeful eyes of a sixteen-year-old, so horrific when termites have finished their secret labours . . . They weren't tears of repentance but of exhaustion; they had burned out, pursuing a ghost. The flesh is in flight, always in flight, impossible to catch because it is so elusive. An inexplicable desire to render what was fleetingly eternal had so eaten them away! They came to the confessional because it was the only place where they could find someone who would listen, who would understand that chilling cry from Paradise lost. They were the only arms that would welcome men who had lusted and been defeated, their lives squeezed dry as a lemon, exploding in a final tempest of tears: they were arms nailed to a crucifix.

I always felt a hidden sympathy for these highly sensual men, perhaps – who knows? – perhaps because I have so little of that. In the stifling greenery of the Caribbean wilds, one recognises a chosen tree by its pale foliage; these men also wear a translucent, dark-grey pallor, alongside the melancholy of the universe in their eyes that mirror the abyss. Soleràs' eyes, set in his pale, angular face, two candles in a mortuary chamber, the astonished eyes of those who do not live but are lived, of those who breathe life like a wind-swept flame, blasted by a storm. They don't live life; they burn it. I suspect I feel so sympathetic towards them because I am so unsensual. Their foreheads never rest on tear-drenched pillows, because they never seek repose or even mere pleasure, but passion that is a cross. They flee happiness; they would think a quiet drink by a happy hearth unbearable. They flee happiness to the day they feel burnt out, when they explode in a final deluge of tears.

When the hand of God squeezes him, woe to the man who is dried-out flax; woe to the man who refuses to surrender and still clutches the flag of defeat, how achingly sad is the old man who remains obstinately faithful to a flag that has lost all its glory! Will all-merciful God have any mercy for those who, like Soleràs, refuse not to surrender, but to grow old – who prefer death to old age? Lord, have mercy on them! Why did You claw us from nothingness if everything within us is drawn towards nothingness? Your hand alone keeps us from the abyss. And that echo reverberates across the generations, from the depths of time; a chill clamour for Paradise lost comes to our throats when we stoop over the well of the past and see not our face but an unknown face reflected there.

And I *did* love! I loved a woman; I did not dream that; I know that is true and yet I often wonder: is it true that I loved? My heart hardly dares ask yesterday's heart, just as my face today dares not confront tomorrow's face reflected in the murky mirror at the bottom of the well. I did love, not from any youthful infatuation, but in my thoughts, as in a dream, of grey hair and December evenings. How our solitude grows throughout life! How our shadow lengthens as the sun goes down! That tall cypress silhouetted against the sky like the cross on the anguished horizon of Calvary, its shadow lengthening as the sun dips on the horizon, just like the cross. The closer nightfall, the longer the cross' shadow, until it has cloaked the world. The cross is all we have to cling to against a descent into the abyss of nothingness that sucks us down.

Night must have fallen because the tree of the cross is casting its shadow over the whole world. And the only voice of consolation comes from Him, from the man nailed to the cross and silhouetted on every horizon . . . Music, divine music from deep within the soul, resigned melancholy –

> Oh, keep there, because, as on that day,
> if I close my eyes, if I hear your gentle voice,
> my sadness melts into melancholy,
> my melancholy into peace.

A distant, soothing, resigned melancholy, the brightness of her eyes, the timbre of her voice, her gestures, her silences . . . her presence alone transfigured a hotel room that was as impersonal as it was sumptuous. She carried her home within her, as she did in Santa Espina, as she always did. The first time she came, if my memory isn't a total blur, was two or three years after that conversation with Lamoneda in his *garconnière*.

She first went to see her father's niche at the top of the cemetery on Montjuïc, from where you could see the whole expanse of the port and the open sea beyond. It is a niche like any other, a drab niche with no inscription, bereft among tens of thousands, though it is immediately recognisable from the mountains of flowers at its foot, flowers discreetly removed and replaced every Sunday by anonymous hands, hands reddened by bleach and worn or calloused by tools, the hands of humble women and old workers who never forget.

Every evening she went to mass in Sant Felip de Neri; her white hair glinted against her black mantilla. She was endowed with that early grey hair that so enhances true beauty. Isn't Antiquity the name given to immortal beauty? Endowed to be at her most beautiful with white hair; she, who was no beauty at twenty, was now at fifty. She missed not a single mass in Sant Felip de Neri after she discovered that the Oratory fathers had never, even in the worst of times, stopped preaching in Catalan; when it became impossible, they became wedded to silence.[8] She did not miss an evening in Sant Felip de Neri, or a Friday on Montjuïc, and lived in that palace as if unaware of the unbridled luxury surrounding her.

But Lluís . . . Lluís lived in that palatial atmosphere like a huge predatory fish in the warm waters of his native sea. He often assumed affected airs of disillusioned irony; as when he tapped

8 In the aftermath of the fascist victory, the use of Basque, Catalan and Galician was forbidden in public acts, at school, college and university. Priests who had once preached in those languages were ordered by their respective bishops to use Spanish.

me on the shoulder and said: "You see how the palace manager bows and scrapes before me; he'd change that to a kick up the backside if the cheque I've just given him bounced." His basic self-satisfaction oozed with the swagger of a man who couldn't give a damn, as did his attachment to the absurd carnival of this world. He rarely spoke about his business in Santiago de Chile; he tried to affect a jocular tone when speaking about it, as if he couldn't care less, and likewise his playful tone concealed smug complacency. You suspected he had allowed himself to be seduced by the wretched philosophy of worldly cynicism that makes people shed almost any sense of the supernatural or even of the natural. He had been seduced by glittering surfaces, yet, all the same, he was a good man, or, more precisely, a good-natured sort. The kind of good-naturedness characterising Epicureans who think they are happy because their wallets fall apart with being so full. He told me, for example, euphoric after a copious meal, of his desire to return to live in Catalonia and with part of his fortune found, as soon as he could, a technical training school for young workers, where they would learn first-rate skills and receive lessons in cooperation: "I will name the school after my father-in-law," he told me with a smile: the Milmany Foundation . . . And that would be so appropriate: Trini's father had always preached the road of working-class self-improvement, that the only positive way forward was an apprenticeship in a good trade and the organisation of efficient cooperatives.

They had been able to make that first visit that they had planned and looked forward to for so long, thanks to the U.S. citizenship Lluís had managed to get (his business included an important branch in Chicago). Previously, they had made life hell for people coming on a foreign passport, but that was beginning to change. A passport like his was a most efficient lightning conductor, now that diplomatic relations had been re-established with the United States, which had hitherto been presented as the mortal enemy of Spain.

They made a second visit in 1959 or 1960, also for a few weeks, and also without Ramonet; on this occasion they brought their other children, three boys and two girls. The oldest girl is very pretty, somewhat in the elongated style of El Greco's Virgins. I asked why Ramonet hadn't come as well and to my astonishment Lluís replied that he had had to stay in Santiago de Chile "to head our business". "You know," he said, "Uncle Eusebi died years ago," adding, with a smirk, "now we have to look after ourselves without him." I really was such a fool: I still thought of Ramonet as the boy I had got to know in Santa Espina, not taking into account the twenty or more years that had passed! In my endless dark tunnel I get into such a mess over the years that have gone by! "How old is Ramonet now? Over twenty?" I asked, and Lluís burst out laughing when he saw my amazed expression, and said he was almost twenty-seven, already married and about to become a father. Good God!

They took over three huge rooms, what was called a suite in those palaces. They liked to be in their parents' bedroom during the day, where they even had their meals served because Trini decided, quite rightly, that the palace's huge, pretentious dining room was off-putting; there was the added disadvantage that you had to dress elegantly for dinner. So they had had installed a table big enough to seat everybody in their suite; Trini always presided in rather an aloof manner over those family scenes and one sensed the unity of the clan as well as that this unity emanated from her. One afternoon, when I was having coffee with them after lunch, the receptionist walked in with a telegram from Ramonet – a business telegram. That girl in the office behind the reception, where you have to report upon entering the palace, had already caught my eye; she was one of those rude, irritable girls you find everywhere. Who knows if today's youngsters are so rude because they have no tomorrow, because they foresee that when they are older everything will have passed them by? She must have been eighteen, the age of Lluís' daughter, who reminds one of an El Greco Virgin; when you spoke to her at the reception, like a robotic figurine, she would shake a deliberately messy mane of hair that was so red it seemed to glow like a flame. And now she had walked in while we were drinking coffee, and strode over to Lluís with almost military arrogance – on the highest of heels and straight out of a comic operetta. When her eyes and Lluís' met, her expression was so turbid, inviting, and provocative even a simpleton like me could not get it wrong. I suddenly realised that in the view of this young woman, weaned on the cinema, who gambled her whole life on the single card of her brazen youth, Lluís with his millions, the grey hair on his temples, and laid-back, disillusioned manner, must have seemed a perfect exemplar of "the interesting, mature man", but Trini didn't notice anything; she was always responding to her children, always gently distant.

Does this astonishingly young, seductive grandmother (Ramonet is now a father for a second time) still notice or suspect nothing . . . or is the only thing that exists for her in this world the family she has moulded, her children and two grandchildren, on whose behalf she denies herself and who she would still adore if they were all quite stupid? And what better husband, father, and grandfather than this Lluís who has earned a colossal fortune and protects them against the contingencies of life? She had embraced religion, a religion as soothing and gentle as herself; she believes in it and clings to it. Her missal smells of musk, like her white leather gloves, like her mantilla. She believes in it and clings to it. A mantilla that so suits her! One night they invited me to dine in their rooms; in my honour, Trini had shut off the central heating and had a wood fire lit in a hearth that surely no previous occupant had used. Lluís had just presented her with a diamond medallion and black lace shawl that had belonged to his great-great-grandmother – the wife of that Carlist colonel from 1833 – which she wore to please him. To create an 1833 atmosphere she also had the electric lights switched off and lit the candles in the candelabra. It was the prettiest lace mantilla I had ever seen; Trini was dazzling, with that shawl over her shoulders and the diamond medallion like a brooch on her breast. Lluís always contrived to drape her in extraordinary, surprise items he knew would appeal to her; his idea of a Milmany Foundation was in the same spirit. By his wife's side he sometimes assumed the affable, obsequious air of a foreign ambassador with a foreign queen he had to keep happy – whatever it cost. How seductive she was in that antique shawl, her grey hair glowing in the light from the candles and wood fire! By contrast, that wretched receptionist was like a Coca-Cola advertisement next to a Rembrandt portrait . . .

And yet . . . *eppur si muove*. Lluís deceived her almost as blatantly with the receptionist from the palace as with a manicurist he had come across somewhere else. Trini didn't deign to see anything. She stuck to her path, life has its requirements; her path was the right one. No doubt, but I loved the rebellious Trini of old a thousand times more, the Trini who refused to resign herself to her husband's infidelities or the opium of a complaisant religion. I loved *that* Trini a thousand times more, because this Trini, who is so gently aloof and melancholy, so imbued with the scent of musk and white leather, with her intriguing grey hair, is so astonishingly seductive . . . and it is so difficult to love a woman who is too seductive!

I almost forgot to say, though it is rather self-evident, that Lluís had made a fortune in Santiago de Chile manufacturing pasta for soup. His factory is now the biggest in the entire southern hemisphere. They had been able to escape from Olivel de la Virgen once Ramonet was cured, cross Francoist territory, and board a plane in Seville that would fly them to South America where his uncle was waiting for them, all thanks to the influence wielded by the *carlana* of Olivel.

Soleràs was made of other clay. He would never have betrayed his youth, fallen on his knees at the feet of mundane Deceit, inhabited a palace, or manufactured macaroni. He was a great sinner, but, Lord, You love this kind of sinner, because they burn out totally and are incapable of betraying their youth; they self-destruct halfway rather than betray! In Your infinite mercy, won't You forgive them for bringing forward the hour of their death?

Why are these sensual types, burnt out by their thirst for beauty, so ugly themselves? They are like the driest tinder and that is why they burn until they are completely consumed by flames, and why death is always mirrored in their eyes. That is why – they feel life is so dizzy-making and fleeting – they are burnt out by a thirst that has no definitive name: love, youth, hot-scented blood, uncertain glory. People exist – Soleràs is one of them – who so love this thirst that they prefer to die of thirst rather than humbly kneel before the fountain and drink . . . They flee happiness as if it were poison! They are not men who love, but men of passion; they seek thirst, not water. But what do we really know about them? What do I know about all that? Only You, Lord, can know what inhabits these souls; they display their sins and hide their repentance, and are so driven, only You can know. I can only glean the palest idea in my confessional. Lord, You alone know the storm withering one such soul when it can go no further; You will forgive him, in Your infinite mercy, for shattering Your gift of the chalice of life . . .

VI

In any case, what exactly did I know about Soleràs, whether he was even dead or alive? Nothing at all!

Lamoneda's hazy account only made it clear that he had returned to the republican ranks in the final days of the war. Could he have followed the defeated brigades in their retreat, crossed the Pyrenees, and found himself, like so many others in the French maquis or ended up heaven knows where, in Africa, the Americas, or the South Pacific? And why not the South Pacific? We have no news of so many who are scattered throughout the world; there are people in the Philippines, Madagascar, and Siberia. Or could he have returned, as others did, once the war in France was over, stubbornly to prosecute the struggle with our maquis, and when it became impossible to remain in the Catalan mountains, could he have gone into hiding, as so many did in Barcelona? Who would ever have found them ensconced in that anthill? I knew some hideouts; I visited them when I could give a helping hand; I always asked after Soleràs, but nobody had news of him. I have not given up hope; why shouldn't he make an unexpected reappearance, hadn't Lluís done so after years of silence? How happy I would be if he were to turn up one day at my mountain rectory! How truly happy!

There is a bus that goes down to Barcelona early in the morning and comes back up in the evening. On an early summer evening I was enjoying the cool on one of the stone seats placed either side of the rectory entrance in the village square. I was watching the village children play and the swifts and martins fly to and fro from the eaves, swooping and mewling; that was life, the heat returning, as it did every year, one more year gone; it was a new summer for those children, swifts, and martins, the first heat waves were reason enough for them to be happy again, so wonderfully exciting, and for me it was a step further along that endless tunnel; what was I doing in that mountain village, what happiness could I now expect from life? And as I sat and mulled over these sad thoughts, the bus drove up; "It's past eight o'clock, another day dying . . ." I muttered to myself, and, lo and behold I spotted him among the country folk getting off the bus with their bundles and baskets, and people were staring at him, intrigued, since it's always an occurrence when a stranger comes to the village; but it wasn't Soleràs, it was Lamoneda.

He walked towards me more of a ghost than ever and I felt icy cold because I would never have expected to see him in the village; it is a ghost, I thought, a repulsive ghost reappearing to haunt you again, years after our last encounter, when I had completely forgotten him. He walked towards me across the square lit up by the slanting rays of the setting sun in late June; his face was a picture in that brightness, but it was the smile of an old man who is down and out and done for. How could Lamoneda be so old?

"They've put me out in the street again," I heard him mumble gruffly, as if I was dreaming, "back in the direst poverty. All slander, you know; as usual."

I asked him to come in, because the kids were crowding round him to get a good look.

"Phew," he sighed, flopping onto one of the two chairs. "I had a hard job finding you in this village. The Curia refused to tell me which village you were priest in. Why did you lie to me?" his voice whined. "You told me you were in Vinebre, don't you know that's a hell of a way to go? I went there by train; nobody could tell me your whereabouts, your name rang no bells . . . I should have guessed! We're old friends and comrades, but you gave me the slip . . . !"

My God, I'm not sure, this was the early sixties, perhaps '62 or '63; I can't handle dates, they're all the same, how can I tell one year from another in the darkness of this tunnel? And Lamoneda immediately started telling me how he had fallen victim to envy, how they had taken advantage of liberalisation to ruin him; yet again he was on his uppers . . .

"You're a priest, couldn't you find me a job?"

A job for someone unequipped to do anything, I thought, and realised he took it for granted that we priests had our hands on the controls; I thought I could infer that he held us largely responsible for the process of liberalisation that had been begun four or five years ago and that constituted the most blatant betrayal of principles in his eyes. Sitting on that straw chair, his exhausted body slumped forward, a bus ticket, not a handkerchief, was poking out from his top pocket.

And while he rehearsed his round of bitter disappointments I stared at that ticket, wondering what, if we explored the depths of his pockets, we would turn out – hundreds of used metro, bus, and tram tickets, silent witnesses to journeys across the huge city, journeys that had died and vanished in the mists engulfing his ghostly life. Lamoneda's past, I thought, as if I daydreamed, my eyes staring at the ticket that was poking out, wasn't a boulevard that autumn carpets in yellowing leaves as it vanishes into the distant haze gilded by a setting sun and divine melancholy; it was an interminable, unspeakably dreary, tarmacked road, covered in used bus, metro, and tram tickets, and disappearing into the distant smog from a double line of black chimneys . . . Lamoneda looked as if he might be carrying on him, packed into his bottomless pockets, all the bus, tram, and metro tickets he had ever bought, and I shivered as if from a first cold snap or a high temperature while he endlessly recounted his round of disappointments. He leapt from one thing to another and reproached me again for deceiving him in saying I lived in Vinebre, but his reproaches weren't embittered, they were almost affectionate, as if he found it perfectly natural that I should have done that: "And why Vinebre of all places?" he repeated, "Do you know where that is?" No, I didn't have a clue, I only had the faintest, almost imaginary idea, and that's why the name had come to mind when he insisted on having my address when we bid farewell in his *garçonnière*. Summer was only beginning but that evening you could feel the heat; I ushered him into the kitchen garden and shade under the vine and he talked and talked, resuming the topics of our conversation from the *garçonnière* as if we had only interrupted it the previous evening, as if all those years had never passed; he even returned to topics from that more distant exchange in the café on the Ronda: "My tenant has made a pile. He's now got two tractors, a threshing machine, a hydraulic press, a van, and a car. Not only does he still live in my house, as always – there was no way the local courts could force him to leave – he's refurbished it, modernised it, as he says; he has had the façade plastered because he reckons the stonework looked cheap and nasty, and walled up that gallery of pointed arches we called the suntrap, and given every bedroom a bathroom. Not that the pig ever washes, but he says it's the modern thing to do. I couldn't find a way to get him out of the house. I'm the one who has no right to step inside! I tried to make his life difficult in every way I could. To no avail. He's a real bright spark. In the years the civil guard used to go round the villages requisitioning harvests, the farmers who didn't declare theirs had a bad time of it. Mine made hay! That sharp operator raked it in; he sold on the black market like in the war, though at even higher prices. I denounced him, not once but several times. The civil guards turned up unannounced and searched everywhere from the attics to the cellar and found no oil, wheat, or hazelnuts! It was an inscrutable mystery; they found them in every farmhouse apart from mine. Was the fellow in cahoots with the civil guard? Were they in on the business? I denounced them as well; they were changed. Futile. It was always futile. They finally found the key to the enigma when liberalisation began, when it was too late because they'd stopped requisitioning. Just listen to this."

Sitting on the wooden bench under the vine, his back turned to the wall at the rear of the garden, he didn't notice what I could see out of the corner of my eye – the sanctimonious old woman peering over the wall: they were always the eyes of that sanctimonious soul, the one forever denouncing me to the bishopric after she discovered I was a "red priest"; the old crone was always spying on what came in and out of the rectory, and everything that happened or was said there. The garden wall looks over an alleyway they call "the house-back" where a pile of stones had been dumped at some point; I should have had them removed, as they are a nuisance, and it's where the old woman climbs up and stands on tiptoe so she can peer over. She thinks I can't see her; meanwhile the ghost droned on: "There's been no priest in the village since the war; a lack of vocations, you may know about that. It's a big talking point: there are lots of villages without a priest or parson; it's the lack of vocations. A rector from another village a long way off comes to say mass; he comes only on a Sunday, and even then not every week. I should say that my tenant is the biggest mass-goer for ten leagues around; he's got the loudest voice when it comes to bawling the Kyrie at high mass and he makes the vaults of the church shake! A blast from his lungs and voice box really echoes! As he is the biggest Jesuit in the parish, the priest has entrusted him with the key: my man has been sacristan from 1940. Well now, the parish church has a crypt where the uncorrupted body of St Pandulfa is kept; I suppose you must have heard about this saint and her miraculous relic. And the cunning sacristan, namely my tenant farmer, as the marble plinth is huge and hollow inside . . ."

Out of the corner of my eye I registered the old woman's shifty gaze; she had pricked up her ears on hearing the story about the saint and her relic.

"I expect you've guessed by now: he kept the oil beneath that mummy, inside the plinth; that was his storehouse. How did the civil guard find it there? Just imagine, my pious tenant farmer invoked the support of St Pandulfa to safeguard his harvest! As for the corn and hazelnuts, he hid the sacks behind the reredos of the big baroque main altar; no, the reds didn't burn it, they burnt nothing at all, because the previous tenant, who was the mayor . . . or perhaps I've already told you about that? It was in the years when the price of corn, oil, and hazelnuts went through the roof; he lined his pockets while I was poverty-stricken! Ten thousand pessetes a year and thank you very much . . . When the ministers began to liberalise the economy, he let slip one Sunday afternoon in a conversation in the village café: 'You all know how I'd liberalised it years ago on my own behalf . . .'"

The old woman didn't miss a trick, as her shifty eyes peered at us. While Lamoneda rehearsed his interminable monologue, I was thinking, with a *frisson* of horror that was giving me goose bumps, that now he had located my hideaway, he might pay me frequent visits. Should I ask to change parish so I could put that obsessive ghost off my track as he was threatening to turn into my shadow? With darkness falling, his face seemed more a madman's than an old man's; though he was a very placid madman, that placid dementia, the tranquil nature of his inexhaustible dementia, was completely unnerving. And those shifty eyes remained in place as the sky turned a darker and darker blue and the Shepherd's Star shone above the wall like another eye also spying on us, and the moment came when I could resist the temptation no longer and politely addressed her: "Good evening, Senyora Guinarda, enjoying the cool air up there?"

She quickly slipped away and Lamoneda droned on without pausing, as if he had heard nothing: "Did you know that Rexy Mura has gone down the plughole? You didn't? Well, it's not as if it's not been in the news . . . If only you knew how many big factories will have to close! On the other hand, the small-time manufacturers, who for years have had a torrid time with inspectors making their lives impossible and forcing them to work clandestinely at night because by day they cut off their electricity . . . those fellows are bearing up with liberalisation, I mean, they're breathing . . . What's that? Yes, the small manufacturers, those busy little bees – and his voice was full of sarcasm – all those keen on work, saving, and free-market competition, shitty bourgeois liberals . . . are all now singing victory hymns! That little shoemaker, you know, is making a killing by exporting women's shoes to the United States, or perhaps you have forgotten all about him?

Yes, that's the man, while Rexy Mura and other big prestigious factories are falling apart . . . shitty little manufacturers . . . always thinking about work, with their mania about two and two making four and only four! Ah, those idiots now breathe freely, though they will never understand the heroic grandeur of our proletarian, imperial style of life . . . What's that? You knew nothing about the collapse of Rexy Mura? It came down with such a crash! The whole of Barcelona shook. A few weeks ago the Marquis of Santas Cruces had to hire himself out as a *maître d'hôtel* in a fancy hotel. Do you remember Mr Kroitz? Yes, Mr Kroitz is now working in a fancy hotel. He's a *maître d'*. Wealthy guests from the United States slaver when they find out it's a real Spanish marquis bowing and scraping to them . . . *c'est la vie*! What pigs those Americans are! Buying their shoes from Freemasons! Ah, Llibert Milmany, I expect you'd like to know what he's doing. What a guy! He saw it coming in time; he was the first to see the first leak in the ship's hold before anyone suspected a thing. Now he's in Jaén, managing another gigantic factory, a factory in Jaén, you ask, what on earth's a factory in Jaén making? Well, what do you expect; something like the extraction of acids from *orujillo*, that's right, *orujillo*, and what might that be? I expect it means mashed olive stones! Yes, he extracts acids from *orujillo*. You want to know who owns the factory? Well, who do you think? That lot will never go bankrupt . . . two and two will always make five when they have to, isn't that what budgets are for? Hey, the great Llibert, he's one who never got his hands dirty! I went all the way to Jaén, just now, when I was thrown back onto the street on my uppers, and, you know, Jaén couldn't be further away, particularly if you have to travel third class. An endless journey, I'd never have thought it! The other end of the world! I went to ask him to hire me to help him extract acids, you know, acids from *orujillo*, you ask me if I could make head or tail of any of that! Do you think anyone did? Do you reckon anyone on the planet could tell you exactly what *orujillo* is and which acids you can extract from it? But Llibert . . . Llibert Milmany . . . the great shyster . . . the eternally indispensable . . . shyster! What a mean bastard! He not only didn't want me in the factory, or want to share the cake with me like a good brother, he issued veiled threats that he would do away with me on the quiet if I let on to anyone about anything. I had insinuated I had in my possession certain papers, you know where I keep them, in that Arab chest, but he doesn't know where my *garçonnière* is . . . I could only get a five hundred note out of him, just enough to pay for my third class return ticket to Barcelona, and when I started shouting: 'Five hundred. A pittance! You mean bastard!' he summoned that gorilla from Medellín to drag me by my collar to the factory entrance. My trip to Jaén was a total waste of time . . . but I do have those papers . . . I hang on to everything! They still haven't located my *garçonnière*; we could create a stir, let all hell loose if you wanted . . . you and I could . . ."

"Could what?"

"Let all hell loose, aren't you too one of the disenchanted? There are so many of us! We could let all hell loose with the practice we've had . . ."

It was very late; I invited him to dinner. I had some potatoes on the embers from the day before that I re-heated over the ashes; I also had a dry goats' cheese local shepherds make and bread that was several days old. I still had a small demijohn of that light, tart wine they make locally. He went at it like a wolf; we dined under

161

the vine in the garden, in the cool darkness of that night at the end of June, and while we chewed dry bread and dry goats' cheese, he pursued his monologue: "That's why I've paid you a visit; we the disenchanted should get our act together . . ."

"Didn't you say you came here because you thought I might find you a job?"

"Yes, that's what I had in mind; I thought that, since you are a priest . . . and, in fact, I am rather surprised: Cruells, how come that, being a priest, you don't rule the roost? There can be only one explanation: some of you priests have been hoodwinked and now face the bitterest of disappointments. Well, we could achieve great things! Fantastic things! We can still kickstart that glorious revolution we have talked about so much, the revolution of the youth, the most glorious of revolutions! Oh, what a revolution we could make! I've still got my contacts, you know, that's really why I came, to establish contacts with disenchanted priests . . . to create a united front, the front of the disenchanted . . . They so let us youngsters down! They fooled us, they tried to get rid of us when they no longer needed us, well, they won't mess us around any more! We hold the secret; we know what to do!"

His nonsense went on interminably. It was very late, so I took him to my room and laid out another straw mattress for him. And what do you think, as I spread it out I felt another set of shivers down my spine, because I seemed to be reliving something I had already experienced; when this happens, when we suddenly relive a scene we have experienced many years ago, when we start repeating the same gestures and saying the same things we did or said in a remote past, when the past suddenly, as if they had set a trap for us . . . in that darkness, each of us on his mattress, he continued rambling incoherently, now telling me about Malvina Canals i Gonzàlez, and I couldn't for the life of me remember who that Malvina was. "My wife," he said, and I gave a start: his wife? Was Lamoneda married? "Don't you remember?" he asked, "that redhead, the one on the Ronda de Sant Pau." This Malvina had evidently made life impossible for him; she kept close track of him and each time Lamoneda found a job, even if it was only temporary, she would turn up with a judge's decree by virtue of which he'd have to give her a large slice of his monthly wage. "She won't let me live!" he whined in the dark, and then told me how he had attempted to start divorce proceedings by invoking adultery but all her friends had come and made statements in her favour, even the altruistic handyman who shared her with the others, like a good brother, swearing by the Gospel that Malvina's behaviour had been beyond reproach ever since she'd got married. Lamoneda lost the legal battle and then, into the bargain, after reading out his sentence, the judge had quipped: "Well, my good man, how on earth did you come to be embroiled with a loose woman?"

He droned on in the dark and I felt I had been set a trap, that someone had substituted Lamoneda for Soleràs – as on that distant night at the front on another straw mattress when Soleràs had confided such surprising things. And now the scene was being repeated, though it wasn't Soleràs but Lamoneda, as if an invisible genie enjoyed swapping one for the other in my sad life. Because I still hoped I might find happiness in this life, that I could still be so happy with a friend who gave me companionship, and could this friend, this unique friend, be anyone other than Soleràs? If one fine day I were to see him reappear, defeated and a failure no doubt, defeated and a failure like myself, "broken and exhausted";

if he were to present himself unexpectedly one day outside my mountain rectory . . . would I not quickly make a place for him at my side? What good company we would be for each other on the downward slope where it is so sad to walk alone! But a mischievous power was having fun putting Lamoneda where Soleràs should have been, and while Soleràs was on my mind from that distant night in a rain-swept autumn when we both lay like this, each on his own mattress, this ghost, who liked to lurch from one topic to another, now decided to talk about Soleràs, as if to resume our earlier conversation in his *garçonnière*, or that even more distant one on the Ronda, as if countless years hadn't slipped by, as if we had interrupted our conversation only yesterday or had managed to stop time ever since that conversation in the café. As he had mentioned Soleràs, I asked: "Have you never had news of him? Can't you tell me what happened to him after he went over to the republican lines? Where is he now?"

"How should I know?" Lamoneda answered. "He went over to the reds, he disappeared. I've received no news of him, how do you expect me to know anything after he went over to them? He was such a fool! Yes, Soleràs was a fool, but can you believe it, he predicted everything that's happening now? 'You'll see your revolution,' he told me (because he always said 'your' revolution, 'your' comrades, as though he'd never been on our side) – 'you'll see this glorious revolution of the youth drown in an ocean of holy water.' And he added: 'Everybody will fuck up you youngsters.' You see, he said 'you youngsters' as if he was already an old man, but he must have been twenty-five or -six when I was well past forty. 'And as for this war,' he went on, 'you'll see the novels foreigners will write about it! Oh, the novels they will write! Total rubbish, of course, but won't they sell! Like hot cakes! The fact is if you try to explain our fun and games to foreigners, they soon lose their way; they don't understand one iota. Not that we understand it much better, but at least we do have some notion of its extremely simple complexities. On the other hand, they want extremely complicated simplicity. Foreigners aren't fond of subtleties; they have decided once and for all that this Spain of ours should be located in the tropics, Capricorn rather than Cancer, and that its inhabitants are gypsies, when they're not toreros. If you try suggesting that, apart from gypsies and toreros, there's the odd paterfamilias who spends his time making socks or shoes or pasta for soup, they find that too intellectual, too complicated, too incredible, and stop listening because that gives them a headache. I've lived abroad and know them and know what it's all about; I know they'd explain your fling with little Miranda their own way; they'd turn you into the most gypsy-like flamenco torero and she'd be the biggest . . . hmm.' 'Look, Soleràs,' I interrupted, 'watch what you say, she's my betrothed!' 'You and your betrothed aren't worth a brass farthing; all these foreigners want is a novel that will sell. I know them, I've lived abroad and know them off by heart.' It's amazing how lucid that fool Soleràs was."

"He was always lucid," I replied. "Who knows what happened to him when he returned to the Catalan brigades . . ."

"What happened to him? How should I know? He was always coming out with such crazy notions . . . Didn't I say he was pickled the night he went over? He was dragging me by my arm; I was looking out of the corner of my eye at my two men following us, and starting to feel scared, we were getting so close to the enemy's advance positions! The moment came when I refused to take another step; we had reached the edge of that wood, where the bare plain began. It was at that point, when we'd come to a stop among the last pine trees, that he blurted out: 'I wonder, Lamoneda,' he said, 'I wonder if you have ever heard of that carpenter.' 'That carpenter?' 'Yes, exactly right: *that* carpenter.' 'A carpenter, at this point in time?' I retorted. 'And why not; why shouldn't we talk about carpenters right now?' he replied. 'But which carpenter?' I asked. 'Oh, one among many, a village carpenter I can't get out of my head.' 'Why worry about a village carpenter . . . ?' 'You know, a villager from the back of beyond, a sort of Olivel de la Virgen.' 'Why start going on about a carpenter in the mess we're in . . . ?' I looked behind me, convinced he'd gone over the edge: my two trusties had stayed hidden in the undergrowth in the woods and weren't letting us out of their sight. 'He was a poor carpenter from a down-at-heel village in the back of beyond; by the name of Jesus, if that means anything to you.' 'So now you're going to start on about Jesus?' 'And why not, you bastard? Who do you expect me to go on about at this moment in time, if not Jesus? Who should I be thinking about, if not Him? Himmler? Hey, you bastard?' 'Don't call me a bastard again, Soleràs. I won't tolerate that.' 'I tell you, I really worry about that carpenter, you now know who I mean, *that* carpenter from the back of beyond . . . If it weren't for Him, what sense would anything have? What sense?' 'You're the one who has no sense,' I replied, 'you don't know what you're saying, you're raving mad!' 'I'm not raving mad at all, Lamoneda; I know only too well what I'm saying. If it weren't for this village carpenter, life would be one huge leg-pull! Lamoneda, are you of the opinion that we should believe in you rather than in Jesus of Nazareth? Must we read your novels rather than the Gospels? I ask you! If they force me to choose between you and Him, I'm with Him all the way. That Mary Magdalene understood men, you know, she was no innocent abroad, that Mary Magdalene, and she didn't follow Stendhal but Him.' 'Don't make me laugh,' I retorted, 'do you think Stendhal lived in Jerusalem at the time of Mary Magdalene?' 'It could be,' he replied, 'anything is possible. You'll find few women as experienced as that Mary Magdalene, and she stuck by Him! Telling a porker like you is pointless, as you won't understand, but I'm dying to tell you, I'll explode if I don't!' 'And what is it you want to tell me?' 'I could never read the gospel according to that Mary Magdalene without tears welling in my eyes, and it's been like that ever since I was twelve.' And he suddenly started wailing at the stars: 'Mary Magdalene, harlot and martyr, don't let go of my hand!' That madman wailed so loudly the advance enemy lines finally heard us and sent a burst of machine-gun fire our way; luckily, though they could hear us, they couldn't see us, because it was pitch dark and we were still among the last few pine trees. From there on the terrain was flat and bare as far as the stockades of the reds; in the bright starlight we caught glimpses of their sandbag parapets in the distance on a ridge. Soleràs had grabbed my arm again and was trying to drag me in their direction, but I tried to wriggle away: 'And now,' he said as I tried to break free from a hand gripping my arm like a steel manacle, 'I'm going to desert before your very eyes, in full knowledge of who you are and what you're up to; I'm deserting because that's what I feel like doing; from the tender age of twelve, I have always, but always, done what I have felt like in defiance of whoever.' That was when I finally broke free of his grip and shoved him to one side; since then . . . I've not heard a word about him. He went off, and I lost sight of him! He walked alone towards those parapets and that was the last I heard of him. Why are you so fascinated by that fool Soleràs? You barely knew him and he was a dolt!"

"You say he disappeared from sight and yet the terrain before you was flat and bare as far as the enemy stockades . . . there was a full moon, I remember you telling me that day in your *garçonnière . . .*"

"A full moon? No, there was no moon, I can assure you; it was a pitch-black night with no moonlight at all; the terrain was undulating. And don't ask me any more questions! All I know is that he deserted. He was a fool and a deserter. I don't want to hear any more nonsense, so no more questions! I'm up to here with all that! And as for all the Soleràsses there've ever been or will be, I'd like to . . . you know, didn't I tell you about Captain Ibrahim? What could you ever expect from an idiot like Soleràs? Let's forget him; I find talking about him exhausts me. I'd rather recite fragments of the novel that is the *summa* of all my novels, and a masterpiece. My life's supreme achievement . . . the epic poem of our immortal deeds! I know whole chapters by heart."

And there and then in the darkness of my bedroom he started reciting monotonous swaths from his dreary novel where a duchess called Atalanta turned up with a young ambassador by the name of Recesvinto from some empire or other, it was deadly boring! Luckily he soon fell asleep and then I only heard his loud, cavernous snores. At the crack of dawn I got him up for the bus, paid for his ticket, and made it clear that I would prefer never to see him again.

VII

Cui prodest?

And in fact it was years before I saw him again.

One autumn evening in 1968, after I had returned from a day spent with Lluís and Trini in Barcelona, I had started sweeping my church; it was Friday, the day for sweeping. The church is bare and empty, like the one in Santa Espina, as its interior was burnt to bits by flying anarchist pickets in '36; only the stone altar still stood. After the war they put a large temporary cross without an image on the bare wall; it was made from two pine trunks that had hardly been smoothed or polished; it was, as I said, a temporary measure, while they commissioned new images to replace the reredos that had been burnt. The years have passed by, thirty by now, and nothing has changed; I prefer this large, rough-and-ready cross to any other that men might make.

So there I was sweeping on that Friday evening and the only light in the church came from the wick in the lamp hanging in front of the Holy of Holies, and the dust thrown up by my broom from the flagstones smelt of the fresh earth that comes with a new grave, a Good Friday smell. And, yes, it was already the autumn of '68 and the years had slipped tediously by, all seeming identical in the darkness of that endless tunnel. In the meantime there had been the prolonged death agony of Auntie Llúcia which lasted for months; she finally died – in '64, '65, or perhaps '66? – and I was left alone in the world; every step we take is one more step towards solitude. I swept and daydreamed while a cold, wily draught blew in through a crack in the ill-fitting door and swung that lamp like a pendulum; it swayed gently as I swept, absorbed in my daydreams.

All of a sudden I noticed a piece of paper on the altar.

How could anyone have slipped into the church and left it on the altar? The church was shut from morning mass to evening rosary. Yet there it was, that sheet, so visible in front of the tabernacle; a pebble from a stream held it in place so the wind wouldn't blow it away. I put it close to the flame so I could read it: 'Bring me bread, I'm in a tight corner, Soleràs.'

A rough map of the path to follow to his hideout filled the rest of the page.

After all of thirty years could I believe he had survived? I confess that my first reaction was one of scepticism – how could it be him? But if it wasn't, who was it? Nobody in the village knew anything about Soleràs, or the friendship that had linked us thirty years ago, and no stranger had been seen in the village recently. What if it really was him? Could he have lived all those years abroad without ever contacting me? Or did he hole up with the maquis and then hide in Barcelona? I knew of others who had joined the maquis in the war in France after ours was over, and, when it finished, they had secretly crossed the Pyrenees and continued resisting in the mountains; by 1948 a few still remained who had not laid down their weapons and were surviving like wolves holed up in the remote wildernesses of Catalonia. Later on, when even that became impossible, they had hidden in the giant anthill that is Barcelona; I know some of them; more than once, I had given them help; might he have acted like them? And if it was him, was he cornered like a wolf in the depths of the forest and was I his only hope in the world?

I knew the spot indicated on the map; I had been there often on my solitary promenades. It is a deep ravine far removed from all habitation, with only the ruins of a paper mill nearby. In the spring, hundreds of pairs of rooks make their nests in the holes that dot its high crags; you see them flying in and out with beaks full of food for their chicks, and their shrill cries, amplified by the crags, bring some life to those shadowy solitudes for a few months. However, once summer is over, the landscape becomes increasingly silent and from the beginning of December the sun never touches the bottom of that high, narrow gorge, where a brook runs.

I walked there at night. Driven on by crazy expectation, I walked for five hours: what if it was Soleràs! If it really was Soleràs, if it was him! If in my growing solitude God had sent me that friend back from the dead! What good company we would keep in the twilight of our lives! What good company!

Day was barely dawning when I reached the Mill Strait, which is what locals call that stretch of land. I dreamt all sorts of things and made wild plans as I walked in the light from the stars and crescent moon; could Soleràs and I live together for the rest of our lives? Defeated failures in this world, could we not live together each on the hopes of the other? Because, if it was him, he must really feel as lonely or more than I did, as or more of a defeated failure than I, as or more lost in the pitch black of a never-ending tunnel, as or more neurotic . . . We could live together in my rectory, who knows, I might even persuade him to be ordained. And if, for whatever reason, he didn't want to be ordained, could he not live with me like a lay brother, as a lay brother much more intelligent and cultured than his clerical counterpart? Didn't they arrange lives so in bygone times, didn't they establish brotherhoods between Christians in search of peace and solitude? Isn't history full of hermits and anchorites? Isn't our century the one that, more than any other, summons us to peace and solitude after all the horrors we have witnessed, and is solitude, my Lord – I kept asking myself – tolerable without companionship? my Lord, give me solitude in the company of a brother, and I will ask You for nothing else in this world!

Day was barely breaking when I saw him from afar; he was sitting on a big rock by the side of a brook with his back turned towards me. It was *his* back, it really was! A stooping back with a backbone that seemed to stand out like a battered nag's, and I trembled at the sight of this man who had come back from the dead. I walked towards him and he didn't turn around although my big, iron-soled shoes clattered on the pebbles by the side of the brook. I could see his emaciated neck, his straggling locks of hair; he was poorly dressed and warming himself in front of a fire he had lit. The crackle of damp green wood muffled the sound of my steps: the spitting, damp green wood and the bubbling brook. Suddenly he heard me and turned quickly round and I saw his yellowish face, pale as the parchment skin of a mummy, with an almost white, bristling, days-old beard, and his eyes – his sad, cunning eyes.

I couldn't stifle a great cry of disappointment: "Lamoneda!"

While he devoured the bread I had brought, a few metres away I saw a pile of pebbles from the stream topped by a cross.

It was made from two small, rusty iron bars, tied loosely together with a length of esparto rope. Upstream along the ravine, almost hidden among the brambles, was a charcoal burners' hut where, as I soon found out, he had chosen to live. At the sight of that cross

I started to weep quietly, damned if I know why; he put down the bread and looked at me suspiciously: "So you're crying now, are you? Are you planning to inform on me? You're devious enough to!"

"Inform on you?"

Inform on him? To whom? And why? What did he mean? The crescent moon was still visible, a waxen yellow amid the pink and blue of dawn, and pointing his finger at it he said: "It's like a face though it's been so nibbled away, as if half has been chewed. It too seems to be spying on me . . ." He started stuffing bread again and for a while we were silent; he stuffed and I watched him stuff.

"You won't inform on me," he said finally, "that's why I have come to hide in the shadow of your soutane. It was my only way out; it's impossible to slip across the Pyrenees, all the passes are being watched. I need to be patient until they tire of searching for me. Admit that if I'd not signed Soleràs, if I'd signed Lamoneda, you wouldn't have come. I'm not exactly welcome here; you made that quite clear the last time we met. Well better still, they won't come looking for me here. It won't occur to them! I've put them off my scent for a while, provided you don't inform on me. You won't do that, you're incapable of such a thing and, besides, you loved my uncle too much!"

At times the expression on his face was completely wan and grief-stricken; he would suddenly stop talking and listen to the wind whistling softly through the tops of the pine trees, so like the sound of those huge mortar shells when they sped high over our heads. He suddenly went faint as if he were about to lose consciousness: behind us we heard the noise of what might be cautious footsteps.

It was only a squirrel, a big red handsome squirrel, and the second he saw we were looking at him he fled in alarm, scattering piles of half-rotten pine nuts. I understood none of this nonsense: Lamoneda possessed the key to some mystery and that was why they were looking for him, but who were *they*? Who was looking for him? And what was the mystery? What was the key?

"And why this cross?" I asked, because it did really intrigue me. That extraordinary cross was there; it was no dream. He looked at me as if he hadn't understood my question: "This cross?" he repeated. Then he stammered: "I found these two small bars among the ruins of the mill further down and that gave me the idea. If a stupid shepherd or hunter came this way, I'd need to explain why I'm here and what I'm up to in this ravine, don't you reckon? I'd have to explain myself; a tale of an anchorite's penitent solitude, some holy baloney, it always works with that kind of person. I even feel inspired to make up a miracle, and why not? Like my uncle. Why not? It's not as difficult as it appears . . ."

He laughed as he looked at me askance: "My uncle! And what if I were to tell you that he wasn't my uncle?"

He stirred the fire as he whispered: "There's no point play-acting with you; we know each other too well."

His fire had finally taken off and I thought all that was very weird. He puffed too close to the flames and I could smell his hair being singed like burnt wool; while he puffed, he glanced at me on the sly.

"If I were to tell you that he wasn't my uncle . . . because, you know, we know each other too well and play-acting won't do. I should certainly tell you why I came and hid here. I bared my canines at them the last time; I always retain my trump card, and they don't know where it is; they still haven't found my *garçonnière*. The problem was I misplaced it; I only wanted some dough; five hundred one thousand notes would have done it, been enough to shut Malvina up. They must have misunderstood; they must have thought I wanted more and took my threats seriously. They decided to eliminate me."

Given he thought he was surrounded by mortal danger – could I be in any doubt he was in the grip of persecution mania? – I asked him why he had lit the fire. He hadn't thought – he said in a state of shock – that the smoke would be visible from a long way off.

Every week, and always at night, I took him his provisions. As autumn advanced, he got filthier and filthier, like an animal growing slothful and starting to hibernate. I always found him at the back of the cabin sprawled on a heap of putrid straw. He always wore the same underwear; he had none to change into. I couldn't get him any because had I asked for some, it would have attracted attention; only quite recently my parishioners had given me a couple of shirts, the only ones I have because I threw the old ones away. In the end he stopped washing, even though the brook was only a few steps from the cabin. He threw his socks away because sweat had ruined them and from then on he wore his shoes on his bare feet; his shoes gave off a steady pong; they were almost new because he never walked anywhere.

I sometimes arrived when it was still pitch black and surprised him reading by the light from an oil-lamp I had taken him; the moment he saw me, he hid the thick manuscript under the straw. It was, he finally confessed, his masterpiece, his life's crowning achievement: "I had to avoid the worst, the loss of my manuscript."

When the first morning frosts began and night started at four in the afternoon, if not sooner, and everything at the bottom of that ravine was so gloomy, he became obsessed yet again with the idea of secretly crossing the Pyrenees; he was convinced he would find in Paris what he had never found in Barcelona – a publisher. To undertake such a journey, he would have needed underwear, socks, a presentable suit, a sturdy overcoat, and money. I could cut his hair and lend him my razor so he could shave, that at least was possible, but what about everything else? How could I buy him a suit, underwear, socks, and an overcoat? He hadn't a sou and neither had I.

As time went on I found him more and more repellent, and yet unfailingly, week in week out, I took him his bread and potatoes; I took him potatoes already roasted in the embers so he wasn't forced to light a fire to cook them. I found him fouler by the day, and yet I went, it was impossible for me to abandon him to his plight and his lunacy, and each time I wondered in astonishment why his face aroused such a desire to . . . you know, erase it, like you erase a bad drawing in order to begin again, until it became the face of Soleràs, because somebody had tricked me and put Lamoneda where Soleràs should have been. Lamoneda was simply a lousy caricature of Soleràs! And what a lousy caricature! Such an ugly face had no right to exist, it was anti-human! If my loathing grew every week, it wasn't so much because of the fat manuscript packed with such recherché rubbish, or even the key to that riddle when I finally guessed what it was; not at all, my loathing would have been as strong anyway because Lamoneda was the anti-Soleràs, was anti-human . . . was Cain! He had no right to be so ugly! Oh, why had such an ugly man become embedded in my life like a tick; why did he have to be transformed into my inseparable ghost? Why, in this world, when we are separated from those we want to be with, must we always tolerate the proximity of those we would prefer to be made remote from by infinite space?

I shouldn't deceive myself. As long as I live, I should be fully conscious that I began to feel that desire, the desire to erase this intolerable caricature, before I'd guessed what the key was to his riddle, before he started reading me chunks from his manuscript. As long as I live, I should be aware that my desire preceded all that, that it was aroused by the way his face disgusted me and I would have felt this way in any case; I need to be conscious of this so I have no illusions about myself.

There is indeed a criminal lurking deep within me.

Especially that night; on the one previous I had dined with Lluís and Trini in their suite in the "palace", and then the following day I had to take him his bread and potatoes. I never failed to go and deceived myself with the old excuse of Christian charity: How can I abandon him to his plight and his lunacy is what I asked myself. But the truth was that I was finding this crass caricature of Soleràs increasingly attractive; the more loathsome he seemed, the more he attracted me; oh, how I was drawn to him, as certain foul women sometimes attract a man who is chaste or ought to be, and, in my hypocrisy, I made the same excuse as the unsullied man who entertains a foul woman – that I was trying to convert him. I shut my eyes when I said I wanted to save him, it was quite the opposite of what I wanted. From the moment the brook froze over, he never emerged from his lair, and the inside of the cabin stank like an old fox's den. I had dined the previous night with Trini and Lluís in their suite at the palace, and now here I was, as the black sky began to turn blue, face to face with the anti-human. It was freezing outside the cabin, we were both in the stench of his old fox den and I could see the rusty iron cross silhouetted against the bright haze outside through the ragged mouth of the doorway. In the dark I heard his monotonous voice reciting from memory long passages from his novel. This was the night after the evening I had dined at the palace, when I had seen Trini in that black lace shawl with the diamond medallion, an intriguing sight with her hair snow-white in the light from the candles and the flames in the hearth. And before that dinner I had been to see my old archbishop, who is is dead now; I had been visiting him more frequently, because, stricken by apoplexy and inconsolable because he had been forced to retire and was no longer our archbishop, the poor fellow craved my company . . . I had been to see him and had wept in his arms. I had cried as I always did when I saw our archbishop who was so fundamentally good yet so dim-witted and incredibly thick, and here I was listening to that tedious drone, a litany of obscure monstrosities, obscure even to me, who had heard plenty of murky filth in the confessional! And it was really dull, boring and mind-rotting to hear all that twaddle about a mature duchess and a simpering marchioness, and that ever so precious aristocracy, when my thoughts were of Trini and the old archbishop; the hero, a young secret agent, of whom Himmler had the greatest expectations and who was indeed scaling the most exalted heights in the Reich's diplomatic circles, was irresistible in the eyes of both the mature duchess and the simpering marchioness; they were all over him, could refuse him nothing. I lost myself in those horrendous labyrinths (yet I'd visited plenty of murk in the confessional!)

and, turned off by his droning voice, my brain flitted to a different story, that he had finally told me one night about his real father. He had finally revealed that Dr Gallifa wasn't his uncle, though in fact he *was*, however much Lamoneda tied himself in knots; he *was* his uncle since his mother was Dr Gallifa's sister, so that unexpected find changed nothing. When I commented in this respect, when I attempted to make him understand that, even so, Dr Gallifa was definitely his uncle, his maternal uncle, he shrugged his shoulders and said: "I couldn't care a hoot about my family."

It was his tenant farmer who had told him the truth that nobody was aware of until then. Nobody except for Dr Gallifa, that is, who had kept it quiet because it involved his sister, and even if that hadn't been the case, guided by Christian charity he would have had powerful reasons to keep the secret. What was surprising wasn't his uncle's silence, but that nobody had suspected anything before the discovery by the tenant farmer, an entirely chance occurrence made only because he was continually instigating building reforms in the Lamonedas' old ancestral home, which he now possessed by dint of a rental agreement in perpetuity – that in effect included the house, according to the tenor of the contract drawn up by his father. The last time Lamoneda had come to collect his ten thousand pessetes annual rent – almost a year ago – he had insulted the fellow, as he always did: "You're nothing but a thief, you've stolen my house and my land." He had insulted him many a time with these or similar words, at least once a year – when he went to collect the rent – since the end of the war; it was nothing new. The tenant farmer simply shrugged his shoulders and grinned like a rabbit. What was different this time was that the tenant farmer retorted in a quiet, mocking tone: "So what if you were a Lamoneda heir just as much as I am?"

"So what if you were a Lamoneda heir just as much as I am?" the tenant farmer had challenged him with a sardonic glint in his eyes, flourishing the bundle of yellowing letters at him without actually handing them over.

You could say that bundle of letters tied with a piece of red thread was a chance discovery, though not so unpredictable if you kept in mind that building work had been going on in the house for the last thirty years, ever since he had taken up residence there towards the end of the war. It would have been odder if he hadn't ended up finding them, for they had only been hidden quite simply in a space between two stone ashlars in one of the attics. He had wanted to convert that attic into a modern dovecote; when the mason was cementing stones that had been badly laid, he noticed the bundle stuck in a crack and took them to the tenant farmer. Moreover, according to Lamoneda, a rumour had spread around the village that he had found a copper chocolate tin full of gold doubloons; it had surfaced, people said, when a stone step was being removed from the little doorway to "heaven" – which was what they called the small space in the loft, next to the attic, where they stored their mature wine, whereas they dubbed the lowest, almost subterranean, part of the house, where they kept the old olive-oil press the tenant had replaced with a hydraulic model, "hell". Lamoneda was sceptical regarding the gold doubloons: "The doubloon chocolate tin," he growled sarcastically, "was that bundle of letters. It's amazing how women can't resist the temptation to keep them; it's stronger than they are."

His mother had died in an accident when she was very young, soon after he was born: she had gone to get some wine one evening, not to "heaven" but to the big cellar downstairs, alias "hell", because when she was setting the table she had realised the demijohn in the kitchen was empty; walking in the dark she had fallen into one of the vats, the trapdoor to which the farmhand had neglected to shut. That happened in November when the vat was full of fermenting must; she died instantly, choked by carbon monoxide. Lamoneda's father had told him the details of her death: "That was all he ever did tell me about her; apart from explaining how she had died, he never mentioned her; it was certainly very odd that she went down in person to fetch some wine when we had servants. It was also very odd that the trapdoor had been left open . . ."

Senyora Lamoneda, who had not reached thirty when she fell into the vat, had hidden the bundle of letters in that crack, thinking it was a temporary hiding place; she must have thought she would find somewhere more secure later; how could she have imagined she would die so unexpectedly? Had she lived, she might have decided to burn them. The fact is they had remained there in that space between two stones in the attic for seventy-plus years, unknown to anyone; seventy-plus was now Lamoneda's age, hadn't more than a quarter of a century passed since our conversation in the café on the Ronda, where he had said he had just made it to fifty "like an idiot"? For seventy-plus years, almost eighty, that bundle of letters had remained embedded, yellowing away, until one fine day – its hour come round at last – the bricklayer saw it and took it to the tenant farmer. "Poor Mama held on to them," muttered Lamoneda, "like Madame Bovary, like Natalya Vasilyevna, like them all! It's stronger than they are, they can't bring themselves to burn them . . ."

*

The tenant farmer began to make a few discreet enquiries once he had been put on the right trail by that unexpected bundle. An old man – almost a hundred years old – lived in a nearby village where his teeth were beginning to grow anew, as sometimes happens when people reach such an advanced age; this venerable old man vaguely remembered something; a wedding had apparently taken place in Barcelona, against the time-immemorial tradition landowning families had of celebrating weddings in the village of the bride's ancestral home; the couple weren't seen in either village, hers or his, for two years after the wedding. They returned with a boy who looked older than two, so much was immediately obvious, and in those days, said the venerable old man whose teeth were growing anew, "we remarked in the villages around here that no doubt 'they had celebrated their Easter before Palm Sunday'. As these things often happen and make no odds, people stopped gossiping about it." "Is that all the gossip there was at the time?" The old man really didn't remember anything else. They didn't know the bride very well in his neck of the woods; she was from a well-known family, but her village was a long way away, and besides she had lived in Barcelona for most of her life: "she was the second-born to a highly respected family from the Plain of Vic," he added, "and brought a good dowry to the Lamonedas; that and little else is what people knew." The tenant wasn't content with that rather vague, inconsequential information; he asked for copies of the marriage and baptism certificates from Barcelona and was able to confirm that the baby's baptism had indeed preceded the parents' marriage. None of that would have been at all scandalous had it not been for the unexpected discovery of that bundle of yellowing letters.

*

He often broke off his account of that story because whole chunks of his novel flooded into his mind; everything I have just recorded came in fits and starts, incoherently, mixed up with peculiar declamations about the doings of the Duchess Atalanta and Count Recesvinto the ambassador; week after week, as the cold bit more sharply in that gloomy ravine, his lunacy deepened. He became like a machine, so mechanically did he stop speaking about one thing to start on another, and the tirades from his saga were such a dreary litany. His style, which he thought surpassed Eugeni d'Ors' – and that did indeed remind you of him – was all metaphors, vacuous ones at that, and he never missed an opportunity: there was no train that didn't snake, no snow-driven city that wasn't like an enormous host, and, in terms of plot, it was all Sodom and Lesbos, de Sade and Masoch (not forgetting old Onan), incest and rape, bestiality and sacrilege, inextricably dosed with morphine and cocaine. You couldn't make head or tail of what Count Recesvinto, Duchess Atalanta, the Marchioness Brunhilda, and other characters of both sexes, or indeterminate sex, were up to. Their entries and exits were as countless and tedious as those inscribed in a telephone directory, but a telephone directory that only accepted the most hifalutin aristocracy and cunning and clever of diplomats. "High society and I are like this," said Count Recesvinto on one occasion, and Duchess Atalanta remarked: "Richelieu was an innocent abroad compared to you, Recesvinto; thanks to you, the sun will never again set on our empire." His droning voice recited whole chapters from memory while I daydreamed of Trini, her shawl in the light from the candles and the fire in the hearth, I saw her snow-white hair, her eyes that were so bright and serene, so full of gentle melancholy and distant dreams. He never stopped his gross litany and I felt an ever-stronger desire to erase his ugly face, a face as ugly as that had no right ever to have existed, Lamoneda was beyond the pale!

One night he didn't recite his novel; he was making plans. He often got such moods and started to speculate about the oddest things: "That scum will need me again someday; they can't dispense with me." On several occasions he had spoken to me, always in the most nebulous terms, of a new "prior catastrophe", and that night he told me more, his seventy-plus monkey face an ugly sight in the dim, freezing light of a December dawn, and that iron cross was still there, its slanted bar tied to the vertical pole by a stretch of half-rotten esparto rope, a black silhouette against the hazy glimmer outside, and thoughts came to me of Soleràs, whose intolerable caricature that monkey was, Soleràs who was made of the driest wood and burnt easily, but his caricature was nothing but putrefaction that fell apart when you touched it and my unease only grew: that obscene caricature of Soleràs must be erased!

I felt the sweat trickling down my spine as he spewed out one project after another; a surprising idea had finally come into my head, I felt it lodged there like a migraine, but then the machine abruptly changed tack and he was reciting his novel once again, in Spanish, as ever, rather than Catalan, the language he used in conversation: "The duchess, a mature woman by this time, whose virtues were given as examples for young women to follow, stopped at nothing in her private life; she had learned to mingle crime and caprice . . ." He recited, and I sweated frustration; he recited nonstop, and I switched off. I didn't realise he had stopped until his changed, imploring voice reached me: "If something remiss happened to me, you would take responsibility, wouldn't you? Do you promise?"

"Responsibility for what?"

"I mean . . ." he looked at me taken aback, "for publishing it!"

One day someone I knew only too well appeared among his characters, although I hadn't realised they were acquainted. "You know, we were in contact before the war," he said, and added immediately when he saw my look of astonishment: "Why are you so surprised? They were very secret contacts; neither he nor we wanted them to be in the open. Did you never suspect anything? Well, that was what it was all about, about nobody suspecting anything. We had agreed that after the prior catastrophe we would incapacitate the cardinal[9] by having him certified as suffering from dementia and that he would be his replacement; he was already taking it for granted, and saw himself in a cardinal's biretta and purple vestments, he'd already sworn he would renounce the primacy *ab aeternum* for him and his successors. Only he had forgotten one small detail: the pope."

"The pope?"

"The pope wouldn't accept any of what we agreed, and refused to contemplate any incapacitating of the cardinal primate! Quite the contrary, he welcomed him in Rome, in exile, with all the honours. The pope died, but his successor was just as worthless; if I had ever suspected that Pius XI was a Mason, I've wondered whether Pius XII, besides being a Mason, wasn't also a Jew."

---

9 Monsenyor Vidal i Barraquer was the only cardinal who did not join in the Spanish Bishops' collective letter of support for Franco in 1936.

"Anything is possible," I muttered, "we know for sure that the first pope was."

"Do you know who coined that sublime saying: 'the youngest of revolutions is the revolution of the young'? Well, it was your relative, Monsenyor Pinell de Bray. Those words alone merited a cardinal's biretta, but, as you know, he never got that far. The pope didn't want to hear a word of what we had planned; even in exile the archbishop cardinal continued in post. At the time of his death, Monsenyor Pinell de Bray's hopes blossomed afresh, but to no avail yet again! For years, the pope refused to fill the vacancy that in the end was taken by someone else. Your relative never got over such a bitter disappointment, it led him to an early grave."

Monsenyor Pinell de Bray had in fact died many years ago – was it 1950, 1952, or 1954? How could I possibly remember or tell one year from the next when they were all the same? I had completely forgotten him and now Lamoneda had reminded me of his existence.

My auntie had died years after her cousin. Her final illness was a dreadfully protracted affair, as the wretched nephew she had made her heir thought he was duty-bound to have recourse to all possible means to prolong her life. A doctor was permanently at her bedside, with an auxiliary and two nurses, always ready to inject her like someone putting a drop of oil in a lamp whenever the flame flickers because it is about to go out. In this way, her frightful agony was artificially prolonged for months. I went to see her several times; she generally gave no signs that she recognised me, but once she did begin to talk about Pope John XXIII and the Second Vatican Council, that was taking place around then, with an intense rancour that stunned me. How could that moribund octogenarian, kept barely alive by injections, be aware of the sessions at the Council and find enough strength in her failed organism to speak of it with such caustic, corrosive energy? "You and evil priests like you are the ones that ruined the Church!" she repeated to me a few days before she died, in another lucid interlude. She said it with such hatred I even thought that she must have lost her faith. God on High, have mercy on her and all us sinners, amen.

So Lamoneda reminded me of that Monsenyor Pinell de Bray I had so soundly forgotten, but how could I recognise Auntie's second cousin, whom I had seen so often in other circumstances, in the inconceivable character he had become in his novel? His amethyst ring was all entangled with the mature duchess' "fly-wing" silk stockings that appeared time and again, obsessively, and with the labyrinthine intrigues of the simpering marchioness and the young count, "who, in effect, became one of the luminaries of the imperial diplomatic corps". He tirelessly recited huge chunks "in rhythmic prose", he said, where all that became entangled like a skein of wool you might have given the cat to play with: "Monsenyor pretends he has forgotten how much he owes me. Atalanta, however, couldn't be more grateful: she knows they owe me everything, unlike the ungrateful Monsenyor who pretends he has never met me. But I am no cleric! I carry the struggle and high diplomacy in my blood, give me tempests and I can breathe comfortably! Me a cleric, God forbid!" As that same city from one of the early chapters resurfaced and was snowbound, this second Eugeni d'Ors had the wit to write: "Years ago I had found it snow-white like an enormous host, now it was more snowed under than ever, like two hosts at least," only immediately to return to the "fly-wing" stockings, that meant heaven knows what – what kind of stockings might be the sort that obsessed him – and it was a painful obsession, his voice choked in his gullet whenever those "fly-wing" stockings cropped up. In the stinking gloom of that den, at the bottom of that narrow ravine where everything had been frozen for days, I felt at times that I was lost in the depths of a chasm where thousands of "fly-wing" stockings were clinging to the stone vaults like bunches of hibernating bats or blackish, transparent cobwebs that disintegrated when touched by a hand.

Sometimes, as if illuminated by a streak of lightning, I thought I glimpsed in that rampant nonsense a kind of wedge, equivocally worded, palpable and despicable lumber amid so much junk covered in dust and cobwebs! He didn't notice – or barely did – but he blended into his tales of duchesses and marchionesses words and whole sentences that were like sudden flashes of lightning in the pitch black of that gorge, illuminating all that astonishing dross: he barely noticed and I barely understood, oh, how I struggled to understand and yet that huge piece of lumber was mixed up with his rambling tales – blood-curdling details of what had happened one night inside the Carmelite monastery. But why did it take me so long to grasp that? It was as if I had been brutalised by so much horror, because horror brutalises and atrophies and I was brutalised and atrophied.

Sometimes in the stifling silence a sound rose like an almost imperceptible wind that hardly sways the blades of grass; sometimes incredible news came as a distant smell might be wafted by an almost imperceptible breeze. Silence created such incredible sounds, the pitch black of the tunnel created such ghosts. One evening I was wandering, as I still used to, along the broad, gloomy, unconstructed road which runs around that shanty town; we so come to love the places where we once suffered, how sad and wan was twilight on that long, slippery, slimy road. I wandered at random as I still did then, in the '50s, whenever I went down to the city; once, in the '50s, seven or eight little children ran up and kissed my hand, so happy to see me again after five, six, or I don't know how many years, because they were now eleven or twelve and had earlier, when six or seven, attended the classes I'd organised among the hovels when I was the local priest. They recognised me but I struggled to recognise them, children change so much between six and seven and eleven and twelve, and they were the ones who told me that incredible story.

How could people exist capable of doing such a thing? Could somebody have stolen a child's eyes without a single voice clamouring to the heavens? Isn't it also truly horrific that all these people believe it happened? Because all in that little shanty town – young and old – believed a story which seemed so far-fetched.

He had disappeared from his hovel: a little boy, the third in one of the most poverty-stricken families in the town. A family with twelve, thirteen, or fourteen children that lived in the bottom corner, in what was now the dry bed of the river, dry most of the year but which suddenly grew and flooded the shanties almost every September; the people there were so used to it they took no notice. The neighbours realised he wasn't around, because he was a very chirpy, noisy eight-year-old whose presence people were always aware of. When the neighbours asked, his parents replied that they had already informed the mayor, not the mayor of Barcelona but the "district" mayor who owned the bar on the corner of the street. They also said he must have run away because he was frightened, as he had already done once before when he had broken a clay cooking pot he was playing with; he would come back under his own steam, as he did before, driven by hunger or thirst.

He was seen again at dawn on a rainy day, standing by the roadside – that same long, muddy road where I sometimes wandered. He stood still under the rain, unable to take a step forward; he was eyeless. He was holding an envelope and remembered nothing, as if he had just woken up from a nightmare. The day he disappeared, he had been amusing himself by shooting at sparrows with a bow he had made, under the plane trees along the road. A big car had stopped, some strangers had enquired about a road in the locality and invited him to get in to show them the way, and that was all he remembered.

The envelope contained eighty one-thousand-pesseta notes.

At least that is what those children told me, all excited, hectically interjecting to add their own piece. As I couldn't believe it, I immediately asked to talk to the family: they were no longer around, I was told; they had left without saying where, and that was the last anybody had heard. The father was half-gypsy and a drunkard; the family's only source of income were the irregular amounts the mother brought in doing the donkey work in other people's houses. When I went to the eye bank to offer mine after my death, I told this strange story to the doctor who was seeing to me. The man gave me a pitying look, as did everyone else I told it to at the time; they made no attempt to spare me their pitying looks, accompanied by a shake of the head, but I wasn't the one who had invented the story. Isn't the fact that people believed it as horrendous as the story itself? They all believed it: that's what I bear witness to, not the story. In what chilling, horrific world did the wretched people in the shanty town believe they were living, under which invisible Moloch did they think they reproduced and pullulated, lived and died? Isn't that the scariest thing of all, much more than the story in itself? The ability of those poor people to invent and believe the most hair-raising stories?

Yes, the silence spawned the craziest rumours as easily as the pitch black spawned ghosts. After that story came the one about the priest whose tongue was severed; how was one ever to find out, in the silence oppressing us, whether it was another myth or true? So many shocking scandals, unfortunately only too real, were hidden that years later one even wonders whether it wasn't all just one big nightmare. Was that priest beckoning to me with his gaping mouth just a dream? Those who survive us will perhaps see him one day by an altar, and once the bushel is lifted the candle will burn bright, but right now I don't know if I dreamt him or saw him. He had devoted himself to another shanty town, perhaps the most dreadful of all, one in the cemetery of Montjuïc where dens of destitution rise up on the very edges of the huge common grave. And they talk to us about the Church of Silence! Hasn't every one of us seen the Church of the Severed Tongue?

To tell the truth, I had by that time retreated into my solitude and sadness, in the sorrowful acceptance of my complete futility . . . One day, a dozen seminarians paid me a surprise visit in my village.

Some still looked almost like children. They came to see "the sadly famous Cruells", the mangy sheep, because they wanted some of my mange; they told me, all excited, that behind them, behind the dozen that had come to see me, were many others, perhaps a hundred, but this was all nothing new to me, my Lord, and while they chattered I started to whimper as I told them: "My sons, don't forget those other horrors, from 1936; you didn't live them, I did."

And they were taken aback when I spoke to them so affectionately about our bishop, that poor fellow who was so dim, so rustic, yet so good; when he was no longer our archbishop, when he lingered on, laid low by old age and apoplexy, above all, by his compulsory early retirement, I often caught myself longing for him. But I could see only too clearly from their faces that I was a disappointment: those poor fifteen- or sixteen-year-olds had climbed the mountain thinking they would find a lion in its den but had only found an old crybaby. Really, what else was I in their eyes?

We have had to behold so much horror in this hapless world! And the Lord's silence often seems to connive, but didn't He warn us of that? He told us He would not return until the Last Day. The mystery of iniquity began with Annas and Caiaphas; remember that, my sons, Caiaphas was "the highest pontifex that year". That was when the mystery of iniquity began and it will last until Judgment Day; the Lord says nothing while the Anti-Christ speaks, because, in truth, the end of the world began when the Lord predicted it would, with the destruction of the Temple – and while I spoke and whimpered, the dozen seminarians looked at each other and shook their heads, but I persisted: "From that time onwards we have been witnessing the very slow end of the world; from that time onwards the Anti-Christ has been in this world, always being reincarnated, sometimes prowling close to the chair of your priest, and always uttering 'outrageous words and blasphemies'. We find all these dark mysteries bewildering and perturbing, my children, and rightly we find them troubling and you now think I am deranged because of what I am saying, but, otherwise, how can one reach an understanding of the mystery of iniquity! It is difficult! Yes, You, Lord, if only You knew how difficult it is to understand! If only You knew, O Lord! Because the Anti-Christ pursues You like Your shadow, and while You are silent he speaks, and You allow him to speak and rule, my Lord and God! We have seen so many atrocities in this wretched world in the course of this criminal century of all centuries, yet You were silent! Who would have thought it, this century of ours will soon be seventy, this century that I first knew, my sons, when it was the youngest of centuries, when it was brand new and wanted to change everything, a century that wanted to erase all the injustice and dross from preceding centuries. And what a sound this century of ours would make, the one we had loved as our own; raging sound and fury, so many great revolutions, so many great wars that everyone fought on behalf of the justice and happiness of future humanity! And now look at our seventy-year-old century, our paranoid century that will soon be only a century in its death throes and then a defunct century and on top of its carcass other, innumerable centuries will come to rest like the slime that comes to rest on the bed of the ocean, millennium after millennium, and who will ever remember our century? How often, hereafter, will another century likewise toll its bells so loudly against all previous centuries, announcing that *le jour de gloire* has finally come, yes, it is always but always *le jour de gloire*, yet what always comes, my sons, is repulsive butchery, Robespierre and Napoleon, Hitler and Stalin, guillotine or gas chamber, concentration camps, an ocean of blood and shit . . ."

Their glances betrayed their disappointment; they said nothing, hunched over, exchanging furtive looks, and I understood those were not the words they had come to hear from my lips, but in my boundless despondency I could utter no others: "My sons, don't let yourselves be moved, if you don't know whose hands are moving you; I could tell you so many mysterious things that we are only now beginning to discover, so many things that seemed one way and were another, so many double games, so much incredible duplicity, so much unbelievable conspiring . . . Don't agitate, my sons, if you can't clearly see who is behind the agitation; don't allow yourselves, in your naivety, to be the tools of dark forces that will make fools of you!" – now the poor little things *were* listening to me – "Keep far away both from black deceit and red deceit; Deceit rules this world and sullies us from under the most unlikely colours! Truth is love and that is how you will always recognise it; spurn anything to do with hatred, the father of deceit. Love your country and love freedom, love them with all your heart and soul, but anyone who says you must have recourse to hatred to serve them deceives you. Love is the illumination that comes from on high. This world would be but a nightmare without that unique illumination that comes from the top of the mountain, 'where the highest cross was erected'. Whatever happens, don't fail to look to the top of the mountain where that cross stands. Or will we also deny Him because Simon did? Because Judas betrayed Him, will we? My children, think of Demas, think of Mary Magdalene, when you see the Apostles betray, deny or forsake Him; if you think of Demas and Mary Magdalene you won't betray, deny or forsake Him!"

The first of those demonstrations that were to be wrongly interpreted by so many took place a few months later: May 11, 1966: here finally is a date I remember quite clearly, the only one I remember from thirty interminable, grey years, such an endless tunnel! That day I glimpsed the first glimmerings, albeit still hazy and distant, that augured an eventual exit.

I found out almost by chance. It was organised by, among others, the dozen who had visited me in the village and they were the ones who spread the word that I had become a reactionary and visionary who couldn't be relied upon; I know that's what they were saying about me, but I don't bear a grudge. After all, it was probably the truth, and nothing but the truth; as well as reactionary and visionary they could have said I was a total neurotic and they wouldn't have been lying, my poor sons. At no point did they let me know what they were preparing, but news of it reached me via other channels. And I turned up out of the blue.

It was just before midday on that Wednesday, May 11, 1966, in the cathedral cloisters. A glorious day in May I shall remember for ever! What you had to do to revive hopes that were moribund by that time! From that day on I began to rediscover in the night sky the great companionship and repose I found in other times – the one that is always there! – and never again did I feel the anguish brought on by the incomprehensible monotony of all those galaxies. What can the wretched of this earth hope to know of Your works? We can only know that they are spread through infinite spaces over countless centuries and are beyond our understanding in their greatness, which is only a shadow of Yours. What companionship Your works now bring me again at night, my Lord, what companionship, ever since hope has been rekindled in my heart!

It was a magnificent day in May and when I arrived a hundred or so priests, mainly young ones, had assembled; they included the twelve who had regarded me with astonishment and suspicion, and you could see they had told the others about me because they all reacted similarly. No matter, I walked into their midst, and then we went to pray in Sant Crist de Lepant. In that huge shadowy chapel where hundreds of candles and tapers burned as usual, brought there every day by so many anonymous hands, we stayed on our knees until the chimes of the Palace of the Generalitat rang for one o'clock; then we returned to the cloisters, where a ray of sun was breaking through the shiny leaves of one of the hundred-year-old magnolia trees, reaching us like a benediction, and there and then, one of the youngest priests addressed us and did so with great humility and gentleness: "We are priests," he said, "our mission is to preach, to pray, to offer, to hallow and to deny ourselves on behalf of others. Everyone is our brother; we must never hate anyone, however much the mere sight of our soutane arouses sarcasm. Truly it would be too easy to be a priest if we were only to inspire love and respect in everyone . . ." This young man, whom I did not know, though now I felt that I had known him for ever, as if he were my son, was speaking so mellifluously, as we all listened in silence, that I had to make an effort not to whimper; I didn't want them to see I was a hopeless neurotic, or for sadness to rack my soul; I didn't want to appear an old coward in the eyes of those young men! "Should we be surprised," continued the young man, "if the paths we have chosen bristle with thorns? It would be surprising if it were not the case. We have gathered here today because we must go and tell our brothers in the police that they commit grave sins when they torture our student and worker brothers." After uttering those words, he paused for a moment before adding: "Perhaps what we are about to do will be misunderstood by many; I am sure that our brothers in the police will not understand and be angry; however, if we didn't do this, our student and working-class brothers will think we didn't love them either. The day will come when we shall make everyone understand. We belong to the Church and must act in line with what it has taught us and what we pass on to others on its behalf, and it has taught us and we have repeated to others that man was created in the image and likeness of God, and hence deserves respect. It is the gravest sin to insult a brother, to spit in his face, and manacle and beat him or worse in order to extract statements; our brothers in the police sin woefully if it is true that they do this to our student and working-class brothers and we must go and tell them so. We may now feel fear, and that is nothing to be ashamed about, Jesus was afraid in the Garden of Gethsemane. Like Him, we will do our duty, despite our fear; let us pray for all our brothers, be they police, students, or workers, and may our meekness show them a beacon of light and peace in the love of Christ and the Church. May God help us. Amen."

After he had spoken these words, we silently left the cloister and walked towards the nearby bishop's palace; the archbishop wasn't there; we left a collective letter for the Vicar-General. Many of the priests who were in the palace courtyard joined our group and some friars and monks did so as well. We were over two hundred when we left that courtyard and headed silently towards Via Laietana. People were leaving their offices and many were walking along on the pavement: everybody stopped to watch, because all those soutanes marching in double file along Via Laietana made a strange sight and we walked two by two until we were in front of *that* building.

Two uniformed police jumped out of their jeep and obstructed our path; one of them bawled at us, demanding to know what we were doing. Meanwhile bystanders were gathering on the pavement opposite. The young man who had spoken in the cloister replied that we only wanted to hand over a letter, but to the Prefect in person, and that when he had received us and accepted the letter from our hands, we would each return in orderly fashion to our homes. He was still speaking when men with truncheons emerged from inside – some uniformed, some not – and they hit us in the face with these or their fists, and some people were knocked unconscious to the ground, where they continued being kicked. We had pledged in the cloisters that we would not run away, whatever happened, and we kept our word; we let them hit us, we didn't budge or offer any resistance. Meanwhile, Via Laietana was now packed with people. Everybody stopped to look and the crowds halted the traffic; people also thronged balconies and windows. We folded our arms, let them hit us, didn't insult them, behaved as we had pledged to, but the crowds looking on shouted angrily at the men who were beating us.

Suddenly I fell to the ground like so many others and managed to get back on my feet in time to dodge a kick to the stomach; I couldn't stop myself gesturing impatiently: I knocked someone's cap off. I was ashamed of myself and shouted to the others: "Let's leave now, my sons, or we'll lose our tempers!" None of the others had in fact reacted in anger; I saw one priest, and not one of the youngest, who, when the policeman beating him dropped his truncheon, simply picked it up and gave it back to him. One of ours shouted: "Let's go to the Jesuits!" because we had agreed that if they dispersed us we would regroup in the Jesuit convent on carrer Casp. As they were hard on our heels, still hitting out, the group split into two: some ran along carrer Jonqueres, others up Laietana, and what a sight that was – billowing soutanes in flight, battered by truncheons – the cries of indignation from the crowd watching turned into a gigantic howl of fury. We ran into a large number of police waiting for us at the entrance to the Jesuits where we were hoping to find refuge: one of them hit me so hard on the skull with his truncheon that I tottered into the church blinded by the blood pouring down.

This was the first of the demonstrations that shocked so many Pharisees. Luckily, Auntie Llúcia was dead by then (may God have forgiven her); because, if not, they would have caused her to lose the little faith that remained in her after the Vatican Council. As for my archbishop, he came to visit me days afterwards in the hospital and really treated me like a father; the poor fellow was older and weaker than ever and his love for me had only increased over the years. However, as I answered his questions, trying to make him understand things that were quite beyond him, he exclaimed in Spanish: "My son, what you have been told beggars belief; I have made my enquiries and know he is a man who takes communion daily."

And yet You had sent us that clear-sighted saint, that brilliant saint our century needed so badly. You had sent him to us and raised him to the highest throne in Your Church. We saw him with our eyes and heard him with our ears, that good Pope John, and the ice quickly melted, but You soon deprived us of that sun that caused it to melt. Didn't Your Church deserve him? Must we always, but always, relapse into the errors of old? Must the mystery of iniquity last until the Day of Judgment, must the shadow of the Anti-Christ hang over us until Your Second Coming?

My archbishop had forbidden me to talk of these dark things that were increasingly preoccupying me, of this riddle of the end of the world that never came, which had started as You had predicted, soon after Your death; I must say in all honesty that he didn't forbid me *motu proprio*, but after consulting some of the best theologians who advised him in these matters. I will even say that initially, before he consulted the theologians, when I first began to bring up these issues of the end of the world and the Anti-Christ, I could see he was hesitating and wavering, that I was within a whisker of winning him over to my point of view. I would say that, in those latter times, the poor fellow was so tired of this world that the greatest happiness I could have given him would be to have told him that his own end was near. The theologians alarmed him when they said, although all that was quite orthodox in the last analysis, "it quite stank of heresy"; terrified by the word "heresy", he ordered, or rather begged me not to mention all that to anyone else, and make a real effort not to think about it. I obeyed while he was my archbishop; then he ceased to be that and now he has been dead for a number of years – are the precepts issued by a dead man still valid? Besides, I now speak to no-one apart from myself and, before he forbade me, when I did discuss it with some of my colleagues, they invariably shook their heads pityingly as they glanced at each other: I could see quite clearly in their eyes what they thought of me. Well, if I am a neurotic, why shouldn't I be? Is one forbidden to be neurotic? And could I be anything else after everything I had been forced to live through? Lamoneda's secret, the blind killing all mixed up in my brain with a shifting forest of legs clad in fly-wing silk stockings, and the unconscionable rubbish he was coming out with – all as if oblivious of my presence. Who knows what that young man with the pointed moustache, 1890s style, was really like, that young man who wrote those passionate letters a bricklayer found eighty years later rolled into a bundle tied with red thread in that hole in the wall? Yes, those yellowing letters, dated 1890 and 1891, left no doubt as to the origins of the baby that was Lamoneda *in illo tempore*. He was born on 17 December, 1891, shortly after his mother married; those letters spoke in Spanish of the infinite regret of the elegantly moustachioed Don Juan (from a photo that appeared with the letters): "If I didn't mention it to you before now," declared Don Juan, "if I hid from you the fact that I was married years ago in the city of my birth in Extremadura, it wasn't with the intention of deceiving you, I swear to God, but because of extremely serious circumstances that compelled me to be silent, circumstances which I cannot reveal to you; one day you will find out everything and will forgive me . . ." The tenant farmer carried out the most exhaustive investigations in order to trace the protagonist of those distant loves; some of the letters that had faded so badly bore the letterhead of police headquarters (which was really strange given that they were love letters) and the young enamoured man signed off as Gumersindo: the only police officer with that name, as the tenant farmer discovered, had died long ago, much to his chagrin; it was all ancient history, though what sadness these tales were to cause years later! Not that he had been under any illusion of such a character still being alive after almost eighty years, but he had hoped he might find the odd trace, some tangible evidence of his existence from a more recent period. The tenant farmer's enquiries proved fruitless: apparently this Gumersindo was just one more policeman, and all it was possible to find out was that he had died in 1925.

Evidently, there was still a bit of a mystery to clear up: why had the Lamoneda heir married her? Did he think the baby was his? That was the only possible explanation, however much one was perplexed by the frivolous behaviour of the young lady (the sister of Dr Gallifa, no less). Another, equally hypothetical explanation would be too sordid, but, naturally, was the one the tenant farmer went for: around 1891 the Lamoneda heir very probably found himself in dire straits as the result of massive loans generated by his vast estate (possibly a consequence of the phylloxera that destroyed Catalan vineyards in 1890), and the dowry brought by Miss Gallifa was cash and a huge amount for the time . . .

"The tenant farmer," Lamoneda told me, "didn't in fact know that a policeman by the name of Gumersindo, and from Extremadura to boot, had acted in cahoots with members of Baron de Koenig's gang between 1914 and 1918. I have researched in depth the secret archives at police headquarters everything related to Baron de Koenig, the brilliant precursor of . . ."

So once again he was telling me about Baron de Koenig, the man he most admired in an era before Himmler put in an appearance; that seemingly fake baron, a dubious character who belonged simultaneously to the secret police and clandestine groups of terrorists. He incited these groups to attack Catalan manufacturers in the name of the class struggle, though strangely only those working for the Allies fell to anarchist bullets, never those who worked for the German Reich. I recalled with what fervent admiration he had spoken to me about Baron de Koenig in those distant days, before the war; before that war, our war, that was now beginning to seem as remote as the one fought in the time of Baron de Koenig.

Be that as it may, Dr Gallifa must have known that his sister had given birth before she got married, and as she was betrothed to the other man (because he had taken the iniquitous comedy as far as betrothal – as one could clearly deduce from the letters – a betrothal that wasn't broken off until her pregnancy could no longer be concealed) he must inevitably have had his own ideas about who the child's father was. He never said a word: she was his sister and, even had she not been, charity would have sealed his lips eternally. Lamoneda would never have suspected a thing if that bundle of letters had not been found, in light of which there could be no doubt. I believe this unexpected discovery contributed to his being locked in that final dementia.

He recited those dreary tirades where everything was a hodgepodge, Duchess Atalanta and Monsenyor Pinell de Bray, Marchioness Brunhilda and Ambassador Recesvinto, Malvina Canals i González and the devious handyman who altruistically shared her with his band of mates, because that Malvina, whom he hadn't mentioned, now surfaced again in his soliloquies and the interminable tirades in that lunatic novel which he rehearsed from memory, mixing it all up with his monologues, and she was now transformed into a secret agent sent by Soviet counter-espionage to queer the pitch of the great Recesvinto. He managed to dodge all the traps the enigmatic redhead set for him and would find out once and for all that her name wasn't Malvina or Canals or González but Olga Dmitrievna Putarov, and my thoughts drifted back to that bundle of mummified, dead letters and what the childhood of that 77-year-old (he was born in December 1891) who was now declaiming from memory those crazy chapters, which were totally bewildering, must have been like; what a dreadful childhood his must have been, without a mother and with a father who may have had – well-founded! – doubts about his paternity . . . Then there was the other son, the one born out of wedlock, whom the father had favoured in his last will and testament with a legacy of half the income from the land (how could he foresee that over thirty years later five hundred pessetes a month would be a pittance?), and declaring him, and not his legitimate son, principal heir in the eventuality that the elder son died without offspring. It was very likely that he loved his other son – the illegitimate one – and how could the legitimate son not suspect this to be so, given the circumstances of his own birth? What a dreadful childhood that hapless fellow's must have been . . .

"You know, Cruells, at the end of the day you are nothing but a clergyman, right?" he suddenly asked me. "That's basically what Soleràs was – and that alone."

"Soleràs?" I exclaimed. "Soleràs was a clergyman?"

"Well, to be sure, he was basically a clergyman. You're so fascinated by Soleràs yet he was basically a clergyman. He didn't give a damn about our principles and, most of all, didn't give a damn about me! He came out with stuff that just knocked you out. For example, I've just thought of a night when we had both drunk far too much, something that often happened during the battle of the Ebro, and he was being really rude about little Miranda, as usual. Then he suddenly changed the topic and started to attack my genealogy: 'What do you know about it with any certainty?' he asked. 'Well, you know,' I retorted, 'the genealogy of the Lamonedas is well documented from the fifteenth century.' 'I'm not asking about the Lamonedas, but about yours.' At the time nobody suspected the existence of a bundle of letters tied by a piece of red thread in the nook of an attic; that was unthinkable. As far as I was concerned, it was like a flash of lightning had struck me; you can imagine how the tenant farmer keeps them, how he relishes them in his moments of leisure . . . he told me he wouldn't sell them to me for less than a million! At that time such a thing was so unthinkable I couldn't grasp where Soleràs' hints were pointing: 'You see,' he went on, 'my behaviour can be easily explained by my genealogy, since everyone in my house was crazy from the very first Soleràs anyone can remember. My grandfather belonged to the Great Orient and do you know why? Well, simply to enrage my grand-mother, who was a lady of the Holy Sepulchre. Let's leave it to posterity to decide who was the maddest of the lot. So my behav-iour is easily explained by heredity, but what about yours? The Lamonedas, like the Gallifas, were, if I have understood right, two landowning families, upstanding patriarchs, sensible people nothing could undermine. They might have been Carlists and they surely were, but that's not what I am questioning, I want to know who you are and that's impossible!' You, Cruells, are fascinated by Soleràs but I tell you he was a highly dangerous character, one of those spirits of contradiction who destroyed everything, red among blacks and black among reds, a maverick! 'There are genealogies that are a real fucking mess,' he concluded that night, 'and if we could sort them out they would provide the key to the mystery of certain kinds of behaviour . . .' Yes, he did say 'genealogies that are a real fucking mess', because he was always looking for the most hurtful things to say to me, and I had to grin and bear it."

"So what about Malvina?" I asked, interrupting him. "Did she ever leave you in peace?"

"No, she hounded me! She wouldn't let me breathe! She had now suggested she would renounce her rights in exchange for compensation; she asked for half a million pessetes. Where was I ever going to find such an amount? That was what I tried to get; if they'd given me that, I would have kept a low profile for a good while. They misunderstood me; they thought I was threatening to blow their cover, when all I wanted was half a million to get Malvina Canals i González off my back so I wouldn't have to worry about her ever again. Perhaps I got carried away; I led them to think that if they didn't loosen the purse strings, I'd take it to the brink, I'd tell all! They decided it would make more sense to wipe me out of the picture for good . . . and all a consequence of that Malvina, do you see, of that whore with the red hair!"

Up to that point, however strange it may seem, I had simply lost my way in the story he was telling, as if it were a fog where lots of ghosts floated, and how can I find the words to describe now the fascination I felt that other night, one of the last, how can I ever? He had gone on and on as he always did and I whimpered so softly he couldn't hear me. And I was whimpering because I finally knew who the man I lay next to in that darkness was, and why that hyena felt more hounded than ever, after thirty years of stinging humiliations and frustrated desires; the shivering hyena was there, curled up under that putrid straw, in that fetid darkness, and his ravings were full of obscene ghosts, his only company. Because he clung more and more to his novel in that loneliness of his – it was all he had left in the world! He confused and entangled it with everything he was saying or explaining, whether true or false; his voice sometimes turned shrill and then choked as if an invisible hand were strangling him, and then it would resume its usual monotonous flow. Oh, Monsenyor Pinell de Bray, bishop *in partibus infidelium*, Auntie Llúcia's illustrious oracle, you who thought you were so subtle and clever, could you suspect everything that is hidden under "the prior disasters necessary before God's kingdom can be re-established"? I would like to think you were a puppet operated from afar by cold, invisible hands; a puppet of another kind perhaps, but in the end a puppet like Lamoneda. And Lamoneda kept on with his rants and that item of lumber with its ambiguous contours became increasing tangible amid so much incoherence; it grew and grew, a huge, shocking object, a terrifying presence in that cavern peopled by ghosts and cobwebs. Now a cavalry colonel finally made his appearance in that turbid torrent of words; for the moment I could hardly distinguish him from my relation, Monsenyor Pinell de Bray, and Ambassador Recesvinto. That never-ending novel was really idiotic and yet I listened, gaping, because a mystery was being revealed; and no, it wasn't the mystery of Llibert Milmany, who was no longer one, as far as I was concerned: Llibert Milmany had also finally appeared in the novel, cropping up more and more often in that frightful potage of plots and personages: "Liberto Milmany, he was another! He was indispensable; he knew the underworld, he knew the language to use to get them on board, he had the 'Open, Sesame' we lacked; without him we would have failed, we had to tolerate him and pay him his weight in gold! He stipulated only one condition: that someone should open fire from a monastery. That was an onerous condition in those days, when the dastardly influence of the Cardinal Primate was so strong!" And once again my relation turned up with his complex machinations to deprive the Primate of his purple so he could wear it; Auntie Llúcia's deceased cousin was now completely integrated into the novel's intrigue as a friend and close advisor to Duchess Atalanta, "Oh such an understanding friend, such an indulgent advisor"; he recited his text in such a deadpan, flat manner, as a machine might have, though it was a fractured machine that now occasionally began to replay and stutter out the same sentences two or three times before continuing: "The Cardinal Primate was mentally defective, unable to grasp the grandeur of the imperial concept driving us onwards and upwards; it was left to me, Count Recesvinto, to find the simple, brilliant device, I was the only one with that ability! The colonel was a man with no imagination, imbued with old, reactionary prejudices . . ." The machine repeated three or four times: "old and reactionary and stupid prejudices", and then continued: "he never understood anything. All the better for it, if he had understood, he would have refused." "He would have refused, would have refused, would have refused", the machine repeated. And then, "Our forces had been defeated but we could still trigger the prior catastrophe we so longed for, if only a mere spark would fall on that powder keg, that anarchist underworld . . ."

The machine stuttered to a halt, as if exhausted by reciting so many passages from the novel by heart; a long silence descended over that darkness, I was by the door and he was crouching at the other end of the cabin, at the back, half tucked under the straw. He then told me in a changed, hoarse, and plaintive voice: "It was after I recited this chapter that Soleràs exclaimed: 'I would give all Stendhal and all Eugeni d'Ors for just one page of you!' And he even added: 'What a pity I'm not a publisher! I would publish it so lovingly! We would amaze a good few, and more!' Yes, he did use those words, that we would amaze lots of people if we published only that chapter . . . He was a fool but you can't deny that he had a nose for fine literature; the fool could have been such a great critic! And that was in those days when the chapter ended there; it was unfinished. It still is; oh, finishing it would be such a labour, just imagine, I want to surpass the renowned passage on the Battle of Waterloo in *The Red and the Black*! Which could also be the title of my novel; it's odd, but no more true for all that, mine could be called that, and much more appropriately than Stendhal's! Every week I churn over this great chapter, the climactic chapter, when Recesvinto and his men, who are but a handful of despairing idealists, are defeated and cornered by nineteenth-century demo-liberal, Judaeo-masonic forces. All the forces of public order and most regiments, with the Captain-General leading the way, were arrayed against them, a handful of despairing, misunderstood men, and therein lay their greatness! That was when Recesvinto drew on all his enormous talent, in circumstances when anyone else would have collapsed and begun to speak of surrender, he and no-one else goaded the bull with a brand of fire! The colonel hadn't a clue; he was a good man who thought that everyone everywhere should be like people in his village, where a regiment had only to set forth behind a brass band for the populace to come and cheer. Early that Sunday morning, when he rode before his regiment as far as the Cinc d'Oros, he stopped and surveyed all the windows and balconies that were shuttered and barricaded despite the oppressive July heat; that unanimous, hostile silence unnerved him.[10] Recesvinto, on the contrary, had anticipated the hostility of his compatriots, he knew them only too well! He knew they wouldn't exactly appreciate the heroism of a minority imposing itself on the general will by brute force! He was aware of that, he knew them only too well! But he also knew that when a bull is

10 Cinc d'Oros: A monument in Barcelona at the crossroads of the Diagonal and Passeig de Gràcia.

too tame it can be enraged by a brand of fire stuck in its flank, and this was the simple but brilliant idea of Count Recesvinto, future glory of the Empire's diplomatic corps! The chapter, the climactic chapter of my novel, will take place in Parzelonenburg, the imaginary capital of sub-Carpathian Pomerania."

"Sub-Carpathian," I repeated, intrigued.

"Yes, sub-Carpathian," he replied, "sub-Carpathian Pomerania."

"Sub-Carpathian," I repeated quietly as I whimpered, repeating myself: sub-Carpathian, I whimpered and he didn't notice. It was as if a November nimbus cloud were floating through my head while he went on outlining the plot he was working on for the final, climactic chapter that would take place in sub-Carpathian Pomerania, precisely in Parzelonenburg, its capital, and the shadows in that hut stank more than ever as I whimpered so softly, crouching next to the doorway as if my head contained one of those huge November clouds that bring rain and more rain and never stop. And then he said: "This chapter must be a *grand tableau d'histoire*, it's such a pity that I won't be able to read it to Soleràs, he would have held it in such high esteem! Such a fool, but such a great critic! He had always advised me against marriage, like Stendhal; if I married, he prophesied I would be cuckolded to a degree that hadn't been witnessed for centuries. 'Geniuses like you and me,' he went on, 'weren't made for marriage.' Sometimes he also said: 'Any idea why you are such a genius, Lamoneda?' or else, 'Lamoneda, don't be such a genius.' Soleràs came out with amazing quips! Such a pity I won't be able to get him to read this chapter! I haven't written it yet but I've planned it all in my head. I will describe the colonel, with Count Recesvinto always at his side dragging two hundred and fifty soldiers through a barricaded and shuttered city that was unanimously hostile and lacking in understanding: canteens rattled in time against sheathed bayonets; the colonel coughed. He was rather nervous and that made him cough; he didn't understand any of what was going on because he found sub-Carpathian Pomerania totally alien and on the other hand he wasn't at all familiar with big cities like Parzelonenburg. That silence, those closed shutters, the scowling reception given by the big city rather than the delirious ovations he expected, which is what he would have received in his village, in the back of beyond in the depths of the steppes of Balkan Transylvania . . . and all of a sudden, they were being shot at from balconies, from terrace roofs, from behind trees. It was the guards of the autonomous government of sub-Carpathian Pomerania whose dark-blue uniforms they recognised; they were firing at them. Some emerged from behind trees, and advanced before lying down and firing again. We began to hear machine guns we couldn't see; our soldiers began to flee or fall. The mules pulling our machine guns were terrified by the rounds of fire; one ran off, crazed, others collapsed on their backs, legs kicking in the air, their entrails spilling out. We had to retreat from tree to tree and street corner to street corner; the soldiers had left their horses behind and they had walked from their barracks; they had only brought the mules for the machine guns. Count Recesvinto acknowledged that the colonel had at least got that right; not one horse would have survived that barrage of fire. They abandoned machine guns and dead mules and retreated to the monastery on the corner. The colonel was dismayed; he now saw what Recesvinto had concealed from him so cunningly until then: the other guards were also against them. He had seen their leather helmets glinting at the end of Grazenstrasse; they were in their customary, impeccably disciplined formations, and obedient as ever to the constituted government. He was dismayed and could only talk about meeting death in the fight to save his honour; yes, he came out with that kind of nonsense. It was then that Count Recesvinto whispered *the idea* in his ear."

Now the machine began spinning in the void as if unable to find the continuation to the chapter; Lamoneda stopped and repeated what he had already said, as though the novel had disappeared from his head; he spoke of the colonel, and his memories of that long night of stifling heat, blood, and flames.

"He only did what I told him to, and he didn't understand what he was doing. He'd been told that I was a totally trustworthy contact and he trusted me. I was wearing a mechanic's overall and a black and red kerchief; the colonel didn't know they were also the anarchist colours, he was so ignorant! Yes, the poor fellow was so ignorant – an innocent lily. I was the one who took all the decisions when everything seemed lost, yes, it was I, Count Recesvinto! That was my idea and mine alone! Only Atalanta remembers; she alone is grateful: 'You are the victor!' she stammers, melting away in admiration and gratitude, because the colonel could never have conceived such a fantastic idea. He was a hapless fellow, a soldier with no imagination; at that moment of supreme anguish the fool could only think of his honour. He talked of killing himself and was ashamed of dragging those two hundred and fifty wretched devils into such a deranged adventure. They were conscripts, almost all from the provinces of Jaén or Almería, and had followed him as Andalusians always follow those who are giving the orders, blindly, never asking where they were being led. 'Poor wretches,' the colonel muttered, 'I dragged them into a slaughterhouse. I could never have imagined what happened.' He seemed so deeply ashamed I was afraid he might blow his brains out before I had time to make the decisive move. We went in. The friars had to open the door; if not, we would have battered it down with the butts of our rifles, and wouldn't we just! Hadn't we decided to go for it once and for all, Monsignor? 'The youngest of all revolutions is the revolution of the young!' However, that worldly prelate smiled as he listened to the duchess' most intimate confidences and he knew how to play two cards at a time when she told him I was the one who battered down the monastery door: 'The youth is wonderful!' he exclaimed, 'What revolution could ever be more glorious than the revolution of the young!'[11] And you know, Monsignor, the youth has its own needs and one day we might tire of rescuing your chestnuts from the fire so that worldly prelates can look at the bulls from the front row, and not get burnt; he was playing two cards! He acted as if he was with us ('in spirit, of course', he made clear) but he was really only interested in the cardinal's biretta and purple: he was made to wait for them for years and in the end he never got there, but meanwhile he reneged on us and acted as if he didn't know me. What had become of all those flattering words he used to encourage us youngsters once? Once 'the prior catastrophe' was past, he acted as if he didn't know us! All those friars were scared stiff by the sight of the machine guns; we had brought a few with us which we had uncoupled from the halters of the mules that had been shot to pieces. But

11 From here on fragments of hard reality fuse with Lamoneda's novel, and the characters now speak in their corresponding mother tongues of Catalan or Spanish. Monsignor and the representative of the Generalitat use Catalan, while the military and anarchists speak in Spanish.

what now? Would you dare put a brake on the chivalric ardour of youth? Days later the duchess showed the count the blue welts left by those garters; she had promised to St Pandolfa that she would wear garters that were too tight for a whole week in an act of self-mortification if the count managed to provoke the prior catastrophe they so longed for. The rumour soon ran throughout the whole of the vast city of Parzelonenburg: 'The Carmelites have opened fire on the people . . .' Gangs of ragamuffins in red-and-black kerchiefs soon began to appear behind the forces of public order besieging us and started to bawl and threaten us with clenched fists. It was nightfall and there we were shut in and besieged in that monastery with bullets whizzing at us through every window . . ."

A cold, wan day was beginning to dawn outside the cabin and the horizontal bar of the rusty cross stood out hazily against the stars like an arm paralysed in a peculiar gesture; the madman still spewed out his foaming, turbid stream of words: "At the time those hypocrites promised us everything, and they gave us bugger all! They've put me out in the street, the man they owe everything to! They shut every door in my face! All I have left is my novel, and nobody else but Atalanta!" The machine spun and spun, returned to grey fly-wing stockings; he shouted hoarsely: "Make way for the youth!", but I was no longer listening. I had got up silently from the straw that was cracking, and quietly, but very quietly headed outside, because I now knew all there was to know.

I finally discovered how Soleràs had died: "Soleràs was dangerous. What else could I do? I liquidated him . . ."

"You liquidated him . . ."

"What else could I do? I signalled to those who were following us and they did the job. That pair had had plenty of practice: I trusted them completely. It was over in a second. Anyway, what does Soleràs mean to you, if you hardly knew him? He was a most dangerous individual . . ."

He could no longer see me from the back of the cabin; I was shaking. The iron arm of the cross was there and seemed to gesture strangely at me, a gesture of encouragement; the idea was there, tangible and simmering; I could vaguely hear the monologue he was pursuing inside the cabin like the buzz of a bumblebee.

"They besieged us all night. They threw hand grenades through the bottom windows and we had a number of dead and seriously wounded; the friars had shut themselves in their chapel. When the new day, Monday, dawned, a captain of the assault guards came to negotiate. The colonel refused to surrender, even though he had just been hit by one final disappointment: as well as the civil and assault guards, in the first light of day we could see distinctly ordinary soldiers among the forces besieging us. So, the army wasn't with us, or at least not the whole army, as we had told him. Beyond the line of guards and soldiers encircling the monastery we could see the crowds filling that broad avenue – the biggest in Parzelonenburg – and lorries overflowing with anarchists who raised their clenched fists and bawled out in chorus – the indispensable Llibert Milmany had ensured they were there, another one who now acts as if he doesn't know me! They all wore red-and-black kerchiefs. For a moment, the colonel, who was closely observing those lorries through his binoculars, put them aside to look at the kerchief that I was wearing. He said nothing. He headed towards the chapel, where the friars were with the dead and wounded, and asked to confess and take communion."

"It's a fly" – that idea suddenly came to me out of the blue; I had managed to leave the cabin without him noticing and I could still hear him buzzing: "It's a fly as big as a man; he hides in this hole and buzzes nonstop because he is a fly but it's winter now when flies hibernate. This fly is a survivor, the only one of the thousands that were born in a flash in 1936 from eggs that were hidden; I must hurry, I must get to work before it lays thousands of eggs, so *that* would spread across the face of the earth again . . ." And the fly buzzed in its hole; it was a fly and it was a robot, its gears out of kilter, buzzing and buzzing as it spun round endlessly: young Recesvinto was by now a jewel of international diplomacy but he liked to travel strictly incognito, he went on reciting all that in the pitch black and everything became entangled in the hum of that out-of-kilter machine, and I touched the esparto rope and the cold, wan sky was further away than ever, was no longer the sky: it was the void.

"He confessed and took communion, then walked out of the chapel and told me in hushed tones as if he didn't want his companions to hear: 'I should have guessed that you were a Judas.' Then he addressed his officers, some of whom had also confessed and taken communion: 'Now, my sons, all that remains is for us to die with dignity.' The guards and soldiers were preparing to attack, the time that the captain had given us to surrender had elapsed. Before the final attack a Civil Guard colonel even came to the front door holding a white flag; he had been sent to give us one last chance. That colonel and ours were the same age and knew each other: 'You should be sensible,' he said, 'it's gone horribly wrong – complete madness.' His expression was tired and a three-day-old beard darkened his face, but his uniform was spotless, the three big stars gleamed on his cuff, and his hair was turning white; our colonel replied that he would surrender on condition that it was to him, that is, to the civil guard. Then the other pointed from the window at an entire section of the civil guard, all correctly uniformed like himself, waiting in formation in front of the monastery; when he saw those impeccable lines, he hesitated no longer and surrendered. The doors opened, and everyone, soldiers and officers, led by the wounded, were about to leave and be taken prisoner, when Count Recesvinto started to wave and bawl from one window, as if he'd climbed up there from the outside, making every effort to ensure his working-man's overall and kerchief were clearly visible: 'This way, to me, companions!' The crowd immediately launched itself like a huge torrent, knocking themselves and everything over in their path. The barrier of guards and soldiers crumbled under the onslaught while the count continued to bellow from the window: 'Death to fascist friars!' Atalanta knows, and will never ever forget; she is aware of everything she owes me and that is why that duchess, a proud descendant of the Romanovs and Hohenstaufen, kneels at my feet like a submissive slave who can refuse me nothing, and one of the friars knelt down and begged: 'Mercy!' while the anarchists slashed and hacked on all sides. However you look at it, Llibert Milmany had been true to his word. The colonel, who was bald and had lost his hat in the immense pell-mell, raised his hands to his head when Gravat, a man whom I knew only too well, was about to bash him with the butt of a shotgun. Lots of women were around; one hissed: 'Top them alive, it's no fun when they're dead!' I saw one using a hammer to finish off a friar who was already mortally wounded and edging along on his knees holding up his entrails; in the church that was still pitch black because the main doors were shut, others were setting fire to a heap of chairs. While they slaughtered everyone in sight, friars and military without distinction, a gentleman in civilian dress elbowed his way through; he wore a jacket and tie and Catalan armband: '*Soc un delegat del govern de Catalunya*, stop immediately! They have surrendered!' He went hoarse shouting, nobody was listening; some assault guards and *mossos d'esquadra* drove a path through the crowd with their rifle butts and stood at his side, but I stood in front of that ridiculous character – and he was ridiculous in his jacket and tie – and spat in his face: '*Tú no eres más que un fascista!*' Gravat immediately echoed me: '*Sí, un fascista!* I saw you in plaza de España yesterday shooting at the people!' Then a huge cry went up: '*Fascista! Fascista!*' They slaughtered the gentleman and the guards at his side; they slaughtered everyone in sight while the fire that had begun in the chapel spread through the monastery and they carried me out aloft, triumphantly, so the crowd outside would cheer me . . ."

Once again the machine started spinning round; once again another tedious tirade from his novel: "That luminary of imperial diplomacy liked to breathe in the midst of tempests, but then he preferred to travel strictly incognito and enjoy the forbidden fruit . . ." And the sky had receded further than ever, and was no longer the sky but the void, and sticky sweat ran down my spine because my shaking fingers were unable to undo the knot. Suddenly he spoke in a different voice, like someone waking up with a start: "Hey, what's the time? What are you doing out there? Saying your rosary prayers? Bah, let that cross be, it means nothing. Nothing exists."

Silence. And then his voice, much quieter: "Or are you planning to kill me?"

I didn't budge. He suddenly said, in a hugely disenchanted tone: "Nothing exists. Not even Duchess Atalanta."

A bead of icy sweat slipped, quivering like quicksilver, over the bottom of my backbone; then he grunted these surprising words: "Nothing exists beyond suffering."

I slumped to my knees; I was exhausted; my hand clung to the iron bar. He mouthed a throttled wail: "I only believe in suffering."

Then he started to whimper so strangely, like a dog.

I was at the airport. The plane carrying Lluís and his family to the other end of the world was disappearing over the horizon like a fly. Rooted to that spot, I could still see her face so bright and her eyes so bright, eyes where a tear had glistened when she shook my hand; a tear, a solitary tear, but how it shone, like that other tear, in another era, at the gala dinner, thirty years ago, my God! That tear in another era was for Soleràs, today's was for me, and You will forgive me because You made us like that, my God, You created us to sin and be passionate.

Lluís had hugged me right at the end and I hadn't noticed him slipping an envelope into the inside pocket of my soutane. I only noticed when I jumped on the bus: it contained ten thousand-pesseta notes. The bus that was to take me back to the village hadn't left yet; I got off and walked the stretch to carrer de l'Arc del Teatre.

Thank you, Lluís, thank You, Lord; I was blissfully happy. I sobbed as I walked and revisited places I hadn't entirely forgotten as I searched for a particular shop in that maze of filthy backstreets. A second-hand shop I remembered so vividly; I sobbed out of joy and moved my lips whispering quietly: thank you, Lluís, and passers-by stared at me but I found the shop I wanted, it gave off the usual stench. It reeked of damp depths, of dankness, of subterranean places where mushrooms are cultivated; I bought a three-piece suit, jacket, trousers, and waistcoat, in lurid check, but wearable, a shabby overcoat that was really warm, a thick scarf and indispensable underwear. Altogether I used three of those notes, because I yielded to temptation; I bought a navy telescope, my very own from an earlier time.

Yes, I had seen it weeks ago, and it was mine. Who will ever know what strange paths had brought it to that second-hand shop after thirty years? It *was* mine, I recognised it from a mark that I myself had made, when I was twelve, with my scout's knife on the brass of the first cylinder; nobody else could have spotted a mark that was supposed to be a clover leaf, though it was so clumsily etched; I am so clumsy, O Lord. It was my telescope, which Lluís and I had used so often in those happy days to look at the moon and planets; I had discovered it a few weeks ago, when I went to that shop to ask about the price of old clothes. I left quite down in the dumps, thinking I would never be able to cobble so much money together . . . three thousand pessetes, O Lord! I had gone there because I had such a vivid memory of it, I remembered it because of the unexpected junk you found there, from amateur telescopes (though how could I ever imagine I would find mine there?) to antique enema equipment, from strange orthopaedic devices to huge barometers from the last century. My telescope from long ago, the only thing I missed from the times when I lived with my auntie! She gave it to me on my twelfth birthday to reward some good marks, some first-class reports, and I had got it back and could observe once more the rings of Saturn and the satellites of Jupiter as I used to, when I so liked to follow them night after night as they came and went around the planet like four peas around a plum, and Venus like a small moon and reddish Mars . . . but then I reflected how now, thirty years later, Venus and Mars wouldn't give me companionship like they once did! My God, then we all thought that Venus and Mars were two other Earths with their own seas and forests, their own trees and animals, with their own inhabitants; the fact is . . . we now know they are two horrendous hells, yet another illusion our century has destroyed forever, a three-thousand-year-old illusion, because Chaldean astrologers had already imagined the stars were inhabited like so many other Earths! From Chaldean astrologers three thousand years ago to now, when we raised our eyes to look at the sky we felt in good company, the company of that unknown humanity sailing in those distant worlds as we did on ours; we now know that the Earth is curiously unique, that humanity is incomprehensibly alone . . . those were my thoughts as I walked along with the bundle of clothes under my arm and the telescope clasped in my other hand, my childhood telescope that I had lost in the last days of the war and had now found again so unexpectedly, and it never occurred to me that a priest who buys a three-piece suit in a second-hand shop might attract attention, even more so if he buys a telescope. I could only think of the planets and that single, wonderful tear as the most distant of stars, I also thought of that wretched woman with whom I had lived in that same district so many, many years ago; I was afraid I might bump into her on a street corner, because she would have recognised me despite the soutane and the years that had gone by. I was afraid I might meet that harmless wretch; I could only think of that absurd danger, because she had recognised me when we did meet up so unexpectedly.

The first time I had left with a cracked skull and a few weeks in hospital, where every day I received a paternal visit from the archbishop with his affable reprimands; on the second, I had ended up in the cellars of that building on Via Laietana. You have to sleep on the cement floor if family or friends don't bring you a mattress, sanctioned by the traditions of the place, and it is amazing how the guards respect these traditions and the rights they confer on detainees. There were six of us in that oven and the news spread like wildfire because six mattresses arrived very soon, one each, with its corresponding blanket. There were other traditions we weren't aware of because we were newcomers, and that was why she and I met so unexpectedly after so many years. On their night patrols the police often arrest some of the wretched women who stand too brazenly on street corners, given that their trade is currently illegal; they usually keep them inside for the three days the law allows and then let them go, till the next time, though they don't hurt or torture them. Nobody tends to remember to send mattresses to these poor girls who are only guilty of being empty-headed; to avoid having to sleep on the cold, hard floor without even a thin blanket they usually beg to share a blanket with a luckier inmate and the tradition of the house allows it, and no eyebrows are raised; the cell guards are a bunch of affable old sea-dogs who have seen everything under the sun and are quite imperturbable. They simply see the humanitarian side and are happy with the modest tip that is similarly stipulated and agreed by hallowed tradition. So there we were, spending our fourth night inside, when we heard whispering and muffled laughter on the other side of the door which half-opened to reveal an old policeman with a drooping white moustache, which gave him the air of a retired Don Quixote, who told us very politely that those ladies "were insisting on their rights".

"We can't refuse them their rights," he apologised in Spanish, "it's up to you whether you accept or not."

Without waiting for our response – and how could we respond if we didn't know what it was all about? – they jostled him and walked in tittering; clearly there had been a sizeable round-up that night and a good dozen had ended up in that basement. Seven or eight had already come to an agreement with other inmates, generally conmen or pickpockets (they always had someone to send them a mattress and a blanket); six had walked into our cell and they couldn't stop tittering when they saw our soutanes. Suddenly, one of the six energetically separated herself from the others, came straight over and stared at me, eyes bulging and mouth gaping; she was the one most caked in make-up, by far the most lurid. She could have been fifty years or fifty centuries old, oh dear, how would I have ever recognised her under that frightful mane of bright red hair, her eyes surrounded by such vivid blue circles?

"Is it really you?" she finally gasped. "How long have you been a vicar?"

And she started to tell her colleagues the absurd yet absolutely true story of those two weeks we lived together – her, her pimp, her pimp's dog, and me – and my very young colleagues looked at me stiff with shock. Because in their eyes I was a venerable old man; yes, at the age of fifty that was what I was in their eyes, a venerable old man and almost a martyr and this is what I told them, more chastened than ashamed: "Yes, my sons, this lady is telling the truth."

"We were always afraid he had a screw loose," she told her colleagues, pointing a finger to her forehead. "But I never had any idea he was a vicar! He took French leave of us, leaving our dog dead as a memento."

We left them our cell and went to sleep in theirs; it was the only solution to that situation – with the strict proviso that they would never tell the people who had so kindly sent us mattresses and blankets. As they were released long before we were, we still got plenty of use out of them. And now I was thinking of her; she must have had a den down one of those backstreets and I would give anything not to see her again.

I could only think of that absurd danger, I feared no eyes but hers. The day after, I returned to the village with all my purchases, so happy I would now be able to persuade him to leave, to leave for ever and once again I would be alone and tranquil in the village, alone and tranquil; because that unexpected neighbour had been too much for me, I couldn't love Lamoneda, my peculiar neighbour – quite the contrary.

His spirits revived when he saw that manna from heaven! He could already picture himself in Paris, he was already dreaming of that top publisher in a swoon after reading his novel: "I'm lucky," he told me, "nobody discovered my hiding place, I've lived here for four months and you were the only person in the know! I am a lucky man!" and he was already picturing himself as a famous novelist in Paris, the royalties pouring in. He started talking about the *parisiennes* and *théâtres à femmes nues* – the only memory he retained from a trip in his youth, half a century ago! Apparently the only time he had ever been in Paris. He caressed the remaining six notes that I gave him to cover the cost of the journey and his first weeks in Paris until he found the wherewithal to survive and his mad old man's face seemed madder and older than ever: "Make

way for the youth!" he repeated, "Make way for the youth!" And
he muttered: "Now I really will shake Malvina off my back!" Dawn
was on the horizon; we decided he should stay hidden in his lair
during the day and set off when it was dark. He would only steal
along at night until he had crossed the Pyrenees.

A week slipped by. I thought he must be in France by now. Early
in the morning, after mass, I set out on the path to the Mill Strait;
I had often taken that track at night and knew all the shortcuts so
it was child's play by the light of day. It took me less than three
hours. I would have happily taken my telescope (ever since it was
retrieved, it went with me on all my hikes), but I had lost it again.
I had lost it a week earlier, could I have left it in the boot of the
bus on my last trip? The bus driver said he hadn't found it, it was a
mystery . . . Lord, I am so absent-minded! But it wasn't my mislaid
telescope that was on mind: it was a turbid desire to revisit that
spot where I sweated from the strangest anguish ever to possess
me, where I had been on the point of surrendering to the most
criminal, most irresistible temptation I had ever felt; I wanted to
savour that peaceful spot, without him – at last.

He was still there.

He was there, sitting upright on the cabin doorstep. His skull
had been smashed in.

The cross-bar of the iron cross had been flung to the ground by
his side.

The cold had preserved him in the state he had been left in when
they struck him. He was wearing that loud check suit and leaning
back on the door jamb, eyes and mouth wide open, his novel on
his knees.

*

We awake from our youth as if from the delirium of an endless, feverish night and, lo and behold, we are over the ridge, and the landscape opening before us is so different, so different from the one we have left behind! We start on the downward slope and feel despairingly that *"nous étions nés pour quelque chose de mieux"*, to conquer the world! Born to conquer the world, the glory that is our end – though not worldly glory.

Not worldly glory – that is vainglory; another glory, the one that is genuine – which we cannot attain by simply using our own energies. What can we do with our own energies? Shameful, often frightful relapses . . . when we awake from that endless delirium, when we see lucidly what we were capable of doing while it lasted; what have we made of our youth, O Lord! What traces will our empty footsteps leave on the sands of the endless desert? Why would we want to endure in the memories of men, when they have none? To endure in the memories of men, who have none and never have had, would we agree to erasure from God's memory?

It is possible to be erased from God's memory: that has always been so under different guises from remotest times, from the very beginning. That has a guise, that exists, and since it exists we should look it in the face now and then. A man can spend his life with his eyes glued to that, his mouth gaping, as if frozen by its breath, that thing which we call nothingness, absurdity, void, nausea, and by a thousand other names, but which always amounts to the same ancient thing. Lots of eyes are frozen by the sight of *that*! Because if one isn't yet an immortal soul, if one isn't yet the work of God, one is a robot: eyes frozen, staring into the absurd, abdicating one's soul to turn into a robot. Then the robot goes out of kilter and spins, spins round endlessly . . .

But if that exists, then so does love, which would still exist even though everyone denied it, even if everyone always denied it everywhere! Its breath cannot blot out the sky – it cannot reach so high.

We have seen so many robots in the world throughout this century! We have seen so many atrocities from one end of the world to the other! And the robots would like men to be only robots, all identical, all doing and saying the same thing; we would end up being able to do only what has already been done millions and millions of times by other robots. Abandoned to being automata, how far might we fall? The fall is endless since there is no floor; the out-of-kilter machine endlessly falls, spinning in the void, and all that spins in the void withers endlessly until a blow from an iron bar stops it whirring.

But had I not behaved like a robot ever since coming to live confined within this mountain village after returning from the Caribbean? The only thing I ever inspired was an instinctive distrust because I behaved towards them like an automaton. I went to their houses and spoke to them, I talked about the threshing, beetroot and sainfoin, as adults speak to children, and tried to establish friendly relationships with non-churchgoing families. And the more I tried the more robotic I became because I did it not out of love but duty, and without love one is nothing but a robot. Didn't Guinarda – that sanctimonious soul who had spied on me so furiously and informed on me so fervently to the bishopric – begin to mistrust me because I only *pretended* to be interested in her problems? Her problems that I found such a bore! As they were childless, her deceased husband had drawn up a nonsensical will; the wretched old woman was at risk of being reduced to abject poverty because it transpired that her husband had left everything to his nephews and hadn't even retained the usufruct for her; I tried to intervene with the best of intentions, since she was illiterate and totally at sea in that gigantic legal mess; if I wasted so much time trying to extract the meaning from that maze of a testament it was – so she deduced – because I expected to get a decent slice. She began to suspect it; then she found out by chance that I was a "red priest" and, ever since, what has she not suspected me of, what has she not said against me? Had she limited herself to writing to the archbishop (or rather getting someone else to write on her behalf, as she doesn't know how): "you have sent us a robot instead of a vicar", she would have simply been stating the truth. And what about the others? The others weren't as devious as Guinarda, or at least didn't appear to be, but I could read in their faces their displeasure at my robotic, simulated concern, the displeasure we trigger in a child when we speak in an affected and infantile language, much more infantile than is warranted! Yes, that was what it was all about: why are we wearers of soutanes so fond of speaking to those who aren't like us, as if we were adults and they children? There was also that invalid who scarpered whenever he saw me; he lived not in the village but in a farmhouse more than an hour's walk away. The poor fellow is dead now. He walked painfully, as if his backbone had been broken; whenever he saw me, he turned abruptly round as if horrified by the sight of a soutane. One day I learnt they had almost broken his spine with a blow from the butt of a gun in a concentration camp, the same one where I ended up after the war was over; another day – these things surfaced every now and then – an old man who had placed his trust in me told me how in those early post-war times a corporal would pass through our village every Sunday and do a roll call at the door of the church and then pay a visit on those who hadn't been to mass: basically wasn't I like that corporal, wasn't I a robot?

Ever since I stopped visiting their houses, I barely talk to them, and now simply pray by myself and roam alone with my telescope tucked under my arm; ever since I decided to burden Your suffering shoulders with everything, Lord, a burden that was crushing me I was so useless . . . Now I do nothing to attract them, they come! Because it is You, Lord, and not I who attracts them, and You don't imitate any childish dialect, You know how to speak to each individual in their unique, secret, and noblest language, the mother tongue of the soul!

I roam these barren wastes with my telescope tucked under my arm in the dying light of day, leaving the sacristan with the task of ringing the Angelus, because I like to hear the Angelus from afar, at that bewitching twilight hour – and on the distant horizon I glimpse that radiant face emerging from some abyss or other! After unburdening my anguish and anxieties, after placing on Your shoulders the load that was crushing me, I wander these barren wastes and woods alone, over hills and valleys, my Lord, but I do glimpse that face above the dying day, that visage of fire and thirst which everything separates me from. It appears as clearly as in a vivid dream; I don't know his name and he makes me cry silently. Who are you, faded scent, forgotten melody, searing sadness, making me cry so silently; distant visage, who are you? The archangel who is coming or going? Life that is fleeing, or death that is approaching? Archangel *sans* name, why do you bear such a glittering star on your forehead; could it be that tear?

*

They've finally tired of harassing me over his death. It was, of course, sanctimonious old Guinarda who informed the police of my toing and froing around the Mill Strait. They even returned the six notes they found in the inside pocket of his check jacket, meaning that the murderers' motive wasn't robbery. I owe this happy outcome to the Baroness of Olivel (the *carlana* was honoured with a baronetcy in 1945), ever prepared to use her influence to help Lluís and his friends. She is now an eighty-year-old lady; her grandson, whose name is also Enric, will inherit the two baronies, Olivel de la Virgen and Castel de Olivo, as his father, that young boy who ran around the grounds with his little brother, married the only daughter of the widowed Baroness of Castel and is negotiating the consolidation of both into one marquessate.

She is now eighty and a lucid lady in splendid health; I had already had recourse to her several times to prevent untold misfortune in the worst of moments, in the first, most difficult years. She has become very devout. She always asks after Lluís.

Twenty years on I found out too late that the baroness could do nothing. What could she have done anyway? One of those maquis groups I have previously mentioned was the "Estany gang" that hid in the densest forests in the Val d'Aran and I often heard about them, though I had never suspected that he was Estany. He was born there, and wanted to die there.

Each band leader had a *nom de guerre*; I had just learnt that his, chosen in homage to science and mispronounced by his men, wasn't Estany but Einstein.

De Gaulle personally honoured him in 1944 with the most glorious of war honours; it would have been so easy for him to go back to France where he was a *compagnon de la Résistance*.

In 1948 only six of the two hundred men who had crossed the high passes of the Pyrenees four years before were still alive; the priest in Ur, who told me all this, spoke to him at the end of autumn: he offered them sanctuary in his parish, where they would be among Catalans.

"Our cause is a just one," retorted Picó.

"It's not just, because they are acts of despair," was the priest's riposte. "Each life sacrificed in these conditions is a crime."

"I won't accept defeat while there's a breath of life left in me."

He sold it dear. When the priest in Ur's negotiations failed, the civil guard organised a round up, the final one. His corpse cost twelve others.

He had never resigned himself to the world of the defeated, that is Yours, O Lord! The only one You sought in this world!

Have pity on his soul.

VIII

Thirty years already, my God . . .

And all that began one Sunday, looking as if it was going to be peaceful enough . . . The heat of the dog days of summer wafted through my wide-open bedroom window. Auntie had gone to her estate in Farena a couple of weeks earlier, where she liked to spend the summer months. I had always accompanied her there; that was the first year when, thinking I was now too old – I was nineteen – to spend three months holidaying like a young rich kid, I had decided to stay and study in the libraries of Barcelona. On free days I would go on excursions with other seminarians who had stayed on in the city like me.

I was alone in the mansion in Sarrià. The alarm clock rang, I was so happy! It was still night time; that Sunday we were going to Montserrat.

It was that most stifling moment in those dog days when, just before dawn, the inland breeze stops blowing and the sea breeze has yet to rise; when ship sails in fishing ports hang listless and flaccid like a chest that can hardly breathe. To my astonishment I found a whole company lined up along the façade of the university.

The great illuminated clock in the tower wasn't yet pointing to four. It wasn't just a stifling stillness that hung in the air; I stopped on the corner of Aribau. I had come down from Sarrià with such a happy heart, as usual when we were going to the holy mountain;

in my thoughts I could already smell the bitter scent of thyme, hear the *Salve* sung by the choir . . . I felt so carefree, I was going to Montserrat, I was nineteen years old and that Sunday seemed so peaceful; from my bedroom window I had seen the city extending down to the sea even in the dark, sleeping so serenely, not a care in the world.

Then I saw a company of assault guards coming down Aribau. I knew nothing, like most of the city: what was the meaning of those soldiers marching down in formation? The stifling atmosphere seemed even thinner in the silent presence of those men. They marched in step, the only sound the rhythmic beat of their boots. When he came out onto the square and saw the soldiers there, the lieutenant of the guards saluted; the other replied; the guards crossed the square in the direction of carrer Pelayo. And suddenly, gunfire.

I hid behind a tree, utterly bewildered. Some guards had fallen and were shouting out, the others were already firing back. I hid behind the tree, like someone relieving himself, while a louder noise rose up in the distance, a solemn barrage of cannon fire; dawn was only a faint glimmer. I had gone to sleep so peacefully the night before, so happy to think we were going to Montserrat in the morning, and now I was frantically running to and fro, besieged by news so incoherent and contradictory! Some regiments had rebelled and nobody knew why; the forces of order had opposed them. By midday there were only three or four centres of resistance and they were scattered and surrounded; the air force was ready to bomb the biggest, the Drassanes barracks, which surrendered on Monday, the following day, at eleven o'clock.

Those barracks no longer exist. They will exist for ever in my memory! They were old and dilapidated and opposite the harbour; a stench of mule sweat and dank air permeated the area. The stalls of the second-hand and antique booksellers were next door; often on a Sunday morning I would stroll from stall to stall and some of the booksellers got to know me. Soon after Auntie gave me that telescope, I bought Camille Flammarion's *Astronomia popular* there; how avidly I read that fat illustrated tome until Auntie took it and burnt it; she had just discovered that in his day Flammarion had been a standard bearer for spiritualism. A hundred soldiers under a lieutenant's orders were still resisting. I was among the passers-by packing the Porta de la Pau and the bottom of the Rambla. Bombed by the air force and artillery and besieged by the assault guards, the barracks tried to surrender; we all saw the white flag. An officer went in with some assault guards; the news soon spread that those inside had laid down their arms and were only waiting to be arrested and taken away. That was the moment when the men with black and red kerchiefs appeared as if by magic; one of them climbed up to a window and, clinging to the bar of the grille, signalled with his free hand that he was a hero, one of the men who had taken the barracks bare-chested – a barracks that had already surrendered! He gesticulated and shouted; naked from the waist up, his broad chest glistened with sweat and displayed – I can see it now! – an enormous tattoo of a woman clad only in stockings. His companions replied by shouting and raising their clenched fists; all of a sudden they overwhelmed the cordon of guards blocking their way and crowded inside. We learnt later they butchered . . .

I remember the lorries that drove around the city, crammed with men chanting rhythmically. What did that chant mean? Who were they? Where had they come from? They trumpeted their own myths: they were the ones, they said, who were the conquerors; bare-chested and unarmed they had taken machine guns and cannon. The most inane myths are the ones we most eagerly swallow, fools that we all are, so hungry for derring-do. The anarchists, held in such contempt till then, now became the heroes of the day! Their lorries drove past and people applauded; I did too, I applauded even though my own eyes had seen the guards, and only the guards, standing firm. The myth was impossible to resist, it was so comforting to believe in Robin Hood, in the loathed anarchist who had saved the country . . . The carnival became more lunatic by the minute; at nightfall I could see only lorries with red-and-black flags driving up and down streets, that rhythmic chant blasting away. The temperature was rising, Barcelona was delirious, completely delirious, all compounded by a noxious stench from horses that had been blown to bits the day before and that lay still scattered over the plaça de Catalunya. Yet another, more subtle stench blended into that hot air charged with smoke and dust, a sly stench, as if from hidden carrion. It wafted our way like a cynical outpouring, and warily concealed itself again; we began to eye one another more and more suspiciously, what did all that mean, where were they taking us? I rushed to and fro, asthmatically breathing air that grew more ominous by the hour. Drenched in sweat, my shirt clung to my back and I was completely nonplussed, though intoxicated by history. My memories are both precise and confused; everything was hot and hazy, grandiose and horrendous. I can't remember dates distinctly but some details stand out extremely sharply. That Monday evening, or perhaps the day after those other characters began to stroll up and down the Rambla disguised as Gandhi, the Negus, and the Apostles; I then saw the "anarchist Christ" everybody was talking about at the time. We had never heard of him earlier; then the radio began to churn out soporific, sentimental lectures. He was very fair, with a long beard and hair down to his shoulders, clad in a white tunic like a Sacred Heart made of plaster. The anarchists had attacked prisons and madhouses; they had commandeered the gallows to serve as platform for the garrotte and dragged it to the High Street in Gràcia where I saw it blocking the middle of the road. They had had hung a placard from it:

THIS IS THE DEVICE USED BY OUR CLASS ENEMIES
TO ELIMINATE OUR COMPANIONS

The garrotte! In fact it hadn't been used for years. It was most unusual; I can remember it being used once against an invert who had cut his lover into small pieces with a kitchen knife and registered the bits to go by train inside a packing case, and the whole of Spain had hung on that case for weeks and months; the king had been within a whisker of reprieving him, it had taken all the pressure of the government and public opinion – horrified by the crime – to persuade him that the entire weight of the law should fall . . . and in the name of the abolition of the death penalty they now carried out massacre after massacre month after month! But we couldn't foresee *that* on that evening. We could only hear a kind of enormous buzz throughout the city, which suddenly went quiet, one of those stifling silences that sometimes descend in the middle of a storm. What strange rumours ran amok through the crowds! My confused memory cannot be sure if it was on the Monday evening or on the one following that I discovered they had opened prisons and madhouses; I do remember it was evening and that someone had informed me of this when we were at the bottom of the Rambla, where smoke was still rising from the Drassanes barracks, and when I looked at the "anarchist Christ" in the arch that gives its name to the carrer de l'Arc del Teatre, he was languidly directing honeyed words at the stupefied women emerging from their lairs for a close-up. So many people had escaped from madhouses and prisons and lots of them were on the Rambla that night. It was like a foaming sea and, there and then, placards appeared like flags waved by shipwrecked individuals floating adrift on the rough waves: VIVA EL AMOR LIBRE! read one banner, hoisted by women with shaven heads, dressed as men and carrying guns. Free love! They were incredibly ugly, O God in heaven, and I asked one of them who had given them those guns: "We took them!' they bawled in Spanish. I got a similar response from some twelve- to fifteen-year-old boys, and you kept seeing them in the centre of the city – the wretched from the shanty towns on the outskirts, poor devils who hadn't a clue about anything, decked out in red-and-black kerchiefs – they could well have been in the opposite colour, it was all much of a muchness; the same people who afterwards, over so many, many years we have seen rushing to rallies, always in a crowd, wearing the same colours and cheering enthusiastically. On Sunday afternoon, or perhaps in the early evening, they began to chorus that huge slander.

As night fell I was back in Auntie's mansion. From the roof terrace I could see through my telescope all Barcelona's monasteries, convents, and churches burning. Dotted across the entire city, black plumes of smoke rose in a July sky red-hot like the copper lid of a boiler. While the fires crackled and spat, flying gangs of assassins already roamed the city and the country; the victory, that had been born legitimately, was turning foul and falling apart. We had been as one from the very first, and were now thrown into terrible disarray and torn asunder; the war we could perhaps have avoided, or at least fought united as offspring of the same mother, was now turning into a struggle of Cains.

It was an old trick, as old as the world. They came in their dozens, in their hundreds; the flies suddenly appeared and crawled everywhere. A Pep Put, a Gravat, a Quimet Solé were caught in the act on those very first days. They thought it was amusing to climb into belfries and shoot at passers-by! That was all they had to do to make the people in the shanty towns believe the incredible news – they seemed prepared to swallow any kind of atrocity, nuns buried alive with their wrists manacled, or parents who sold their children's eyes to rich foreigners! When Quimet Solé was caught in the act and executed, the anarchists let all hell loose: they swore he had always been one of theirs! Well, it is so easy to be a man for all seasons . . . In those early days it was still possible to judge and execute Quimet Solé; later, the anarchist tide submerged every-thing. Lamoneda was able to slip away at the end of September. The country lived under the red-and-black terror for seven months; we heard about that at the front, but couldn't really imagine what it was like. I had gone to the front in early August, after spending a couple of weeks giving blood and then working as a nurse in Barcelona hospitals. Once at the front, the rearguard was really remote, news from behind the lines reached us late and was fragmentary and confused . . . And our desire not to believe any of it, or at least that it could not be so horrendous, was overwhelming!

*

But that other fellow, Lord, did exactly what I had done and then there is that strange detail: I found the telescope again. That's how I came to have it back. I found it behind the cabin, among the brambles. That's why I had it again; that's why I am no longer so forlorn on my solitary promenades.

Yes, that unfortunate telescope I thought I had lost yet again was there, a few feet away from the corpse, and at night, restless in bed, I felt unbearably oppressed. It was all so incredible! I even doubted that Lamoneda ever existed – perhaps he was a monstrous creation of my dreams?

But if he really did exist, if he wasn't a phantom of my imagination, his death was so mysterious! Because he was crucified.

He died by means of a cross; a blow to the skull from that iron arm of the cross. And he was *his* nephew, Lord! Lord, at times Your grace follows such entangled paths, what can we know of the paths the roots of a tree mark out underground? How could his uncle not have loved that new-born babe who had no mother and was perhaps hated by his father – if only out of pity? How can we doubt that Dr Gallifa felt compassion towards the child-without-grace that Lamoneda must have been? Who will ever know what Lamoneda's childhood was like – a childhood of those fated not to be loved and to be branded with the stigma of Cain?

On the orders of the presiding magistrate they had now returned to me the six notes intact that were found in the inside pocket of his check jacket. And you know what? They burnt my fingers, because they were no longer mine; they had ceased to be mine, they belonged to Lamoneda! I am at peace now: I have just sent a postal order to that unhappy soul (she gave me her address when we met so unexpectedly in those cellars). The poor woman must be suffering since they prohibited her trade, she is so incapable of doing anything else . . . At that time I was surprised by her devotion to St Pancras, the saint who the devout pray to for good health and work; it was futile telling her that in her case there might be an obstacle or two, she was so stupid! The poor woman was so stupid! But she wasn't evil; with the money I gave her she had bought a plaster reproduction of the saint's image and each night she prayed to it before getting into bed.

What can we know of the paths the roots of a tree mark out underground? We can know nothing at all! As we approach death – something we experience acutely every second of our life – our faith must grow if we don't want death to submerge us, because only faith – it also goes by the name of love and hope – is the anti-death. Our faith must grow as much as our death, must grow as much as our shadow as we come closer to the night. But what do we know of all that, of faith, of death, of shadows and the night? What do we know of our faith and the faith of others? In the eyes of the Infinite, faith in a little plaster saint can be worth as much, and who knows if not more, than the faith of the subtlest of the Doctors of the Church.

How shocked she looked when she recognised me among the others in those cellars! I would never have recognised her, the most caked in face paint of all those who had been rounded up that night; my colleagues in the cell looked at me silently, and shook their heads, and one, quite instinctively, quite unawares, tapped his forehead with a finger, but from then on they forgave me all my eccentricities; compassion opened their eyes. They no longer look at me so distrustfully now I have shared that cell with them;

they have warmed to me; they are all such good lads, those poor children!

And the night is immense and its countless galaxies no longer fill me with anguish since my faith and hope have been restored; it now brings me the companionship it brought before, the companionship of the infinite that would pass understanding if it weren't Your work, the ineffable companionship of the stars that are our brothers and sisters since they are Your children.

Faith . . . faith comes to us through contact! Like a flame. And that is all we know. A lit candle can light others that have gone out. Jesus passed the flame to the Apostles, who in turn spread it across the world. When we wander life's paths and find one of those candles that derive from the original flame, its flame will touch us if we do not reject contact with its fire. There are torches that illuminate the night and fight off darkness; we have seen one in our time and his name was John and he was a Pope. There are also small lights, and even humbler oil lamps, and there are even wicks that are almost imperceptible, but that burn all the same in their out-of-the-way corners, ignored by everyone.

Faith isn't proved; it is communicated. Like a flame. And that was what Dr Gallifa was, a flaming candle. Even now, beyond death, it lights up other candles, other extinguished candles light up what seemed cold and dead for ever. And could it not have lit him up at that last moment when the arm of the cross split his skull open? What do I know? What does anybody know of these things that are so enigmatic?

Because isn't belief in suffering already belief in the Cross?

*

And for people like myself, who are useless for anything else, the only glory in this world is to burn like a wick imperceptible in the endless night, fully conscious that the flame is not ours and that a puff can blow it out. At the time . . .

We sometimes foresee the force which that darkness is always about to use to open its maw and swallow us! I make a great effort to wake up when I am restless in bed, but then I fall back into the deepest sleep, I have suffered from nightmares throughout my life! I would wake up quite ashamed of having seen those monstrous or criminal visions. Now . . . now I am alone; frighteningly alone. However strange it may seem, Lamoneda kept me company.

The last I will have in this world! Because the old archbishop is dead; all I have left in this world are infrequent visits by Lluís and Trini. If one discovers friendly faces in the darkness of the Tunnel, in the glimmers of light that now begin to herald the other end, they are the faces of the young, who can understand none of what I have experienced and suffered – friendly faces, no doubt, but ones that look at me and shake their heads when I ask them: what unexpected territory will suddenly dazzle our eyes at the other end of the Tunnel? Yet again will we encounter horrors, horrors deploying other slogans, but horrors all the same?

Oh, if only that earthly paradise from our dreams were to appear, like a reflected glow of the one in heaven! Truly innocent dreams that are, nonetheless, so rooted in our hearts . . . If only we could rediscover our country and freedom like someone rediscovering the house of his grandparents after wandering aimlessly for years and years without a roof above his head! There are times when I believe this; yesterday's hopes will return like birds rediscovering nests they had forgotten; the embers burn on under the huge pile of ash!

I saw Lluís transfigured . . . the same Lluís you would have said was always blind to all faith! His eyes recovered their youthful sparkle the minute he breathed that air; a puff of air and the embers revived . . . They were both in Barcelona at the time and, you know, what many didn't realise is that my old archbishop, who couldn't resign himself to no longer being one and had been inconsolable ever since he was replaced, wanted me to keep him up to date on what was happening on a daily basis, and he was the one most spurring us on: "Don't give up, my sons!" By dint of living in our midst he had finally ended up thinking he was as much one of us as anyone. "A foreigner will never understand us," he would say, and what nobody knows is that I was the one who suggested to him the slogan which was to bear such fruit: "We want Catalan bishops"; yes, he did believe that he was one of us after living in our midst for so many years; he had forgotten he had come twenty-five years ago thinking that Catalan and heretic were one and the same! The crowds gathered in that broad, most bourgeois of avenues in front of that convent full of foreigners, where the intruder had chosen to reside; placards with those three words were raised above thousands of heads when, there and then, the cavalry charged and sabre thrusts began and we all burst out singing the "Virolai". I was with Lluís and Trini, and their eyes shone! Those of Lluís as much as Trini's! How Lluís sang with that powerful voice of his, he seemed so transfigured, he was twenty again! When he embraced me before climbing on the plane that would take him to the other hemisphere, expelled as an undesirable foreigner, his head bandaged, he said: "I will come back, Cruells! I will come back, and be here always from now on! I will recover my citizenship so I can come back whenever I want to; the next time they can throw me in jail, but not expel me!" And there really was an air of resurrection about his eyes and voice.

But in my case . . . perhaps it is too late. When we reach the other end of the Tunnel, something will have died within me for ever that will never revive. The seminarians are now very warm towards me; they forgive me for being such a worn-out old man, a neurotic, a visionary, and even a reactionary; the poor children forgive me everything. Not that they look upon me as a father – not at all! Never as a father. They see me as a grandfather! Like a grandfather who is now on the way out but had his heroic moments in his youth – in those bygone days! – and lived a dignified, mature life. They surround me and love me; they are such good lads! Why should I disillusion them by saying my youth wasn't in the least heroic and my mature years were anything but dignified? It would not be right for a grandfather to disillusion his grandchildren, but often I do not even understand their language; I sometimes feel I am listening to them from afar, from another shore, perhaps even from another world. I watch them and listen to them with greater love than they imagine; grandchildren can and will never imagine all the love of a grandfather; they are absorbed in games the worn-out old man cannot join in. And that is life. Because that is what I am in their eyes at the age of fifty, a worn-out old man who is on his last legs: "He's out of it now, the poor fellow," they say, "but as a young man he fought in the war, the whole war, was a volunteer from the first day to the last." That's what the fifteen-year-old seminarians say and they see everything through eyes of hope, they know nothing of my life and see everything through eyes of hope, and knowing that they say that, I don't feel so ashamed to have aged so quickly and seem thirty years older than I really am!

Who could ever take away those thirty extra years?

And sometimes I would like to warn them off the rose-tinted spectacles of a fifteen-year-old; because I see them look so trusting, my poor sons, of the virtues of the good people and of the purest light of *le jour de gloire* that they hope for . . . they have so little idea about those other horrors, that other nightmare. If they sometimes think of martyrdom, it is always clean, simple and straightforward!

Lord, cure us once and for all of all vainglory; it really would be too beautiful to die simply for our faith or country, for justice or freedom! It would be too beautiful to be the soldier who died for a just cause, with no reservations. What new barren wastes await us still? What new fire of Rome? Won't the flies reappear with the heat of the dog days of another summer? Who knows if we won't have to accept death – that would be sweet if it were only for You – but also infamy, didn't they crucify You for blasphemy, O Lord? Annas and Caiaphas stifled any other voices, the Church of the Strident Mouth crushed the Church of the Severed Tongue. Will they persecute us yet again like plague-ridden animals, like so many rabid dogs?

I rushed this way and that amid the smoke from the fires and the crackle of gunfire and shouted: "It's a lie!", but my hoarse cry was lost in the tumult from the flow; the rumour was already circulating: the friars have shot at the people! And I shouted: "It's a lie!" and my voice was like the death rattle of a wounded man under a pile of dead bodies. That monstrous slander let loose a pack blinded by the scent of blood![12]

O Lord, ensure that peace, love, fraternity, country, and freedom finally appear at the other end of the Tunnel; allow us to see, even if only from afar, the Land that was ever Promised and never attained! However, if Your will is another, and since You allowed yourself to be crucified for blasphemy, cannot we also accept infamy alongside death? O Lord, release me from this anguish that sometimes stifles me, that made the ancient prophet once ask: "What will be the profit from the blood I have shed?"

Mihi autem absit gloriari nisi in Cruce Domini nostri Iesu Christi.

God forbid that I should glory save in the Cross of Our Lord Jesus Christ.

---

12 In fact, the friars did not shoot at the people, but their church *had* been occupied by people who did: a fact not known by Joan Sales at the time. Otherwise, the *frares trabucaires* (*guerrillero* friars) were familiar in Catalan and Spanish late eighteenth- and nineteenth-century history, as Goya's etchings bear testimony.

AFTERWORD

The last part of the 1956 edition of *Incerta glòria* (*Uncertain Glory*) ended with a chapter called "Últimes notícies" (Latest news) which Joan Sales began to expand when working on the French translation with his translator Bernard Lafargues in the early 1960s. Horrified by the complacency of the Francoist regime's celebration of "25 Years of Peace", and the rest of Europe's blind acceptance of the dictator, he began to describe the years of hunger and repression when lorries loaded with corpses drove through Barcelona at night and children and adults were continuously "disappeared". By the 1969 edition the new section was complete as the final part of *Uncertain Glory*. Two years before his death Sales made a small but significant change to the 1981 edition: the final section was now prefaced by a page declaring it was *El vent de la nit, novel·la* (*Winds of the Night,* a novel). The granddaughter of Joan Sales, Maria Bohigas, later argued that the writer recognised the two novels had a quite distinct tone and perspective but couldn't bring himself to separate them. In 2012 she published *Winds of the Night* as a separate, self-contained novel.

Uncertain Glory portrayed the complexities of war through the conflicting narratives of three of its protagonists, one-time radical students Lluís de Brocà, a leftist although heir to a pasta factory; Lluís' partner, Trini Milmany, daughter of utopian anarchist teachers, who is impelled by the horror of anarchist atrocities to convert to Catholicism; and by Cruells, a twenty-year-old studying for the priesthood who is in love with Trini. All three admire the

247

wild and irreverent Juli Soleràs, who also loves Trini. In support of Maria Bohigas's perception is the comment of Cruells, now the central narrator of the sequel: "how sad it is to wake up after a night of feverish delirium. Perhaps the worst of war is the peace that follows . . . You wake up from your youth and think you have been feverish and delirious, yet you cling to the memory of that delirious madness, of those stormy shadows, as if they were the only worthwhile things this world possessed. I am but a survivor, a ghost; my only life, my memories."

Winds of the Night presents a dark commentary on the consequences of Franco's victory from two men who have been made mentally ill by the horrors of the war and subsequent phoney peace. After the fascist insurrection in July 1936, Cruells, a seminarist, had broken off his training for the priesthood to enrol in the republican ranks; Rodolph Lamoneda worked as a fascist agent provocateur inciting the anarchists into more arson attacks on churches and more murders of priests in Barcelona and beyond. Now, in post-war Spain, after a time in a French concentration camp, Cruells has become a liberal priest racked with doubts. Lamoneda is an even more deranged member of the fascist Falange, disillusioned by the way he has been passed over in the scramble for power and influence by men he considers to be mercenary opportunists and closet "liberal-freemasons".

According to Sales himself, in an autobiographical note, Cruells is "a Catalan priest, feeling his way through the long night after the disaster [of the Civil War], through the endless tunnel, a lost neurotic, feeling his way in the dark, while the wind of schizophrenia blows dust in his face. It is the story of a sick mind. A mind made ill because of the immense scandal of National-Catholicism [the pro-Franco Church]; because of the mystery of the iniquity that he cannot understand; because of those interfering bishops who came to Catalonia chosen only for their hatred and who appeared at public events giving the Nazi salute; so many things that we want to forget but can't. The unfortunate Cruells lived in an era similar to that lived by Goya but which lasted four times longer, four ominous decades instead of one." Lamoneda, despite being on the winning side is also a lost soul in Franco's Spain. Franco's victory has turned out not to be a Falangist victory. The Falange has been neutered, converted into the massive bureaucracy known as the Movimiento Nacional. As the regime became ever more stultified and corrupt, Falangist idealists longed to complete their illusory "social revolution". Lamoneda no more fits into Franco's Spain than does Cruells.

Cruells is disorientated by the Francoist victory, his faith severely challenged by the injustices of the ferociously clerical Franco regime. Through his narrative, we get a grim account of the sordid living conditions of the defeated Republicans in post-war Barcelona, many on the verge of starvation. Despite his Catholic faith, Cruells remains something of a rebel. At first, he is working in the slums of Barcelona although he later ends up being sent to a rural parish. He is made to feel guilty by his aunt, who is a traditional Catholic and deeply disappointed that he has not shown enough ambition to emulate her brother, the Bishop Pinell de Bray. Torn with doubts, at one point he sees a shabbily clothed and emaciated prostitute standing in a doorway. To his own surprise, he pays her for sex and merely achieves total humiliation: he ends up briefly living, indeed drowning in filth, with said prostitute and her pimp. "And I felt a burning desire to hurl myself down an endless abyss, as we sometimes do in dreams, hurtling terminally down a kaleidoscopic abyss, a cold wind constantly on the back of my neck and an inner voice tyrannically ordering me to do what I had in mind when I ran away from home; I needed to see it through to the end and I did so, as if it was the vilest of tasks, the most unpleasant of duties, as the cold wind of night hit my neck. That wretched woman had just ridiculed me with her mocking contempt: 'Is it really the first time? You're a big boy now, you know!' I was well into my thirties, nevertheless I lived with her for two weeks." His loss of faith is relatively brief and he returns to his mission to the immigrant workers in the shanty towns growing up on the outskirts of Barcelona. Eventually, his heterodox views lead to him being sent to a remote rural parish in the Catalan mountains.

The book has an underlying Catalanist agenda. Very early on, Cruells movingly recounts the imprisonment, trial and execution of the President of the Generalitat, Lluís Companys, as recounted to him by a nun, Companys' sister. Later, the Catalanist Sales uses Cruells to show that the majority of the younger Catalan clergy were not fanatical pro-Francoists like most of their elders in the ecclesiastical hierarchy. This is demonstrated in the occasional visits that Cruells makes to Barcelona. At times he bumps into Lamoneda and tolerates his ravings because he hopes to find what happened to Soleràs at the end of the war. At others, he stumbles upon significant historical moments such as the famous tram strike of March 1951 which escalated into a general strike involving 300,000 workers that paralysed the Catalan capital or a demonstration a decade later by young priests in protest against regime brutality. He also has meetings with the character referred to as "the colonel-archbishop – a military colonel – who had arrived with so much energy and so little understanding shortly after the end of the war." This character is based on the Francoist cleric from Aragon, Gregorio Modrego Casaus who had been Bishop of Toledo until made Bishop of Barcelona in 1940. His blithe certainties are contrasted with the agonised doubts of Cruells. Yet Cruells reluctantly admits that, as he became more neurotic, he "came to love him like a son . . . He truly provoked a peculiar mix of filial love and contempt that was beyond my control."

During the tram strike, Cruells ends up in the bachelor flat of Lamoneda, forced to listen to him rambling about his sexual conquests and reading incoherent passages from his coded novel about the Spanish Civil War. It takes place in Barcelona, rendered as "Parzelonenburg", the imaginary capital of sub-Carpathian Pomerania (Catalonia). In it, Count Recesvinto (Lamoneda) is a double agent who pulls the strings of the civil war. Lamoneda declares that he is "better than Stendhal!" His self-aggrandisement reaches its height when a Duchess says to him: "Richelieu was an innocent abroad compared to you, Recesvinto; thanks to you, the sun will never again set on our empire." Through its absurdities, Sales is mounting a critique of the empty bombast of the Francoists and in particular, the flowery rhetorical prose of the Catalan intellectual and novelist Eugenio d'Ors, who abandoned Barcelona for a stint as Franco's Minister of Culture.

It has been suggested that Lamoneda was based on a sinister Prussian, Friedrich Stallman, who went by the fake title of Baron de Koenig. In the turmoil of the period at the end of the First World War, Koenig led a gang of agents provocateurs and was denominated by the conservative politician Francisco Bastos Ansart, "a prince of rogues". Koenig was subsidised by the French secret service as well as by the industrialists who paid him to murder trade union leaders. In addition, he also blackmailed the industrialists with a protection racket and was finally expelled from Spain in May 18, 1920. One clue is in the single reference to Lamoneda's full name, in his civil marriage certificate, Rodolf Lamoneda i Gallifa. One of the many pseudonyms used by Koenig/Stallman was Rodolphe Lemoine. Another clue may be seen in Lamoneda's frequent admiring references to Koenig, "a man ahead of his times", with whom he shared anti-clerical views. It finally transpires that Lamoneda is the illegitimate son of a corrupt policeman on Koenig's payroll.

The extremists of the Falange were fiercely opposed to the oligarchy and one of Lamoneda's rages is provoked by the success of Llibert Milmany, Trini's brother. An anarchist contact of Lamoneda during the war, Llibert has become manager of a previously collectivised factory that, under the name Rexy Mura, manufactures skin-care lotions and perfume. Llibert achieves great sales of these products by applying techniques of war propaganda in advertising them: "Llibert Milmany, the potentate, the manager of Rexy Mura," and Lamoneda winked: "Did you ever crack the secrets of Rexy Mura? The same concoction makes men's hair grow and removes women's, you can go a long way with a fantastic recipe like that!" Some critics have suggested that Llibert is based on Jaume Miravitlles, a one-time Trotskyist of the tiny Bloc Obrer i Camperol who by 1936 had joined the left Catalanist party, the Esquerra Republicana de Catalunya, and risen to be the propaganda chief in the war-time Catalan government, the Generalitat. The brief references to the get-rich-quick bourgeoisie help pin the novel in the post-war period. Although *Winds of the Night* is not a *roman à clef*, the same could be said for the reference to a guerrilla chieftain, Estany, who was probably based on Ramon Vila Capdevila (Caracremada), an anarchist guerrillero who, like Estany, fought in the French resistance.

Similarly, the numerous references by Lamoneda to the visits of Heinrich Himmler to Spain have the same function of locating his neurotic ramblings in real Francoist history. In late 1938, at the behest of the Falangist Director General of Security, the Conde de Mayalde, Himmler was awarded the regime's highest decoration, the Grand Cross of the Imperial Order of the Yoke and Arrows in recognition of his role in the fight against the enemies of Franco's Spain. The Reichsführer was a hero to many Falangists, and Lamoneda claims bizarrely that Himmler reciprocated personally, recognising him as a brilliant secret agent during the war. Four days after the death of Companys, Heinrich Himmler arrived in Spain at the invitation of Mayalde to discuss collaboration between the Gestapo and Franco's security services. Cruells recalls reading in the paper that Lamoneda was in the welcoming party, something that Lamoneda would drone on about "as one of the most glorious memories of his existence".

The title of *Uncertain Glory* comes from lines in Shakespeare's "Two Gentlemen of Verona": "O, how this spring of love resembleth the uncertain glory of an April day; which now shows all the beauty of the sun. And by and by a cloud takes all away." The day in question was April 14, 1931 when the Second Republic was established in Spain and people danced in the streets of the major cities in celebration of the better life that it promised. The cloud that would take all away was the right-wing conspiracy that set off the Civil War. *Uncertain Glory* teems with insight into how that cloud darkened the lives of millions of Spaniards.

Its implicit question as to whether the blood and sacrifice was worthwhile is resoundingly answered in the negative by the reality of the Franco dictatorship as filtered through the grim commentary of *Winds of the Night*. Yet despite those horrors, both losers, Cruells and Lamoneda, are nostalgic for the war. Cruells laments: "Lord, my guilty heart longs for that war and that woman. And my guilty heart still longs for my lost youth; I know I will never experience life like that again! Here I am in my fifties, my entire youth lost in this endless tunnel . . . Could it have been otherwise? Every part of me replies that it could; I was only fourteen in that 'spring that was so spring-like', that 'spring as perhaps there would be no other in this world', when the whole of our country emerged from a long, long winter to breathe the scent of thyme blossom. I was only fourteen but I will always remember that marvellous aroma of resurrection and hope." It goes without saying that *Winds of the Night* benefits from a prior acquaintance with *Uncertain Glory* but even without that prior knowledge, it can be appreciated for its exquisite prose, so beautifully captured in Peter Bush's translation.

Paul Preston

OTHER NEW YORK REVIEW CLASSICS

For a complete list of titles, visit www.nyrb.com.